In Search of a Vision

In Search of a Vision

FIRST EDITION

A Boner Book by
The Nazca Plains Corporation
Las Vegas, Nevada
2006

ISBN:1-887895-24-8

Published by,

The Nazca Plains Corporation ®
4640 Paradise Rd, Suite 141
Las Vegas NV 89109-8000

PUBLISHER'S NOTE
In Search of a Vision is a work of fiction created wholly by the
author's imagination. All characters are fictional and any
resemblance to any persons living or deceased is purely by
accident. No portion of this book reflects any real person or
events.

Editor, Blake Stephens
Cover Sketch Art by John Dennis
Cover Color Art by Ross Johnston
Art Direction, Robert Steele

Dedication

Many people, both real and imaginary, contributed to this book.

It's impossible to thank them all.

So thanks everyone.

In Search of a Vision

FIRST EDITION

A Boner Book

THE LAST SON

Rogers ran down the dark path as the rain poured down and lightning flashed. He had gotten disoriented in the dark. Each path, each clearing, looked like the last. He knew that his pursuer was somewhere close. He just didn't know how close. All he knew was that he had to get away.

Gurney stood on the verandah and watched the rain advance across the lake. He could hear the wind generators on the roof rotating; the blades began to pick-up speed as they charged the storage batteries. He could smell the rain. He liked it. It was fresh and clean. He knew that if it rained all night, he'd sleep well.

"Sir, if you don't get dressed, you'll be late for the ceremony," Kirby, his assistant said to him.

"Yes Kirby, I know," Gurney sighed. "You know how I hate these things."

"I know sir, but if we want to keep Spencer's business," Kirby replied. "You have to attend them." The rain had now passed the beach and Gurney could hear it pattering on the tile roof of the horse barn. Soon it would reach the house.

"I hate these piercing ceremonies," Gurney protested again.

"I know, sir," Kirby replied.

The rain had reached the house. Even with the overhang of the roof, Gurney could feel some mist on his face. The pattering noise rose and fell in a slow, uneven rhythm on the tiled roofs. He could hear it surge and gush through the gutters and downspouts into the cisterns.

"I've got your clothes all laid out, sir."

"Thank you, Kirby," Gurney left the verandah and walked back into his suite.

"One moment, sir," Kirby said, "Let me take a look at you."

"You treat me like I'm a little boy, Kirby."

"That's why you pay me the big bucks, sir," Kirby smiled.

"Yeah, right," Gurney grinned back, "But I don't think it was a big BUCK you were asking for the other night."

"Quite true, sir. Now let me take a look at your head, sir." Gurney stood silently as Kirby ran his hand over Gurney's shaved scalp.

"Quite acceptable, sir. Now, let me check the goatee." Gurney lifted his head so Kirby could be sure his goatee was even.

"You know, it's going to be dark there. Who's gonna know if it's a little off?"

"I will, sir," Kirby replied. "I still think you should let me dye these gray hairs, sir."

Gurney sighed. "I figured it will be hot, so I thought the leather shorts under the chaps, short black work boots, leather vest, and a traditional red and black Buffalo plaid shirt." "Fine," Gurney replied.

"Of course your flat top cap, gauntlets, and leather jacket, as usual, sir. It's also raining a bit you know," Kirby said.

"Of course I know."

Kirby took Gurney's robe and laid it on the bench at the foot of the bed as Gurney began to get dressed. First, he put on the shirt, which had been freshly washed and ironed. Followed by the shorts, socks, boots, chaps, and vest.

"All done," Kirby asked. "Let me have a look, then, sir." Gurney rolled his eyes as Kirby walked around him, checking to see if everything was in the proper position.

"Just one adjustment," Kirby grinned, pulled on Gurney's leather.

"I'm not going on a DATE ya know!" Gurney exclaimed. Before Kirby could answer there was a knock the door,

"Come," Gurney called.

"Sir, it's time for us to get going. We don't want to be late do we?" Kadrovich, Captain of Gurney's personal guard and chief of security, asked. His broad shoulders filled the doorway.

"Is everyone trying to be my mother tonight?"

"No, Sir. Sorry," Kadrovich replied. "I just thought we needed to be there early, that's all, sir."

"Well, I'm ready as soon as I get my jacket on," Gurney grumbled.

Kirby helped him into his jacket and handed Gurney his hat and gauntlets.

Gurney walked back out on to the verandah. To the right, across the lake to the west, he could see the flickering lights of Breederstown. Across Crater Lake to the south, he could see the lights of Labrys come and go as the rain shifted back and forth. Between Breederstown and Lthrtown the garish lights of Chiffon were a minor distraction. He thought he could see small lights flickering in the woods at Cruiseville, too. "A busy night," he thought.

"Sir?" It was Kadrovich.

"Coming," Gurney replied. Kadrovich led the way down the stairs.

Gurney walked behind him, pulling on his gauntlets. Despite his protests, Gurney enjoyed the feel of the leather. He felt a stirring in his groin.

When they arrived in the great hall, Gurney stopped. A full squad stood there at attention. "I don't think this is necessary, Kadrovich."

"Sir?"

"This is a piercing ceremony, not a high leather night."

"But, sir," Kadrovich protested.

"You, Bruno, Schmidt, and Griffith. That should be enough," Gurney said, picking out his favorites. Like Kadrovich they were all young and well built. Their muscles were from hard work, not decorative gym muscles. Kadrovich himself was about half Gurney's age.

"Yes, sir," Kadrovich dismissed the rest of the squad. Gurney led the way as they walked out into the main courtyard. The rain had moved on but smell was still strong. The wind was fresh and clean. Kadrovich and Bruno led the way. Gurney walked in the middle. Schmidt and Griffith followed.

The guards snapped to attention as they approached the gate. The leather and chrome they wore reflected the dim light. Somewhere, Gurney could hear a dog barking. Gurney and his escort walked the short distance across the meticulously manicured grounds, out the gate and down Market Street to Spencer's in silence.

The guards were alert and ready for action. Gurney was pensive. To the right he could see the masts of the Provincetown, ready for her first voyage around the lake. He wondered sometimes if it was worth it to be the managing director of one of the biggest collectives in Lthrtown.

He had so many decisions to make everyday. There were all the details of running the collective, with so many men who depended on him. Sometimes the strain was too much. But, Kirby and the rest of the staff knew what to do, and Gurney had confidence in them and in their abilities. The Nimbus Collective was NOT a one-man show, after all!

The street was deserted. It was as if no one dared to be out when Gurney and his escort were there. But actually, it was quite the opposite. It was a sign of respect for his position as the Director of the Collective and his position in the Temple. But, Gurney didn't really think about the lack of men on the street. He was trying to get himself into the mood to pretend that he was having a good time at Spencer's ceremony.

"Barbaric," he thought, "Still piercing genitals. But, it's up to the men who enter Spencer's service if they want to make that commitment, so who am I to make a judgment about it?" As they rounded the corner of Market and Castro, they could see the lights from Spencer's estate.

"Kadrovich."

"Sir?"

"Come and walk beside me," Gurney said.

"Yes, sir."

"Tell me, Kadrovich, what do you think of these ceremonies?"

"I am glad WE do not do them, sir."

"Why?"

"Well, sir. For one thing I feel it's risky even in the best of times. And, it limits your options. I feel it marks you as a full time bottom."

"It seems to indicate that to me, also,"

"I find no problem with ear rings and nipple rings, but other that than, sir? No, sir." They continued on in silence.

"Are you gonna cut this for me, or do I have to do it myself?" Troy asked Pat.

"Honey, are you sure this is what you want to do? Can't I change your mind?" Pat's eyes were red and swollen from tears.

"I can't live like this anymore," Troy gestured at the garish furnishings of the room.

"But, you're a big star, honey! Everybody LOVES you!"

"Yeah, well there's more to life than being a drag queen!" Troy shot back. He rubbed the back of his hand against his new beard.

"But, but."

"Now, either you cut my hair like I want it so I look good for my interview tomorrow, or I do it myself and look bad," Troy glared at him "It's up to you!"

Pat wiped his eyes. "OK," he whispered.

Troy sat down and Pat got the scissors and razor.

"Are you sure, honey?"

"Yes, damn it!"

"All this beautiful, long red hair."

"Save it and sell it to my adoring public."

"I'll save it, but I don't think I'll sell it," Pat said, and then got to work.

"You remember, last week? When I was in Labrys, I said it was my final show?"

"I thought you just meant there, honey," Pat replied.

"So did everyone else."

"You know I love you, honey. If this it what it takes to make you happy, OK."

"Good. Now get on with it. I need to get some sleep for tomorrow."

Spencer's guards snapped to attention when Gurney and his escort approached them. "We are expected," Kadrovich told them.

"Yes, sir," the captain of the guard replied. "We've been expecting you." Gurney and his escort continued on without stopping. Burning torches brightly lit the courtyard. A double row of guards led the way to Spencer's main hall. Leather-clad men milled around outside the double doors.

As Gurney and his party approached they moved to either side and allowed them to pass. Gurney used his best swagger as he passed through the crowd. He didn't look to either side. Kadrovich would tell him who was there when they were inside.

Those outside were the independent merchants and directors of small collectives. All of them were eager to make a good connection. Some were looking for business and some were looking for pleasure. The inside of the hall was dark except for the area around the altar that had been set up for the ceremony. There was a soft chanting in the background. Gurney stood, his guards towering behind him. Slowly, he looked around the dark hall. He could see many faces that he recognized in the dim light. Bigger merchants were there as well as the heads of some of the other collectives. Someone approached Gurney. Gurney was aware of Kadrovich off his right shoulder.

"You honor our master's house with your presence, sir!" the man exclaimed, giving Gurney a short, at the waist, bow.

"Tell your master we are honored to be here," Gurney replied, even though he wished he were anywhere but there.

"Yes, sir!" He bowed again, turned and left. Gurney just wanted the ceremony to be over. Moments later a strapping young man in chains was led in into the center of the room. His freshly shaven body glistened in the light. The only thing he wore was a leather snap front jockstrap. Gurney heard one of his guards mumbling an oath of some kind in the background. The chanting continued as Spencer approached the young man. No words were exchanged. Spencer unsnapped the front of the jock and grasped the man's penis. Gurney closed his eyes. He knew what was coming next. He knew from the gasp of his guards when the deed was done. He opened his eyes. Spencer stood there with blood on his hands. Gurney's stomach rolled.

"Sir?" It was Kadrovich.

Gurney waved him off. "I'm all right."

"Yes, sir."

The crowd slowly filed out the doors. The rain had started again.

Pike, Spencer's assistant, met Gurney at the door.

"Sir, my master requests that you and your party join him in his private chambers."

"Very well," Gurney replied.

"This way please, sir," Pike led the way. Gurney and his guards followed.

They entered a door and walked down a black painted hall with dark, rough, wood beams and posts. Torches flickered in holders.

"He certainly is playing THIS up for all it's worth," Gurney thought.

Pike turned and opened a door. "Sir. Managing Director Gurney of the Nimbus Collective!"

"Gurney, you old dog!" Spencer exclaimed. As he approached he offered his hand to Gurney.

"Spencer," Gurney ignored the offered hand.

"So, what do you think of my latest acquisition?" Spencer took a swallow from his drink.

Gurney smiled, "You know what I think of this kind of practice."

Spencer shrugged. "To each his own." He eyed Kadrovich and the others. "Still growing them big, eh?"

"They have their uses."

"I'm sure they do!" Spencer leered.

Kadrovich growled, low in his throat.

"They're very protective of me."

"I see that," Spencer backed up a step.

Gurney's guards stared at Spencer.

"Well, down to business," Spencer said. "When does the Provincetown sail?"

"A day or two. Why?" Gurney questioned.

"I want to be on her," Spencer replied.

'Not possible," Gurney replied curtly.

"Why not?" Spencer asked, walking over to the bar along the wall.

"It's the shakedown cruise. Labrys, Breederstown, Chiffon, and back," Gurney replied, "No passengers this trip."

"That's not what I've heard."

"Oh?"

"I've heard a story that you're going exploring," Spencer said. "Can I get you a drink?" He walked over to the bar.

"You've heard wrong then, I guess," Gurney ignoring the question.

"I see"

"Sir," It was Kadrovich.

Gurney turned his head slightly.

"Sir, we have a situation. You're needed at the compound," Kadrovich told him.

"Anything to get out of here," Gurney thought.

Spencer stood; drink in hand, watching Gurney.

"As much as I've enjoyed being here, I have to go," Gurney informed Spencer.

"Let me know if you change your mind," Spencer said, with a slight nod of his head.

Gurney spun on his heel and followed Kadrovich out of the room.

"Now, what is this situation, Kadrovich?" Gurney asked, once they were back on Castro.

"Someone has been hurt, sir."

"Who? How?"

"Sir, that's all the call said, sir."

"Then let's pick up the pace, Kadrovich."

"Yes, sir."

Kirby met them at the gate. "They're in MedCenter," He said.

"What's happened?" Gurney asked?

"Salvetti's been assaulted."

"What? Who did it?" Gurney almost stopped in the middle of the pathway.

"Don't know. He was found cuffed to a fence." Kirby replied.

"But, he'll recover," Gurney said.

"I think so. Doc's with him, now." They hurried through the small MedCenter to the emergency room.

Doc turned as they came in.

He pushed them back towards the door. "He'll be OK. He's sleeping."

When they were in the hall, Gurney asked, "Did he say who did this to him?"

"No, sir," Doc sat down on a wooden bench. "I'm not even sure if he knows who did it. From the bruising, I'd say he was grabbed from behind."

"Where did this happen?" Gurney asked.

"Down Market, just past Castro."

"And, no witnesses."

"None that we know of, sir."

"Is it still raining?" Gurney asked Kadrovich.

"On and off, sir."

"Let's go take a look and see if we can find anything."

"Yes, sir."

"Meanwhile, double the guards around the collective," Gurney instructed.

"I already did, sir," Kadrovich replied.

"Of course."

"If there's any change, I'll call you," Doc said.

"Let's go take a look at the scene, Kadrovich."

"Yes, sir."

Gurney and his guards retraced their steps from earlier in the evening until they reached Castro. They approached a small crowd.

"This way, sir," Kadrovich said.

The bloody cuffs still hung on the fence. It was just a short distance from the street.

"We've looked for any evidence, sir. The rain has apparently washed away anything there might have been."

"Post a guard overnight and take another look in the morning."

"Yes, sir," Kadrovich pointed at a pair of guards and they began to clear the area.

"Let's go home, Kadrovich."

"Yes, sir."

Troy approached the gate of the city. He'd been here before, but this was different. Before, he had been in drag. Now, he was himself.

He was surprised to see security guards at the gate. Usually you could come and go as you pleased, as far as he knew, anyway.

"Can I see your identification, please?" One of the guards asked.

"I lost it. I got mugged in the woods."

"I see," the guard eyed Troy suspiciously. The second guard rested his hand on his weapon.

"I'm here looking for work."

"Well, I can give you a temporary ID. Come into the office."

Troy followed the first guard as the second watched.

"I suggest you find a job and a place to stay as soon as possible," the guard said, after having Troy fill out some forms.

"Yes, sir. I'll certainly try."

"We don't like panhandlers or hustlers here."

"Where is the employment office?"

"The closest is Nimbus. Just down the street, on the left."

"I'll go right there then."

"See that you do," The guard handed him his ID card.

Troy walked out of the office. The guard was right behind him.

"Thank you for your assistance," Troy said as he walked away.

The guards watched him walk down the street.

Troy looked down the long street. Colorful banners and flags hung everywhere. He could see collective flags on some of the storefronts.

The office was easy to find. The Nimbus banner hung over the door.

Troy opened the door and walked in.

"Can I help you?" the man behind the desk asked.

"I'm looking for a job," Troy replied.

"Well, then I guess you've come to the right place," he smiled. "Fill out some papers for me here, and then we'll talk a little about you and what Nimbus expects from its members."

"All right," Troy sat down

"Let me get the papers together."

Troy found this man very attractive. A nice build, shaved head, a nice thick goatee. He didn't seem to have an attitude like the guards had had.

"Here you go," he handed Troy some papers.

Troy busied himself filling out the papers as the recruiter read some papers.

"I guess I'm all done."

"Already?"

"Not really a lot to put on here."

"I see," the recruiter took the papers.

Troy looked around the office as the recruiter looked at his papers. It was comfortable and well furnished, but in an understated way. Tasteful art hung on the walls, live plants and fresh flowers were scattered around the room.

"Do you understand how an organization like the Nimbus Collective works?"

"Not completely."

"OK, I'll explain it to you."

"All right."

"As a member of the collective, you work for the collective. Depending on your position you might be in a barracks, a dorm or with one other man. Unless you have a partner."

"No, I'm single," Troy replied.

"OK. You get paid in credits that you can use at Nimbus businesses, but you also get a clothing allowance and meals are taken care of. Plus, all the other collectives will take your credits, too. So, you're not required to spend all you make back into the collective."

"I see."

"If you want to check out some of the other collectives or some of the businesses I can give you a booklet that goes into more detail."

"Well, I did just arrive in town."

"No problem. Think about it and come back in if you're interested."

"Thanks for your time," Troy offered his hand and the recruiter shook it with a very firm grip.

"My pleasure."

Troy stood up, took one last look around the office and walked out the door.

A few minutes later the door opened again.

"Sir, thank you for giving me the time to go to MedCenter, sir"

"That's quite all right," Gurney replied. "Only one guy came in. I have a feeling he'll be back."

"Yes, sir," Parker, the recruiter, said as he took Gurneys place behind the desk.

Gurney left the office to find some lunch.

Troy was down the street looking to the store windows.

"Hello," Gurney said, "Can I buy you some lunch?"

"Uh, sure. I don't have any credits. I didn't think about that when I came here."

"Not a problem. One of my favorite spots is just around the corner."

"Thank you."

"It's a nice, quiet place, good food. Attentive staff."

They walked around the corner and walked down a tree-lined street.

"Here we are."

The name on the awning said, Como's. A red and yellow pennant hung over the entrance.

"Sir, welcome," the doorman said. "You usual table is ready."

"Thank you."

The doorman looked at Troy.

"Bring my guest a menu, please."

"Yes, sir."

The doorman led the way to a table overlooking the patio. It was cool and quiet. A fountain gently splashed somewhere.

Like everything else Troy had seen, everything here was spotless.

"I'd recommend the Fettuccine Alfredo."

"Sounds fine to me."

A moment later the waiter appeared. "Sir, are you ready to order?"

"Yes, we'll have the Fettuccine Alfredo, salad with the house dressing. What would you like to drink?" Gurney asked Troy.

"Water is fine."

"Bring a pitcher."

"Yes, sir." The waiter backed away.

Gurney looked at Troy. His red beard was darker inside the restaurant. His green eyes reflected the light of the wall sconces.

Troy looked back at Gurney. He had the urge to kiss this man, but he didn't even know his name. Or, why he was even buying his lunch. He liked his quiet, controlled manner.

"So, tell me what's not on your application."

"What do you mean?"

The waiter silently served their salads and ice water.

"What are your interests?"

"I know a bit about music and stage production."

"I see," Gurney began to eat his salad.

They ate in silence.

"There's not much in the way of live theater in town."

"No?"

"A few bands in the bars, but that's about it."

"I see."

They finished their salads and the waiter, once again, silently appeared and took away the plates.

A moment later he reappeared with a breadbasket and two large plates of steaming Fettuccine Alfredo.

"This is the best in town," Gurney told Troy, as the waiter sprinkled grated cheese on his Fettuccine.

"I'll take your word for it," Troy replied.

"Sir?" The waiter stood poised with the grated cheese.

"Yes, please."

They ate in silence after the waiter left.

"This is delicious," Troy said.

"Told you so. Made fresh every day."

"I can tell."

They lapsed into silence again.

"I'm stuffed," Troy said.

"Good." They left the restaurant.

"Will you be back at the office later?" Troy asked.

"Oh, you'll see me around," Gurney replied.

"Oh. Well, thanks for lunch."

"Your quite welcome," Gurney shook Troy's hand.

Troy stood and watched Gurney disappear down the crowded street.

"Strange," he thought. "I guess I'd better make a decision."

A few minutes later he found himself standing outside the Nimbus office.

"Here goes," He opened the door and went in.

"Can I help you?" The man behind the desk asked. He had a blond brush cut and a bushy mustache.

"I was here earlier and talked to Mr. Parker."

"You may have been here earlier, but I didn't talk to you."

"You're Mr. Parker?"

"Just Parker."

"I'm confused."

"Have a seat."

"You're the recruiter?"

"Yes, I am."

"Then who was the man I talked to?"

"You must be Troy."

"Yes, I am."

"Good. I have a job offer for you. In the social activities department."

"But, who did I talk to?"

"It pays a nice salary and you'd have a private suite," Parker ignored his question.

"But."

"Are you interested?" Parker asked him.

"Sure," Troy finally replied.

"Good. Here's your contract. Sign here and here."

Troy signed the papers. He sat silently as Parker did his paper work.

"Here you go," Parker handed him his ID card. "Here's a copy of everything for you."

"Now what do I do?" Troy asked.

"Go to the main gate of the compound and the guards will tell you how to get to your suite," Parker stroked his mustache.

"But, who did I talk to when I was here before?"

"I've been instructed to tell you nothing about anything other than the job," Parker replied.

"This is very strange."

"You'll be given more instructions when you get to the compound. You also find a book of rules, regulations and protocols in your suite, as well as one on customs and etiquette. I suggest you study it tonight. Good luck."

"Uh, thanks," Troy stood up. Obviously the interview was over. He looked at the papers in his hand.

Parker calmly watched him.

"Where do I go?"

"Left out the door. Just continue down Market and you'll see the main gate."

Troy walked out in a daze.

A few minutes after Troy left, Parker took his phone out of his desk drawer and made a call.

"Yes, sir. He's on his way."

"You'll have a little bonus this week."

"Thank you sir. Glad to have been of service," Parker hung up the phone and went back to work.

Troy walked down the street to the main gate of the Nimbus compound. The roofs of many of the buildings were only slightly slanted. This allowed them to catch as much rain in the warm seasons and snow in the cold seasons as possible.

"Welcome to Nimbus, sir," the guard greeted him. "Your assistant will be here in a moment."

"Assistant?"

"Yes, sir."

Troy waited impatiently. He didn't understand what was going on.

"Sorry I'm late, sir."

"Uh, that's OK," Troy replied.

"I'm Perry. I'll be your assistant," He stuck out his hand.

Troy shook it. He was surprised by the strength of Perry's grip. Perry was only about 5'2" and slimly built.

"If you'll follow me I'll take you to your suite."

"Do you have any idea what's going on here?" Troy asked.

"What do you mean, sir?"

"I had an interview with someone who wasn't the recruiter. Someone who took me to lunch and never told me who he was. I go back to the office and get offered a well paying job."

"I couldn't really say, sir."

"It's very strange."

"Sir, it's my job to see to it that you understand Nimbus protocols and procedures. I'm sure everything will be explained when the time is right."

"I see."

"We'll get you settled in your suite and then we can go over the rules and regulations."

"All I have is what's in my backpack."

"No problem, sir. You have a clothing allowance. We'll get you everything you need."

"I see."

"Your suite is on the second floor. Managing Director Gurney is on the third floor."

Troy had noticed that the roof on the apartment on the third floor had a barrel roof sheathed in copper that was now green with verdigris. They went through the double doors into the great hall. Going up the stairs, they walked along the galleria to Troy's suite.

"Here we are, sir," Perry said, opening the door, allowing Troy to enter first.

"Wow!" Troy exclaimed.

"Is everything all right, sir?"

"Yes," Troy replied. "Very nice." He looked around the living room. The furnishings were tasteful. The art on the walls was contemporary.

"Very good, sir. If there's something you don't like, let me know and I'll see to it that it's changed."

"Look's fine to me."

"If you'd like to freshen up, the bathroom is the door to the left."

"I could use a shower."

"Very good, sir. Do you need any assistance?"

"I think I can manage."

"Very well, sir. I'll unpack your backpack while you freshen up."

Troy went into the bathroom. It had a large whirlpool tub and a large shower. The tub overlooked a balcony. Troy could see a garden courtyard. The towels were thick and plush. Everything was first class. Troy was impressed.

He came out of the shower to find a robe lay out on the foot of the bed.

Troy went through the other door into the bedroom.

"Sir," Perry said. "Managing Director Gurney's office called with a dinner invitation. I took the liberty of accepting for you."

"That's fine. Maybe I'll get the answers to some of my questions."

"I'd better give you some pointers, sir."

"Such as?" Troy asked.

"Always address the director as sir, unless he tells you otherwise. Your position is considered part of the staff. But, unless he says otherwise, the proper form of address is always sir."

"I see."

"Gurney is very liberal and may ask your opinion on any matter. He likes to get other points of view before he makes a decision."

"Since I've only just arrived how much of an opinion can I give?"

"Hard to say, sir," Perry replied.

"So, what else does your job entail?"

"I'm your assistant and valet. Anything you want, it's my job to take care of it for you."

"Such as laying out my clothes for tonight?" Troy glanced at the bed, where a change of clothes was laid out.

"Yes, sir," Perry replied.

"When's dinner?"

"Not for a couple of hours. Would you like to rest?"

"I think I need a cram course on the rules and etiquette here."

"As you wish, sir."

"Any word on Salvetti?" Gurney asked.

"No, but I can check, if you'd like," Kirby replied.

"Please."

"So, who's the new guy?"

"Oh, Troy? You'll meet him at dinner."

"I hear he's kind of hot."

"You're not jealous are you?"

"Moi? Please. I'm your assistant and valet. You're certainly allowed to sleep with whomever you like. After all, you ARE in charge."

"I'm glad you remember that," Gurney smiled.

"I'll check on Salvetti and let you know how he's doing before dinner."

"Good. I'll be in my office."

"Yes, sir."

"I still think Gurney's lying," Spencer said.

"Well, sir," Pike said, "From what we can tell the Provincetown doesn't have a lot of supplies on board."

"I want someone watching 24 hours a day."

"We're already doing that, sir"

"Did you find out why he left so quickly last night?"

"One of his men was assaulted."

"Really."

"He'll recover."

"Any idea who could have done it?"

"Not so far as I can tell, sir."

"Interesting," Spencer sat back in his chair and stroked his goatee.

"Sir? It's time to get dressed for dinner," Perry told Troy.

Troy looked up from his book. "This is pretty complicated."

"I'm sure you'll catch on quickly, sir."

"Well, don't hesitate to correct me if I make a mistake."

"Yes, sir."

"I guess we'd better get going. This is going to take some getting used to, I guess," Troy said, as he headed for the bedroom.

"Salvetti is recovering nicely," Kirby told Gurney.

"Good, I plan on talking to him soon."

"Should I let Doc know?"

"No, I don't think he'll have a problem with it."

"Yes, sir."

"It everything ready?"

"Yes, sir. You just need to get dressed."

"See to it that Troy is comfortable. Then, you can leave."

"Yes, sir," Kirby replied. "Your clothes are all laid out."

"Thank you, Kirby."

"My pleasure, sir."

"Are you sure this is the right thing to wear?" Troy asked.

"Yes, sir, besides the black T shirt is tight enough to show off the muscles in your chest and arms."

"Alright, if you say so."

"Trust me, sir."

"I will."

"I'll take you to the Managing Directors private dining room. He'll meet you there, sir."

"Lead on, McDuff."

"This way, sir." They left Troy's suite and went to the third floor.

"Here we are," Perry said, opening the door. "Have a nice evening, sir. I'll see you in the morning."

"Thank you, Perry."

"No problem, sir," Perry turned and went back the way they had come.

The room was well furnished like every other room Troy had seen. The table was set for two.

"Hello, sir. I'm Kirby, Managing Director Gurney's assistant. Can I get you anything?"

"No, thank you, I'm fine."

"Very well, sir. Gurney will be here shortly."

"Thank you."

Kirby left Troy alone.

Troy walked around the room, looking at the paintings and other artwork.

"Hello, Troy. How is everything?"

Troy turned at the sound of a familiar voice. "You're Managing Director Gurney?"

"Yes, I am."

"Why didn't you tell me who you were?"

"It was more fun this way," Gurney smiled.

"I see," Troy said. "I've got a lot of questions."

"I'm sure you do," Gurney replied. "Can I get you something to drink?"

"I don't drink," Troy replied.

"Good to hear."

"Care to tell me what this is all about?"

"Why don't we have dinner? I'll give you a history lesson about Nimbus and answer all your questions."

"Sound's good to me."

"Fine," Gurney pressed a button.

"Sir?" a man appeared from a doorway Troy had not noticed before.

"You can start serving dinner, Rommel."

"Yes, sir," Rommel went back the way he had come.

"Have a seat," Gurney said to Troy.

They sat at the small, round table. Once again, the silver and glassware impressed Troy.

Rommel returned a moment later with their salads.

"Do you eat like this every night?"

"No. I usually eat in the main dinning hall with the rest of the staff."

"I see."

"I knew you'd be curious as to what was happening."

"You can say that again."

"Basically, I want to get a cultural arts program started. I thought you'd be the man for the job."

"I see," Troy took a bite of his salad. "What do you have in mind?"

"Various types of music programs. Perhaps a theater group." Gurney poured water into their glasses.

"Do you think there's enough interest?"

"Yes, I do. We have a parcel of land where we can build a performing arts center. You'd be given complete control of the program."

"That's an awful lot of responsibility."

"Are you telling me you can't handle it?" Gurney asked.

"I didn't say that," Troy replied. "I'm sure I can come up with some ideas. I can have them at your office in a day or two."

"Sounds good to me."

"Fine."

They finished their salads and Rommel reappeared and took the plates away.

"I hope you like chicken," Gurney said.

Rommel wheeled in a cart with covered dishes on it. He served Gurney first.

"This is a chicken breast with Risotto. It was diced potatoes and rice. There's grated cheese and a pepper mill, if you need them."

"It smells wonderful."

Rommel waited patiently.

"My compliments to the chef," Troy said, "This is very good."

"Thank you, sir. I'll pass your comments along," Rommel said.

"That will be all for tonight, Rommel," Gurney said.

"Thank you, sir. Have a nice evening, sirs."

Gurney and Troy ate in silence.

As he finished the last of his chicken, Troy said, "You said you were going to give me a history lesson?"

"Yes, I did say that, didn't I?"

"Yes, you did."

"Well, as you know, our society has been structured the way it is for a long time. The mostly male group, a woman's group, the breeders and the, ah, others, who don't fit any mold.

"Everyone knows that's the way it's been for as long as anyone can remember."

"Many young men come to Lthrtown to learn a trade and return to Breederstown. It's the same in Labrys with the women."

"Excuse me, but everyone knows that too," Troy said.

"True enough," Gurney replied.

"I know Nimbus is one of the biggest collectives in Lthrtown," Troy took a swallow from his glass of water.

"We have a hand in almost every major industry in town. We're the only collective to have our own sailing ships. We also do a lot of salvage. The thing's I've seen would amaze you."

"You mean in the Outlands?" Troy was surprised.

"Yes," Gurney replied. "We've found quite a few interesting items."

"I had no idea!" Troy exclaimed.

"Maybe I'll show you some of them in the next few days."

"I'd certainly like to see them," Troy replied.

"I'm sure you'd find them to be of interest."

Troy couldn't believe what Gurney had just told him. Salvage items from the Outlands. What wonders there must be! He'd heard stories, but what was really out there? No one knew for sure. At least no one he'd ever known.

"The view from the verandah is very nice," Gurney said. "Would you like to see it?"

"Yes, I would," Troy replied.

The sun had set. The lights of Labrys, Chiffon and Breederstown could be seen in the distance.

"Nice view," Troy said.

"Yes. It is," Gurney replied. He stood close behind Troy.

"Very," Troy murmured, turning to face Gurney.

Gurney pulled Troy to him. They stood there for a few minutes.

"Come on," Gurney took Troy's hand and led him into the next room.

"That was wonderful," Troy said

"You weren't so bad yourself."

"You're a hot man."

"Thanks," Gurney rolled onto his side and kissed Troy. He could feel his passion rising again. "So are you."

Kelvin's head pounded. It took him a moment to remember where he was. Down by the Nimbus docks. Pike had sent him to watch the Provincetown. But his head pounded. Something had happened, but he couldn't remember what it was. All he knew was that he needed help.

"Sir!" Kirby shook Gurney.

"Huh? What's the matter?" Gurney replied, instantly awake. "You know better than to come in here now."

Troy rolled over, still asleep.

"We have a situation down by the docks."

"What do you mean by a situation?"

"One of Spencer's men was found there. Apparently he had been spying on the Provencetown."

"I figured he had someone doing that. So, what's the problem? Just remove him," Gurney rolled out of bed and took the robe Kirby held out to him.

"The problem is he's been assaulted."

"What? How?" Gurney asked.

"That's what we need to figure out," Kirby replied.

"Does Spencer know about this yet?"

"No, I wanted to talk to you first."

"Contact him. Tell him there's been an accident."

"Yes, sir," Kirby replied and quickly left the room.

Gurney turned to Troy.

"I'm not asleep," Troy said. "What are you going to do?"

"Talk to this guy and see if he remembers anything for starters, I guess."

"Is it like this here all the time?" Troy stretched.

"No. Something's going on. Something strange," Gurney headed for the shower.

"He doesn't remember a thing, sir," Doc told Gurney.

"Nothing at all?" Gurney paced up and down the hall.

"No, sir. The last thing he remembers is watching the docks, but nothing after that. He doesn't even remember getting grabbed."

"Nothing?"

"I can tell he was grabbed from behind, but that's about it, sir. He's also got a concussion."

Gurney's link vibrated. He listened for a moment. "I'll be right there," he said. "Keep me informed, Doc."

"Yes, sir."

Gurney left MedCenter and headed back to his office.

"Spencer is in your office, sir," Kirby said.

"Great. Just what I need!" Gurney growled. He stormed into his office. Spencer was sitting behind Gurneys mahogany desk.

"What the hell are you doing?" Gurney barked.

"I see you're still as anal as ever," Spencer said, running his hands over the expanse of the desk's top. There wasn't a paper on it.

"Is that why you're here? To talk about that?"

"You know why I'm here. I want to know what the hell one of your bullies did to Kelvin." Spencer said.

"What the hell was Kelvin doing spying on the Provencetown?" Gurney shot back.

"I don't believe your story that you're not going exploring," Spencer glared at Gurney.

"Well, it's too bad your stupidity is to blame for all this."

"What?" Spencer sputtered.

"You heard me."

"How dare you talk to me that way, you bastard!"

"I'm too busy to play games with you right now. When Kelvin has stabilized we'll get him back to you."

"Why, you...."

"I'm sure Bruno would be happy to show you the door," Gurney said.

Bruno, stroking his big, black mustache, stared at Spencer.

Without another word, Spencer got up from behind the desk and stomped out of Gurney's office, slamming the door behind him.

"Where's Kadrovich?" Gurney asked.

"He's on the docks, sir," Bruno replied.

"Contact him and tell him I want to know if he finds anything. Anything at all."

"Yes, sir," Bruno left for the outer office.

"KIRBY," Gurney called.

"Yes, sir?" Kirby came into the office.

"As soon as Kadrovich gets here, send him in," Gurney dropped into his high-backed leather chair. He checked the drawers. They were still locked.

"Yes, sir. Anything else?" Kirby replied.

"Find out how soon Provencetown will be ready to sail."

"Yes, sir," Kirby backed out of Gurney's office.

"Bring me a cup of tea, too," Gurney called after Kirby.

"Right away," Kirby replied.

Gurney sat and stared out the window across the lake to Labrys. "Something's not right," he thought to himself. "But what is it? What's going on?"

There was a knock at the door and Kadrovich came in. Kirby followed with

Gurney's tea.

"You wanted to see me, sir?" Kadrovich said as Kirby slipped out the door.

"Yes, I did," Gurney replied. "We're going on the Provencetown's shakedown cruise. Before we go I want you to get in touch with all your contacts in the other towns."

"When will we be leaving, sir?" Kadrovich asked.

"As soon as Provencetown is ready to sail. Get a few of your best men and equipment ready as soon as possible."

"Yes, sir. I'll get the usual group, sir. Right away, sir."

"And try not to attract too much attention."

"Very good sir. Anything else, sir?"

"Yes. Check around town and see if there has been an increase in violence lately."

"Yes, sir."

"Dismissed," Gurney took a swallow of his tea as Kadrovich turned and left the office.

"Sir, the Provencetown will be ready to sail tomorrow," Kirby told Gurney.

"Good," Gurney replied. "I want to get aboard as soon as possible."

"Anything special we need to take?" Kirby asked.

"We?" Gurney answered.

"I'm not going?" Kirby questioned him.

"No. This isn't an official visit of any kind. Just pack me the usual traveling gear. Nothing special. Besides, someone needs to mind the store while I'm gone."

"Yes, sir. I'll have it taken aboard as quickly as I can."

Gurney was on board the Provencetown before dawn.

Captain Walker showed him to his cabin. "I'm sure you'll like this, sir."

"Thank you, Captain. I'm sure it'll do fine," If it hadn't been for the motion of the ship it would have been hard for Gurney to tell he was on a ship and not in an apartment in Lthrtown.

"We'll be in Labrys tomorrow afternoon. If you need anything be sure and let me know."

"Thank you, Captain," Gurney replied as Kadrovich came in through the open door.

Walker left. He knew he had been dismissed, even without Gurney saying so.

"Hello," Troy said as he entered Gurney's outer office.

"Troy," Kirby replied as he looked up from the papers on his desk. "What can I do for you?"

"I have my proposal for Managing Director Gurney. Is he available?" he asked.

"He sailed on the Provencetown this morning," Kirby leaned back in his chair.

"He didn't mention anything to me the other night," Troy sat down in the chair in front of Kirby's desk.

"Somehow, I'm not surprised," Kirby replied. "Besides, it was kind of a last minute deal."

"What do you mean?" Troy was puzzled.

"I think it's time we had a little talk about Gurney," Kirby leaned forward in his chair.

"What about Gurney?" Troy asked.

"I'm sure you think you've got something going with him, don't you?" Kirby asked him.

"I think that's a pretty personal question. And not really any of your business," Troy replied.

"You're just the latest in a long line to share Gurney's bed."

"That's to be expected. He's an attractive and powerful man," Troy replied.

"But, you're hoping for more, aren't you?" Kirby asked.

"Well, sure," Troy replied.

"Gurney, thanks to his position and his, ah, physical attributes, has probably bedded the hottest men in town, both inside Nimbus and out. And, I'm sure a lot of them thought that something more meaningful would develop between Gurney and themselves."

"Well, yeah. I'd hope that would happen," Troy replied.

"I'm just telling you this for your own good. You're new here. You don't know how the system works," Troy walked around to the front of his desk and sat on the edge. "Or, how Gurney is."

"What exactly are you telling me then?" Troy questioned.

"If you're looking for a lover, forget it. Gurney isn't capable of it. I thought the same things you're thinking now. That we'd be a couple and run Nimbus for years, side by side."

"And what happened?" Troy asked him.

"I'm not sure. Somewhere along the way, before I really got to know him, someone hurt him, badly. I'm not sure who or when. But, I know he's hurting inside. It took him a long time to climb to the top. He had to fight for everything he's got today. Maybe that had something to do with it. I wish I knew."

"Did you ever ask him?"

"No. I'd never ask him. Sometimes he's hard to read. He seems to suppress his emotions when something isn't going right. He gets cold and unfeeling. When it comes to making a decision about Nimbus he decides what would be best for the largest number of members. But when you're in bed with him, he's completely different. If and when he wants to talk about it, he will. I'm content to share his bed once in a while. I enjoy being his assistant. At least I'm around him. Besides you're young enough to be his son."

"And you love him," Troy said. "Even knowing the way he is."

Kirby walked around his desk and sat down in his chair. "And, so do you," he paused, "even knowing what you know now."

The sun had risen into a cloudless sky. The morning fog was quickly burned off. It was replaced by a bright bowl of blue sky.

Gurney stood on the gently rolling deck of the Provincetown and watched the water birds. Gulls, ducks, geese, and swans, all passed by. When they had been closer to shore Gurney had seen cranes and egrets standing like statues in the shallow water.

"Sir," Kadrovich walked up to Gurney.

"Kadrovich, enjoying our little trip?"

"Well, sir, I'd rather be on dry land, I'm afraid."

"You'll get used to it," Gurney smiled.

"You like to sail, sir?"

"My instructor said I had a natural touch for it in smaller boats," Gurney replied. "The first time I took the tiller, I had the boat going faster than he had been able to get her to do."

"Really, sir," Kadrovich was impressed.

"Besides, all this fresh air is good for you. Helps me to sleep, makes me hungry and horny too!" Gurney laughed.

"Me too, sir," Kadrovich smiled. "I'm just not sure I'll be able to keep anything down."

Gurney laughed.

"I'm not kidding," Kadrovich grinned.

"Now, do you have any new information?" Gurney was all business again.

"The only thing I have is about a man named Rogers, from Icon, sir."

"Continue," Gurney said.

"He left for Cruiseville the night Salvetti was attacked. Never came back."

"But, as we both know, men leave Lthrtown all the time and never come back."

"The difference in this case is that he had a very good position at Icon. Everything was going well for him. He was well liked by many people."

"Is it possible he attacked Salvetti for some reason?" Gurney asked.

"Doubtful, sir, Doc is pretty sure whoever attacked Salvetti was a much bigger man. Rogers wasn't much bigger that Salvetti, if at all," Kadrovich replied.

"Well, keep at it, Kadrovich. Once we've gotten the information we need we'll see what if any of them have had similar reports. Somewhere there's got to be a connection between these attacks."

"Yes, sir," Kadrovich replied. "I'm sure you're right in that something strange is going on. There are always fights and the like, but usually they're around festival time."

"Well, we can work on it later. Let's go get some breakfast," Gurney said walking towards the stern of the ship.

"I'll try, sir," Kadrovich replied. "No guarantees it's going to stay in my stomach though."

Gurney laughed again.

Kadrovich laughed too. He was happy to hear Gurney laugh. It didn't seem to happen very often any more.

"What do you mean the Provincetown's gone?" Spencer hollered, knocking over his breakfast tray.

"She sailed this morning," Pike replied. "At dawn."

"Damn Gurney. He was on board wasn't he?" Spencer raged.

"We don't know that for sure," Pike replied.

"Well, damn it, find out!" Spencer said, throwing his breakfast in Pike's direction.

"Yes, sir," Pike replied. He quickly backed out of Spencer's bedroom. "Damn the man," He thought.

When the sun set the velvet black of the sky was splashed with bright stars. The only sounds were the muffled voices of the crew laughing below decks and the slap and splash of the Provincetown cutting through the water. The rigging creaked as the sails strained against the wind.

Gurney stood at the stern of the Provincetown. He could see the lights of Lthrtown receding across the water.

"Excuse me, sir."

"Yes, Captain Walker?" Gurney replied.

"I just thought I'd let you know we're making excellent time, sir. We'll be in Labrys sometime in the morning."

"Any problems with the Provincetown so far," Gurney asked.

"No, sir," Walker replied. "She's performing better than we expected."

Gurney could detect the pride in Walker's voice. "Very good, Captain."

"Have a good night, sir," Walker saluted Gurney.

"Thank you, Captain," Gurney replied.

Walker excused himself and went below.

Gurney walked to the bow of the ship. He could just make out the blur of light that he knew was Labrys. Tomorrow morning they would be there. He hoped they would find some answers to his questions.

"I have conformation that Gurney was on the Provincetown," Pike told Spencer.

"What the hell is he up to?" Spencer asked.

"I don't have any more information, I'm afraid," Pike replied.

"Is there anyway we can get a message to one of our agents before he gets there?"

"I'm afraid not, sir," Pike replied.

"Damn that man!" Spencer threw his glass against the wall. "What's he doing"?

Pike had no answer.

The Provincetown entered the harbor at Labrys in the middle of the morning, flags flying. The Nimbus flag hung at the stern. Gurney's red and yellow pennant hung from the main mast. Rainbow bunting hung the length of the Provincetown's hull, making her look quite festive.

"Looks like a good crowd on hand to welcome us, sir," Kadrovich said.

"It certainly looks that way," Gurney replied as he surveyed the town. Most of the buildings were two or three stories tall, the roofs nearly flat, just like in Lthrtown. A dome that was the highest structure in town topped the largest building.

Captain Walker said to Gurney, "Sir, we'll have to take a small boat to the dock. There isn't enough room for the Provincetown."

"Very well, Captain," Gurney replied. "Whenever you're ready."

A few minutes later a small boat was lowered over the side. Walker and a few crewmen steadied the boat as Gurney and his escort climbed down the ladder.

With a strong stroke they were soon pulling up to the wharf.

The crowd was, as Gurney expected, all women. They warily eyed the men as the boat approached the dock.

Gurney searched the crowd, looking for a familiar face.

"GURNEY!" someone called.

Gurney saw her as the woman waved at him. "M'Lena!"

"Throw me the rope," she said.

The crewman in the bow of the boat threw her the line, which she caught and fastened to the dock.

Kadrovich climbed up the ladder first.

The women backed up to give Gurney and the others room as they joined Kadrovich on the dock.

"Gurney," M'Lena called. "It's good to see you!"

Kadrovich was pushed out of the way as the black woman grabbed Gurney in a bear hug.

"Sister," Gurney replied, "It's good to see you, too!"

"What's going on? Why are you here?" She asked.

"All in good time, sister," he replied.

Kadrovich looked at the rest of Gurney's escort and shrugged. He had no idea who this bald headed woman was. But, obviously Gurney did.

Most of the crowd had already begun to drift away.

"You'll stay with me, of course," M'Lena said. "Your men are also welcome to stay."

"There are too many of us," Gurney replied. "Of course the crewmen can return to the ship."

"Great!" M'Lena took Gurney's arm and they headed off through the maze of alleyways and streets.

Kadrovich and the others got the gear from the boat and hurried to follow. They didn't want to be left behind it a strange town full of women.

"So, what are you doing here?" M'Lena asked again when they had reached her house, which was on a quiet side street.

"I just wanted to go on the shakedown cruise of the Provincetown," Gurney replied, looking at her over the rim of his mug of herbal tea.

"Liar," she snorted. "I know something has to be going on for you to be here."

Kadrovich gasped. He waited for Gurney's reply. How could he let a woman talk to him that way?

"I need your help, sister," Gurney finally said.

"You know I'll help you in any way I can," she replied.

"Actually, I'll let Kadrovich explain what's happening," Gurney said. He laughed inwardly at Kadrovich's obvious discomfort at having to explain something to a woman.

M'Lena listened in silence as Kadrovich told her about the incidents in Lthrtown.

"How can I help you?" she finally asked.

"I'd like you to make some discreet inquiries and see if anything similar has been reported here," Gurney told her. "I'm looking to see if there is a pattern to any of this."

"No problem," M'Lena replied. "But it will take a couple of days to get the information."

"I guess we can wait a couple of days," Gurney said. He noticed that Kadrovich and the others looked a little uncomfortable.

"Perhaps your men would like to rest?" M'Lena asked. She could see how nervous Kadrovich and the others were, too.

"I think that would be a good idea," Gurney answered.

"This way, gentlemen," M'Lena led the group down the hall to a room that overlooked a courtyard garden.

"Thank you," Kadrovich said.

"Don't worry. I'll keep an eye on Gurney," she told him. "You boys get some rest."

Kadrovich nodded. "Thank you."

M'Lena returned to the large, yet cozy, kitchen where Gurney waited patiently.

"Kadrovich seemed to be a little jumpy," she told Gurney.

"Well, they don't spend much time around women you know," Gurney replied, "I guess they're not sure what to expect. And, most of them haven't been to Breederstown to do their duty."

M'Lena refilled Gurney's mug.

"Besides, they tend to be a little overprotective. This little trip might do them some good," Gurney told her.

"Well, now to your problem," M'Lena said. She led Gurney to her study. "It'll take a couple of days to get you the information you want. I can also get in touch with my contacts in Breederstown and Chiffon. That might save you some time."

"I could use a rest," Gurney told her.

"Things are rough?" she asked, sitting down in an overstuffed chair that overlooked the courtyard.

"Except for these two attacks, nothing unusual," he replied.

"Just the two?" she questioned him.

"There's someone from Icon missing, but that kind of thing happens all the time. Somebody gets pissed off about something and takes off."

"Oh?" M'Lena picked up the teapot.

Gurney shook his head no. "Kadrovich doesn't think that's what happened with the missing man though."

"Why's that?" she poured herself another mug.

"Good position, popular, well liked," he said.

"A rival doing him in maybe?"

"Well, if that's the case it would be the first time I can remember that happening," he told her.

"I don't mean to doubt you, but that seems hard to believe. I know how some men can be, violent, crude, and greedy."

"And, of course, women aren't like that," he replied. He drained his mug.

"Ah, well. I didn't say that. You did," M'Lena grinned.

"Oh, please," Gurney groaned.

"Let me get going on the info you want and then we can take a walk around town," she told him.

"If you look down this street you can see the Shrine of the Goddess. When it's done we plan to cover it with gold leaf," M'Lena said proudly. "It'll be the tallest building in Labrys."

Gurney didn't have the heart to tell her the Shrine of the Rock in Lthrtown was ten stories tall.

"Excuse me for a moment," M'Lena said, "Nature calls."

Gurney wandered down the street, looking in the windows of the shops. He stopped in front of one that sold religious items. Foot tall statues of the Goddess in her various manifestations filled the window. One was in black leather wearing a mask and holding a whip. Another was clothed in black lace and had blond hair. Still another was in a bright pink dress with sparkling gems around the wrists and neck. There were so many different statues Gurney couldn't make them all out.

Someone bumped into Gurney as he stood in front of the window. "Watch it, buddy."

"Huh? I wasn't moving," Gurney said, turning to confront the person who had bumped him. The street wasn't crowded. Very few women seemed to be out early.

"Says you," the woman snarled at Gurney. She was at least six inches taller than he was and outweighed him by thirty pounds or more.

"Sorry," he replied. The last thing he wanted was a scene.

"Hey! You're that Gurney guy aren't you? From across the lake?"

"Yes, I am," he replied.

"If I were you, I'd get back there," she said. "Things aren't safe for you here."

"What do you mean?" Gurney asked.

"Just take my advice and get back home," And with that she turned and stomped down the street, disappearing down a side alley.

"Well, are you keeping out of trouble?" M'Lena asked, suddenly reappearing.

"I'm not sure," Gurney replied. He related the incident to her.

"Sounds like a nut to me," she replied, "Of course, we do have some real man haters here. But, they usually travel in packs. Even during the day."

"She was big enough to be her own pack," Gurney replied. "She could have been an agent for Spencer, too."

"Well, that's always a possibility," M'Lena laughed. "Let's get some lunch."

They walked down the street towards the center of town.

Gurney could hear the noise level rise as they made their way through the twisting streets.

"Feel like doing some shopping?" M'Lena asked.

"You know me too well, sister," Gurney replied.

They made another turn and were hit by a wall of sound as they entered the central market.

Strange smells and sounds assaulted Gurney's senses. The merchants called out their wares trying to attract buyers. The buyers either accepted the price or argued with the seller. Street entertainers did their thing. Women were dressed in various costumes; from being almost completely covered to bare breasted. Gurney had had some dealings with some of the women before and he wasn't uncomfortable around them like Kadrovich and his other men were.

M'Lena was always close by in case there was a problem. But, there were no incidents.

"Are you shopped out yet, brother?" M'Lena asked Gurney as they stood in a café having a mug of green tea and a chicken sandwich.

"I think I made a few good deals, sister," Gurney replied. "But, I guess I'm ready to get out of here."

"Dinner awaits," M'Lena said, linking arms with Gurney.

"I've already got some info for you," M'Lena told Gurney the next afternoon.

"Already?"

"It seems there were a number of assaults south of town a couple of weeks ago. No permanent damage," she scanned the paper.

"That's it? No idea who did it?" Gurney asked.

"No," she replied, "Like the attacks in Lthrtown they were from behind."

"That's it?"

"So far. Be patient. It'll take a couple of days for all my contacts to get back to me," she told him. "Have some tea."

"I think I'll send the Provincetown on her way," Gurney said. "We can go back on one of the other ships later."

"Do you want me to send them the message for you?" she asked.

"No. I'll have Kadrovich send someone," he replied.

"I'm not sure I like the idea of leaving Gurney here," Walker told Bruno.

"Nevertheless, those are his orders," Bruno said. "You're expected to obey them."

"Very well," Walker replied. "I guess we'll see you back in Lthrtown."

"Given the short time frame, I've gotten as much as information for you as I can for Labrys and Breederstown," M'Lena said.

"So now all we need is the info from Chiffon," he said.

"Right. We'll probably have it tomorrow," M'Lena answered.

The next afternoon Gurney joined M'Lena in her study.

"I've plotted all the incidents on the map," she said. She waved her hand and a map was projected into the air over her desk. "As you can see they start from south of Labrys and follow a path around the lake towards Lthrtown. The red spots are definite contacts. The yellows are probable contacts. There are more than I expected."

"We don't know if anything has happened in Cruiseville, though," Gurney said.

"I'll bet there have been. Probably unreported, too," M'Lena replied. "Knowing what kind of area it is anyway."

"But, since no one lives in Cruiseville it's going to be hard to track," Gurney countered. "Lots of men go there. Finding someone who's willing to report being assaulted might be impossible to locate."

"And the area is too big for a complete ground search," M'Lena said.

"Right. It's a few square miles," Gurney said. "Unless,"

"Unless what?" she asked.

"I'm thinking that if someone was assaulted there, it would be in a fairly high traffic area."

"Why's that?" M'Lena asked.

"Because even though there's a large area available, most of the activity is pretty much concentrated in a few areas," Gurney said, pointing at a few areas on the map. He spun the map so Cruiseville was in front of him.   "Here, here and here, along the main trail."

"Well then I'd say to concentrate your search in those areas," M'Lena refilled their mugs.

"Sound's like a plan," Gurney took a swallow from his mug.

There was a knock at the door. M'Lena waved her hand and the map disap-peared.

"Come in," she called.

"Sir," Kadrovich said, "Sorry to interrupt, but you said to let you know when a ship would be docking."

"Someone's here already?" Gurney asked.

"The San Francisco will be arriving from Breederstown around sunset, leav-ing for Lthrtown some time tomorrow."

"Very well. When she docks contact the Captain and tell him we'll need pas-sage to Lthrtown."

"Yes, sir," Kadrovich said.

"As I said before, your men are well trained," M'Lena told Gurney, after Kadrovich left.

"Sometimes too well. What will they do if something happens to me?   I can't always be there to make all the decisions for them," Gurney sat down heavily into the chair in front of the desk.

"I'm sure they'll be OK," she replied. "I don't think you really have to worry about them."

"You're probably right," he replied.

Gurney awoke with a start. The sheets were drenched with his sweat. He'd had the dream again. Except for him, it wasn't a dream. It was the past come back to haunt him. He went into the bathroom and splashed some water on his face.

"Gurney?" he heard M'Lena call softly.

"Just a minute," he replied, slipping into his robe.

"You had the dream again," she said, after he let her into his room.

"Yes," he nodded.

"Do you think," she didn't finish.

"That's what I'm beginning to think," He replied, "Someone from the

Outlands."

"But who and why?" M'Lena asked.

"I'm not sure I want to know," Gurney replied.

"Neither am I," M'Lena told him. "But, this could be a threat to everything you've built."

They sat in the dim light, silently regarding each other.

The following morning Gurney, Kadrovich, Bruno and the others stood at the end of the gangplank with M'Lena.

"If I get any new information I'll get it to you as soon as possible," M'Lena told Gurney.

"We'll check out Cruiseville when we get back," Gurney replied.

"Have a safe trip," M'Lena said.

"Ready to go, sir," Kadrovich asked.

"Go ahead Kadrovich," Gurney said, "I'll be right behind you."

"Yes, sir," Kadrovich answered. He motioned to the other men and they began to board the San Francisco.

"Be careful, sister."

"You too, brother," They hugged.

"We'll be in touch," Gurney turned and went aboard.

"Welcome aboard, sir," Captain Kelso greeted Gurney.

"Thank you, Captain," Gurney replied.

"I'll have someone show you to your cabin," Kelso said.

"When will we be back in Lthrtown?" Gurney asked.

"Before sunset," Kelso replied.

"Then I'll have no need for a cabin. I'll stay on deck with the men," Gurney said.

"Very well, sir. If you'll excuse me I'll get us underway," Kelso replied.

"Certainly, Captain."

Ten minutes later the San Francisco had cleared the harbor entrance and set off across the lake to Lthrtown.

Gurney stood at the stern of the ship watching Labrys slowly disappear into the hazy distance. He could just see the entrance to the River Styx to the east. The Outlands lay beyond, farther east. Gurney knew that it was a land of wonders and terrors. He had experienced both.

The land was hard and barren. There wasn't even a hint of a breeze. Scrub brush and stunted trees dominated Gurney's field of vision as he stood on the crest of the hill. He took a sip from his canteen. He had to find water soon. "I must be nuts," he thought. "Coming out here alone, what am I trying to prove anyway?" Sunlight reflected off something in the distance. "I might as well check it out. Things certainly can't get any worse than they already are."

The scrub and trees gave way to a landscape strewn with boulders of every size, shape and color. Gurney saw no signs of life. The still air was oppressive. Nothing moved except for Gurney as he tried to find the source of the reflection.

The sun began to slide towards the horizon. Gurney found a small cave in the rocks. He took just enough water to moisten his mouth. He was almost out. He knew it was going to be a rough night.

The rocks didn't stay warm long. The heat vanished almost as fast as the sun. Gurney huddled in the cave. He shivered inside his sleeping bag. He only slept a few minutes at a time. The shaking of his own body would awaken him.

The next morning the sun quickly heated the rocks as it climbed through a cloudless sky, just like it had the day before. Gurney's water was now all but gone.

He began to wander aimlessly, the strange reflection all but forgotten.

The sun baked the already scorched landscape. Somewhere along the way Gurney had lost his hat and most of his equipment.

He fell down and didn't get up. He expected he would be dead soon, but he was beyond caring.

Gurney awoke with a start. There was a cool compress on his forehead.

"Ah," a black woman's face appeared in his line of vision, "Good. You're awake. Feeling better?" She held up his head with one hand as she gave him some water.

He choked as he tried to swallow.

"Easy. Easy," she told him. "You'll be OK. Just take it easy."

Gurney tried to talk but no sound came out.

"Try a little more," she urged him.

Gurney took another swallow. It was better.

"Get some rest. I'll be right here," the woman said.

Gurney slept.

"Where, where am I?" Gurney croaked.

"You're in the middle of nowhere, my friend," was the reply.

Gurney groaned. "Is this hell? Am I dead?"

"Oh, no, you're very much alive. Of course, if I hadn't happened along when I did, you would be dead."

"What happened?" Gurney asked.

"I found you in the middle of the Outlands."

"You rescued me?" he asked.

"Well, I certainly couldn't let you die could I? Even if you are a man," the woman grinned.

Gurney struggled to sit up without much success.

"You're still very weak," the woman said, pushing him back down.

"How long has it been?" he asked.

"A couple of days," she replied, suddenly appearing in his field of vision.

"I'm Gurney."

"My name is M'Lena," she told him as she replaced the compress with another.

"Thank you, M'Lena."

"You're welcome, Gurney."

"I got lost. I came exploring. I was running low on water when I saw a reflection. I tried to find it, hoping it might be something useful. But, I couldn't find it."

"Well, you're safe now," M'Lena gave him something more to drink.
Gurney slept again.

"How long has it been?" Gurney asked M'Lena as she stoked the fire.
"A few days now," she replied. "Time doesn't seem to have much meaning out here."
"I know. Nothing seems to change," Gurney sat up. He was quite a bit stronger thanks to M'lena's efforts.
"The sky, the ground, not a sign of another living thing," M'Lena said.
"You haven't told me what you're doing out here," Gurney said.
"Same as you are/ exploring and Trying to find something useful or valuable."
"I'm not sure I'd know something useful if it jumped up and bit me on the ass," Gurney told her.
M'Lena laughed, "I know what you mean!"
"I wonder what it is about a fire that's so comforting," Gurney said as he moved closer to the blaze.
"It keeps the demons at bay," M'Lena replied.
They sat and watched the flames together.
"I think I'll be strong enough to travel tomorrow. That is if you want to stick together," Gurney looked at M'Lena on the other side of the fire.
"Yes. I think it's time to move on," she replied. "Besides, we have things to discover."

"Sir? Excuse me."
"What? Oh, Kadrovich. What is it?" Gurney was back on the deck of the San Francisco.
"Are you all right, sir?" Kadrovich looked concerned.
"I was just thinking about something. Something that happened a long time ago."
"Sir, the Captain sends his compliments and would like you to join him for lunch."
"Tell him I'd be happy to, Kadrovich," Gurney took a last look in the direction of Labrys and went below to freshen up.

"Take your men and return to the compound," Gurney told Kadrovich. "I'll be there shortly."
"Yes, sir," Kadrovich replied. "Should I notify Kirby we've returned?"
"No!" Gurney snapped, momentarily irritated. "He'll know as soon as he sees you."
"Of course, sir," Kadrovich turned and signaled the men to go down the gang-plank. He could tell by Gurney's tone of voice that he had asked the wrong question at the wrong time.
"Kadrovich," Gurney said, softly.
"Sir?" Kadrovich turned back to face Gurney.
"It's all right," Gurney reached up and squeezed the younger man's hard

biceps. "You didn't do anything. It's me."

"Yes, sir. Thank you, sir."

"It's been an unsettling trip. Things didn't go exactly like I'd hoped they would. But, everything will be alright," Gurney looked him in the eye.

"Yes, sir," Kadrovich smiled.

"Now, Get going," Gurney slapped the younger man's shoulder.

Kadrovich hurried after the rest of the men.

"Where's Gurney?" Kirby asked Kadrovich.

"He didn't tell me where he was going. I assumed he would be following us back," he replied.

"That man can be so infuriating," Kirby said.

Kadrovich said nothing.

"It's been a couple of hours."

"Yes, sir."

Gurney walked along the shore of the lake. The wind was cool. Waves slapped against the seawall. Gulls wheeled and cried out overhead.

He continued to follow the lakeshore past the edge of town onto the beach. There was a headland ahead that marked the eastern edge of Cruiseville.

He stood and watched the sun go down. The sky was full of reds and yellows and oranges that slowly faded into purples and blues. As the sun slowly vanished the stars came out in a blinding array of light and color.

"It's better if we travel at night," M'Lena told him.

"You're right," Gurney replied, as they stood on the crest of a ridge.

"Let's see how far we can get before sunrise," They set off across the tortured landscape.

"Do you think we'll really find anything out there?" Gurney asked, after they had walked awhile.

"I hope so. Otherwise we're certainly wasting our time, aren't we? But, I suppose it depends on what you're looking for. Who's to say?"

They walked on in silence.

"Still no word?" Troy asked Kirby.

"Not a thing. It's not like him to go off on his own like this," Kirby replied. They sat in Kirby's office. A hot pot of herbal tea steamed between them.

"What did Kadrovich say?"

"Nothing, He thought Gurney was following them back to the compound."

"Do you think something happened to him in Labrys that might have affected him?" Troy waved off Kirby's offer of another cup of tea.

"It's hard to say," Kirby shrugged.

"Well, I'm going to try and get some sleep. Will you let me know if anything happens?" Troy said, standing to go.

"Sure. I'll let you know," Kirby offered his hand to Troy. "He'll turn up."

Troy wordlessly shook Kirby's hand and walked out of the office.

Kirby sat back and waited. Gurney's link was either out of commission or he wouldn't answer.

"This looks like a cave entrance," M'Lena said to Gurney.

"Well it certainly looks too even to be natural," he replied as he ran his hands over the stone.

"What do you think?" M'Lena asked.

"It's worth checking out," he replied.

They walked a few yards into the cave.

Gurney knelt down and examined the floor of the cave. "I'd say this is worked stone, too."

"This may be the mother lode." M'Lena said. "Pardon the expression."

Gurney laughed at her joke.

They continued on into the depths of the cave in silence.

"I think I see light," M'Lena said.

"At the end of the tunnel?" Gurney answered, dryly.

"Smart ass," M'Lena took a swing at him playfully.

"Thank you," Gurney dodged out of the way.

The cave quickly opened up into a cavern that, once again, Gurney declared was not natural. "I think you're right. We may be on to something here."

"I just noticed something," M'Lena said.

"No bats?"

"No bats. I wonder why?"

"It could be that they're up farther than we can see," Gurney finally replied. "Or, there just aren't any. We really don't know a lot about the ecosystem out here."

"Pretty big word for somebody so young to be using," M'Lena said as they continued to cross the floor of the cavern.

"I read a lot," Gurney replied.

"When we're done here, you'll have to come with me to Labrys. We have a nice library."

"I didn't think I would be welcome there," Gurney said.

"Despite what you may have heard, not all women hate men. I certainly don't. If I did, you'd be dead.".

"Have I thanked you for saving my life?" he asked her.

"A few times," she smiled.

"Sir," Kadrovich shook Kirby's shoulder.

"What is it?" Kirby had fallen asleep at his desk. The pot of tea was ice cold.

"Managing Director Gurney still isn't back. I've had my men looking all over town."

"Then I suggest you start looking outside of town. How about Cruiseville," Kirby asked, rousing himself.

"Now that you mention it, I remember hearing him say something about Cruiseville to M'Lena when we were leaving Labrys."

"Did he say anything else about it?" Kirby asked, as he headed for the door.

"Not that I heard." Kadrovich replied.

"Get your best men and met me at the compound gates in five minutes. I have to tell Troy what's happening."

Kadrovich hurried along the gallery and down the main staircase. The early morning sun was already streaming through the stained and cut glass windows into the great hall. He trotted across the parquet floor and out the doors.

Kirby knocked on Troy's door. He was shocked by Troy's appearance. He looked as though he had slept in his clothes and he needed a shave. "Are you alright?"

"I've been up most of the night," Troy replied.

"Well, pull yourself together. We're going to Cruiseville." Kirby grabbed Troy's arm.

"Isn't it a little early for that sort of thing?" Troy resisted Kirby's pull.

"Kadrovich thinks Gurney may have gone there."

"But, why," Troy asked, finally beginning to move.

"Something he overheard Gurney say to M'Lena about going there," Kirby led Troy down the stairs.

"Who's M'Lena?" Troy asked.

"Our agent in Labrys," Kirby replied. "She's an old friend of Gurney's."

Kadrovich, Bruno, Schmidt and Griffith were at the main gate. Bruno and Schmidt held reins to the horses.

"I figured we could make better time and cover more ground on horseback," Kadrovich explained.

"Good man," Kirby said, climbing into the saddle. "Let's ride."

Gurney stood facing the east. His hat was pulled down low over his eyes. The brisk morning wind off of the lake made the thick hair on his arms stand up. As the sun began to rise over the Russian River the sky seemed to shimmer and the rings became visible for a moment. The multicolored bands were clearly visible.

But, just as quickly, the sun overpowered them and the rings disappeared again.

He was disappointed. During some parts of the year the rings were visible every night. He never tired of looking at them and the night sky. The world was so full of wonders he knew he would never see with his own eyes. There was so much he wanted to see and do. Somehow he felt he never would. Somehow he felt his time was short. Would anyone remember? Or, would they care that he had been there at all? Gurney hoped so. It seemed to him that he had fought all his life. Always tried to do the right thing. Was there no rest for him anywhere? No end to the struggle?

"LET HIM GO!" shouted M'Lena.

The group of hooded men silently looked at her.

Gurney struggled in the grip of two very tall men. Their muscles strained to hold him still.

"Do not damage him," someone said.

"What do you want?" Gurney asked. His arms ached as he tried to break free of his captors.

"Bring them," the same voice said. Gurney and M'Lena were dragged further into the cavern.

Gurney stopped struggling and let them carry him along. It was obvious they were not going to get away very easily, if at all.

Finally they entered another smaller cavern. The group stood as if awaiting orders.

"Put him on the table." Gurney was strapped face down on a cold metal table.

"What do you want from me?" Gurney asked as the table rotated into a more upright position.

"Very little," the voice replied. One of the giants began to cut Gurney's pants off him.

Gurney looked behind him. The sight he saw horrified him. The giants all stood ready and waiting. "NO. NO!" Gurney yelled.

The closest advanced.

A cloth was shoved into Gurney's face and his world exploded into a confusion of colors and flashing lights. Then, everything went black.

"Everything's OK now," M'Lena said as she whipped the sweat off of Gurney's face.

"What, what happened? What did they do to me?" he moaned.

"They took some tissue samples," she replied.

"That's it?" he was incredulous.

"Apparently."

"I thought they were going to gang rape me. I've never seen anything so big."

"Well, you were probed but by something quite a bit smaller." M'Lena sat back.

"Where are we now?" Gurney looked around the spartan, but clean, room they were in.

"I'm not sure. But, they gave us food and water. They never touched me."

"I can't remember the last time I had a decent meal," Gurney said, sitting up.

"Let's eat then," A small table in the corner had fruit, cold meat and water.

"What do you think this place is?" Gurney asked.

"I have no idea. I've never heard of anything like this before." M'Lena replied.

"It seemed to me that they all looked alike. At least what little I saw of them." Gurney continued to eat.

"You're right, now that you mention it. I didn't really look that closely but even the body hair patterns seemed to be the same." M'Lena drank some water from her mug.

"You're quite right." It was the voice they had heard earlier.

Gurney and M'Lena looked around. They were alone.

"Who are you and where are we?" Gurney asked.

"That is not important," was the reply. "Your arrival was foretold by legend."

"By legend," Gurney asked.

"Legend says that a young man would come out of the desert to deliver rejuvenation to us."

"But, how," M'Lena asked.

"By supplying us with new genetic material you have saved us."

"I don't understand," M'Lena said.

"I think I do," Gurney said.

"Your descendants will live long lives and provide us with new energy and a continuation of our society."

"But, we've seen no women," Gurney said. He had an idea what the answer would be.

"We have no need of women."

"Clones," Gurney said. "Genetic copies."

"You will live forever," the voice said.

"What about us?" Gurney asked.

"You may stay or you may go. If you stay you will have the best of everything that we can offer you."

"And if we go?"

"If you go, you pass into legend. We will provide you with provisions and directions out of the desert."

"I want more than that," Gurney said.

"Ask, and it is yours."

"We have heard there are places of great wealth in the desert. I want a map showing locations of those places."

"You shall have it, then. They are of no use to us."

Gurney stood on the side of the road watching the group of horsemen approach. He waved his hat at them.

When they saw him they hollered and rushed to him. They were all flushed and excited at finally finding him.

"Are you alright, Gurney?" Kirby asked, resisting the urge to hug him.

"I'm fine. I just needed some time to think," Gurney replied, smiling, but Kirby and Troy could see the pain in his eyes.

"We've all been so worried," Troy said.

"We certainly were, sir," Kadrovich said, grinning broadly, as were Bruno, Schmidt and Griffith.

"It was just a spur of the moment thing. I'm sorry I didn't tell you. I certainly appreciate your concern in any case," Gurney felt his mental control slipping.

"Did you find what you were looking for?" Kirby asked.

"Unfortunately, I did. Follow me," Gurney led them down a trail to a small pond.

A man's body floated face down in the stagnate water.

"Rogers?" Kadrovich asked.

"I think so. Check the area for clues. And have someone take the body to MedCenter." Gurney was all business again.

"Yes, sir," Kadrovich replied.

"Don't notify anyone at Icon until Doc has done an autopsy," Gurney instructed.

"Yes, sir, I understand, sir," Kadrovich replied.

"It's possible it might have been an accident. There have been enough problems lately. No reason to start any more rumors," Gurney said.

Gurney, Kirby and Troy watched as Kadrovich and the others pulled the body from the water.

Hot water ran down Gurney's back as he stood under the shower. He was tired and needed to get some rest. He felt drained emotionally and physically. When he got out of the shower and walked into his bedroom he saw that Kirby had brought him some cold chicken and hot tea. He ignored the chicken and drank the tea. He knew it would be the special, sleep-inducing, blend of Kirby's own making.

Gurney walked out onto the verandah. Across the lake he could see the faint lights of Labrys.

He returned to the bedroom and crawled between the fresh, clean, cotton sheets. They felt good against his skin. He was soon asleep.

"Are you sure we shouldn't see if he needs anything?" Troy asked Kirby. "What about Doc's report? Won't he want to know about that?"

"I'm pretty sure he already knows the results. And, I took some chicken and tea to his room. He was in the shower," Kirby replied. "He'll probably skip the chicken, drink the tea and go to bed."

"How do you know that?" Kirby quizzed him.

"Please, I haven't been with him this long to not know how he'll react in certain situations," Kirby answered. "When he's had a very stressful situation that's what he does."

"Well, OK," Troy said. "I guess I'll get to bed then."

"Yeah, I'll be going to bed soon, too. We all need some rest," Kirby answered.

Gurney was almost home. He had gone on a solo expedition to the Outlands and had made a good haul. He was eager to get back and show his partner, Spencer, what he had found. He was making a good living as an independent trader. Everything was going well. He was even coming back a day early.

The small business that housed the store was dark. The flat above the store where they lived only had one light on.

He took the packhorses to the barn and quickly unloaded them.

Then, he hurried to get inside the other building. It looked like it might rain.

Gurney hurried up the stairs two at a time. He was happy to be back home. He was crazy about Spencer and was sure they'd be together for a long time to come. Their commitment ceremony was coming up soon.

When he opened the door the flat was quiet and dark. "Spencer must already be in bed," Gurney thought.

As Gurney approached the bedroom door he heard the faint but unmistakable sounds of people talking. He threw open the door. Spencer lay in bed with another man. The sheets were pulled up to their waists.

"Gurney! Wha, what are you doing home?" Spencer blurted out.

"Get out! Both of you," Gurney rasped. He felt like he was going to be sick.

"But," Spencer began.

"I'm not interested in anything you have to say. Just get the hell out of my home," Gurney's face was pale under his beard.

"But, Gurney," Spencer began to plead.

"Get OUT! NOW!" Gurney was livid. His ears burned a sure sign that he was furious. He couldn't remember ever being so angry. "I don't ever want to see you again!"

Spencer and the stranger quickly scrambled into their clothes.

"Gurney, Please," Spencer pleaded.

Gurney turned his back on them, stared out the window and said nothing.

A few minutes later he heard the door close. He turned and looked at the rumpled bed. He sat on the edge of the bed and covered his face with his hands as he began to sob. Tears ran down his cheeks into his beard.

The next morning Gurney threw all of Spencer's personal things on the sidewalk. He saw Spencer in town, but he'd heard he was working for one of the collectives. They kept clear of each other.

Gurney dedicated all his time between developing his body and mind and building Nimbus into a successful business. Soon, he had a steady line of men ready and willing to share his bed or work for him. He used them and they used him. Everyone got what he wanted.

It took months, but he eventually got over Spencer's betrayal. Or at least that's what he told himself. He didn't think he could ever love anyone again. He locked his feelings away and became distant, cold and unfeeling. He built up as many barriers as he could around his heart. He didn't want to go through the pain he had felt again. He kept everyone at arms length, even the men he slept with and his close business associates. It was years before he was willing to even take a chance at loving someone again. Now he was afraid it was too late. He certainly wasn't getting any younger.

Gurney met Kirby and the rest of his staff for breakfast. Gurney preferred the more casual meetings they had then. The others were often more relaxed and candid.

"There is nothing out of the ordinary to report," Kirby told Gurney. "Profit levels are good. We've had no problems of any kind."

"Security is maintaining an around the clock guard. Nothing unusual has been reported, sir," Kadrovich reported.

"Good to hear," Gurney said. He felt like he hadn't had a decent meal in a week. He tried not to shovel his scrambled eggs into his mouth.

"The only thing coming up is High Leather Night," Kirby said. "You'll need a new outfit."

"See me later. We'll discuss it," Gurney answered.

"Yes, sir," Kirby said.

"Troy, have you written up your program for me?" Gurney asked.

"Yes, sir. I did. It's on your desk, sir," Troy replied.

"Come by my office for lunch and I'll go over it with you," Gurney pushed his chair back from the table, stood up and walked out of the room.

Troy looked at Kirby and Kadrovich. "Are you sure he's alright?"

"He's in one of his moods," Kirby told him.

Kadrovich nodded his head in agreement.

"How often does this happen?" Troy asked.

"No telling," Kirby replied. "There's no pattern."

Troy shook his head.

"You'll get used to it," Kirby grinned.

Gurney sat at his desk and looked at Troy's proposal. He made a few notes and set the papers aside.

Nimbus owned a piece of land that Gurney wanted the theater to be built on. He had already had some preliminary plans drawn up. He'd show them to Troy and get his input.

Gurney sat back in his chair and closed his eyes. Ideas and random thoughts swirled in his brain. He wished there was some way to turn them off.

"Maybe I'll go out tonight," he thought, "I haven't been out on the town in weeks."

He opened his eyes when he heard a noise.

"You said to come for lunch?" Troy said.

"It's lunch time?" Gurney replied.

"Uh, yes, it is, sir," Troy said.

"I guess I must have dozed off," Gurney replied sheepishly.

"Are you feeling alright?"

"Yes. Yes, I'm fine. I guess this trip and then finding Rogers body has been a bit much," Gurney said.

"Maybe you need to rest for a few days. Go out on the town or something," Troy suggested.

"I think you're right," Gurney said. "I've made a few suggestions on your notes," he said, changing the subject.

"Hmm," Troy looked at the papers Gurney handed him. "Looks OK to me."

"And, here are some plans I had drawn up. Take a look and let me know what you think," Gurney told him, "They can break ground in a few days."

"Is there someone I can see about having a model built?"

"Sure. Kirby can get someone to handle that."

"OK. I guess that's the next step then," Troy stood up. "Will I see you at dinner tonight?"

"Probably, I've been gone for a while. I guess I need to make an appearance," Gurney replied.

"What are you going to do the rest of the day then?"

"I guess I'll walk around town. Go see Parker at the recruiting office. Have some lunch."

"I remember our first lunch," Troy grinned.

"So do I," Gurney replied. "It seems like a long time ago."

"Gurney, Sir. I, I need to tell you something," Troy stammered.

"No. Please, Troy. Not now," Gurney stopped him.

"Yes, sir," Troy looked away. He was getting a little emotional.

"We'll have plenty of time to talk later," Gurney said, quietly.

"Yes, sir," Troy felt that he and Gurney were miles apart. He got up and headed for the door.

"Troy," Gurney said, "It's me. It's not you. Believe me."

"Yes, sir," Troy hurried past Kirby's desk and out onto the galleria.

"What was all that?" Kirby asked, coming into Gurney's office.

"It's nothing," Gurney replied. "Have the architect get in touch with Troy to discuss the plans for the theater."

"Yes, sir," Kirby knew better than to pry into Gurney's personal life, especially when he was in one of his moods.

Gurney walked down Market Street window-shopping. Kirby always saw to it that Gurney had everything he needed, but he felt he needed to buy something for himself, by himself. However, nothing really caught his eye. He decided to go to Como's for lunch.

"Good afternoon, sir. Your usual table?" the waiter asked.

"How about something on the sidewalk," Gurney said.

"Certainly, sir," The waiter led Gurney through the restaurant to the sidewalk dining area.

"Do you need a menu, sir?"

"A salad is all I want today," Gurney replied.

"Yes, sir," the waiter nodded and went back inside the restaurant.

Gurney's salad arrived quickly.

"You might as well come and join me, Schmidt," Gurney said, as he took a bite.

Schmidt approached Gurney's table a little sheepishly. "I guess I need to work on my surveillance skills, sir," He said.

"Well, my boy. You don't exactly blend into the scenery."

"No, sir, I guess not, sir," Schmidt replied. He stroked his close-cropped mustache.

"How old are you, Schmidt?" Gurney asked.

"Twenty-two, sir," he replied.

Gurney shook his head. "Do you know I'm old enough to be your father, Schmidt?"

"Yes, sir," Schmidt replied. He wasn't sure what Gurney was getting at, but he knew enough not to ask any questions.

"Do you like your position, Schmidt?"

"Yes, sir, it's a great honor to serve you. It's the goal of all Nimbus security men to be part of your personal guard."

"How are the men feeling? You can be honest with me, Schmidt," Gurney said.

"Everyone is concerned about recent events, sir. But, everyone I know is very loyal to you, sir. They would do anything you asked of them, sir," Schmidt looked Gurney in the eye.

"That's good to know," Gurney replied.

"Can I tell you something, sir?" Schmidt asked, looking down at the table.

"You can tell me anything you'd like," Gurney told him.

"Well, sir. A lot of us look up to you like a father. We all try and follow your example," Schmidt said. "We're all concerned about you."

Gurney reached over and patted Schmidt's shoulder. "Thing's will work out.   I've always believed in doing the things that will benefit the men and the collective the most. I always try and weigh the options. Even if it means doing something I don't like myself."

"Yes, sir, we all know that."

"Sometimes we have to make decisions that we don't particularly like. That's the way things are. All you can do is make what you hope is the right one."

"But, how do you know if it's the right decision, sir?" Schmidt asked.

"That's the hard part, son," Gurney told him. "You can never be one hundred percent sure."

"Yes, sir, I understand," Schmidt smiled.

"Be your own man. When you make a mistake don't be afraid to admit it. Always be willing to meet the other person halfway. Do you understand me, Schmidt?"

"Yes, sir, I understand. I'll do my best."

"Good. Now get out of here and let me eat in peace," Gurney returned Schmidt's smile.

"Yes, sir," Schmidt stood up and walked away, leaving Gurney to his private thoughts.

What little conversation there was at dinner seemed strained. Gurney had little to say. Troy sat to his left, Kirby to the right. They too, had little to say.

"Well, if you gentlemen will excuse me," Gurney pushed his chair back from the table. "I'll be in my office."

Everyone stood as Gurney did. He knew they were all watching him as he walked out of the room.

Troy looked at Kirby.

All Kirby did was shrug his shoulders.

Gurney decided it was time to visit the Shrine of the Rock. It had been too long since he had last been there.

He found all his leather and picked out his favorite pieces. He carefully dressed himself. He stood in front of the mirror and looked at his reflection. "I look tired," he thought. "Even to myself, I'm getting too old for this sort of thing. Maybe it's time to retire."

He slowly walked down the main staircase. His leather creaked. Even at this hour there was always someone up doing some kind of work. He wanted as small a number of the staff to know he was going out this late unguarded as possible.

The guards at the gate snapped to attention when he approached.

"Harrison, Lucas, you saw nothing. Do you understand me?" Gurney said.

"Yes, sir," they replied in unison.

"Good." Gurney walked out the gate and down the street.

The streets were deserted at this late hour. Even the bars were closed and deserted. Gurney saw no one as he walked. But, he could hear noises coming from some of the open windows he passed. Men together, making love the only way one man could love another.

The Dome of the Rock was well lighted on the outside. It was the tallest building in Lthrtown and visible from anywhere in town. The walkway was paved in glazed rainbow colored bricks. Rainbow flags hung slack in the still night air.

Gurney walked through the unlocked doors into the dimly lit interior. He wasn't sure who, if anyone, was on duty at this late hour.

He passed into the inner sanctum. A giant marble phallus, the life symbol, glowed in the lights that were suspended from the ceiling.

"Welcome, my son," he heard from behind him.

"Hello, Father," Gurney replied.

"Gurney, I haven't seen you in some time," Father William said.

"It has been a long time since I've been here," Gurney replied.

"I can tell something is bothering you, my son," Father William stroked his white beard.

"I guess it's just that I always wonder if I'm making a difference. Does anything I'm doing matter at all? Will anyone remember that I've been here?"

"I don't think you find the answers here, my son," Father William said. "Not praying to a big marble statue, anyway."

"I don't have anyone close that I can really talk to, Father. I've got a certain image to maintain. Always the man with the answers who knows how to handle anything that happens."

"And, you don't have them," Father William said.

"Of course not, No one does," Gurney replied.

"Well, I think there are only two places to find the answers you need, Gurney. Here and here," Father William pointed to his head and his heart. "Do what these tell you? You'll never go wrong."

"I'm just full of conflicting emotions," Gurney told him. "I want to be really close to someone special, but I'm so afraid of getting hurt again."

"Don't let the past rule the present. I know it's not easy but you have to let go," Father William took Gurney by the arm and led him back to the door. "You have to kiss a lot of frogs before you find the right man."

"I'm trying, Father, I really am," Gurney said.

"But, it's not easy, is it?"

"No, it's not. I'm really have a hard time. Even after all this time, I'm still bothered by Spencer's cheating on me."

"It wasn't your fault. Just remember that. It's been a long time. Try not to let the past run the future. If you're meant to be together perhaps, sometime, in the future you will be."

"I'll try, Father. I'll try," Gurney said.

"You have to do more than try, you have to do it." Father William said as they paused in front of the doors.

"Yes, Father," Gurney and Father William hugged.

"I'll see you soon, Gurney," Father William disappeared into the darkness.

Gurney slowly walked back to the Nimbus compound. Harrison and Lucas were still on duty as Gurney walked through the gates.

"We need to take a trip to Breederstown," Gurney told Kadrovich. "Would it be faster by water or on horseback?"

"If we take a smaller ship I guess we could be there faster that way, sir,"

Kadrovich replied. "I'll have to check and see who's in port right now."

"Let me know. I want to get started as soon as possible," Gurney told him.

"Yes, sir," Kadrovich replied. He went to the docks to check himself.

"You're going to Breederstown?" Kirby asked Gurney.

"Yes, I am," Gurney answered. "There are some things I want to check for myself. Besides, I haven't been there for a while."

"What about High Leather Night?" Kirby asked.

"I'll be back in time for that. I'll only be a day or two at the most" Gurney replied.

"Very good, sir."

The Somerville rushed across Crater Lake. Gurney sat comfortably in the open cockpit. Kadrovich hung on for dear life.

"I'll make a sailor of you yet, Kadrovich," Gurney laughed.

"Yes, sir," Kadrovich gulped.

Gurney laughed again. The fresh air and the water splashing against the Somerville's hull exhilarated him.

The Somerville was one of three small sailboats used for fast mail service. The other two, the Bronski and the Communard were also very quick and dedicated to fast mail and passenger service.

"When we land we'll go to the police station. I'm formulating a theory about these attacks, but I'm missing some information," Gurney said.

Kadrovich didn't answer. His head was over the railing as his stomach heaved again.

It was strange to Gurney, and especially Kadrovich, to see men and women on the streets together.

"Gurney," Police Chief Brown said, rising out of his chair. "I haven't seen you in a long time."

"It has been a while," Gurney replied.

"I hear you've been having some problems," he offered Gurney a chair.

"That's why we're here. I'm looking for some kind of connection. There have been a number of assaults here too, I understand," Gurney took the cup of hot tea Brown offered him.

"Very isolated cases. We just put them down to some kind of gang problem."

"Can I see the files?" Gurney asked, taking a sip from his cup.

"Certainly," Brown went out into the squad room. He came back a few minutes later. "If there's anything you'd like copies of, let me know."

"I'd appreciate it," Gurney replied. He quickly skimmed the papers.

"Find what you needed?" Brown asked.

"Yes, I did. Thanks for your help, Chief."

"Any time," Brown escorted Gurney to the front door.

"Well, Kadrovich, we can head back right away," Gurney said. Kadrovich had waited outside the police station.

"Sir, I think you had better take a look at this, sir," Kadrovich held out a piece of paper to Gurney. He had a strange look on his face.

"What is it?" Gurney took the paper. "Some drag queen disappeared? Of what interest is that to me"?

"She looks a little familiar to me, sir."

Gurney took a closer look at the picture. "It, it can't be."

"She disappeared right before Troy showed up in town, sir. I remember reading on the daily report that he had come through Cruiseville, sir. No identification. No money of any kind, sir"

Gurney was stunned. It certainly looked like Troy in the picture.

"Are we going home now, sir?" Kadrovich asked.

"Yes, Kadrovich, Yes, we're going home," Gurney replied.

The pair of them walked the short distance to the dock. The Somerville left immediately.

Gurney sat in the small cabin, staring at the picture. He hoped this was all a bad dream and he'd wake up soon. "Was everything a lie?" he thought.

Gurney didn't even wait for the Somerville to tie up at the dock. He jumped onto the dock and hurried to the compound.

"That was a quick trip," Kirby said, when Gurney walked into the office.

"Look at this," Gurney held out the paper to him.

"I don't believe it," Kirby said after a few moments of stunned silence. "It's got to be a bad joke or just someone who looks like him."

"Have someone find him and get him up here to my office," Gurney said.

"Right away, sir," Kirby replied. He was in shock himself.

Gurney stood on the verandah and looked across the lake towards Labrys. Just the Shrine of the Goddess was visible.

There was a knock at the door. "Come," Gurney called.

"You wanted to see me, sir?" Troy asked.

"I went to Breederstown this morning," Gurney told him. "While I was there Kadrovich found this," he held out the paper.

"What's this?" Troy took the paper from Gurney and looked at it.

"I'd say there's a bit of a resemblance, wouldn't you?" Gurney asked.

"I, I don't know what to say," Troy slowly sat down.

"How about the truth?" Gurney said.

"I came here to get away from my past," Troy said. "I never expected to meet someone like you."

"Someone like me? What do you mean?" Gurney asked.

"Someone I could, or would, fall in love with," Troy replied. He looked at Gurney.

"So you lied to everyone, including me," Gurney glared at Troy.

"I never meant to hurt you," Troy replied. "You've got to believe me, Gurney."

"Oh, Troy, Troy. You've got to know that I'm old enough to be your father."

"That doesn't matter to me," Troy replied.

"I'm just a father figure to you, that's all. In time you'll find someone closer to your own age," Gurney said.

"I don't want someone my age," Tears rolled down Troy's face. "I want you."

"No," Gurney shook his head. "You'll find someone. They always do."

"What do you mean?" Troy whipped his face.

"Wanting something is often better than actually having it," Gurney said.

"But, what does that mean?" Troy asked.

"It means that the anticipation is better than actually possessing it. Besides, this isn't the first time I've been lied to. But, every time it happens, it still hurts all the same."

"I don't understand," Troy said.

"A long time ago, someone betrayed my trust. I keep saying I'm over it, but I guess I'm not, really." Gurney sat down heavily into a chair and closed his eyes. "Every time I drop the shields I get hurt again."

"I'm sorry. I never meant to cause you more pain."

"Well, it's a little late for that, isn't it?" Gurney snapped at him.

"Yes, I guess it is. Is there anything I can do to make you feel any better?"

"Just go away and leave me alone for a while," Gurney turned his chair around and looked out the window. "I need some time to think."

Troy quietly left the room.

High Leather Night was the biggest festival of the year. The streets were full of leather-clad men. The central market square was crowded. There were even women from Labrys in the crowd. The air was full of the smell of new leather, food and noise. Men walked holding hands or arm in arm. Some masters led their slaves on leashes.

Gurney walked through the crowd. Kadrovich was in close attendance. It was afternoon and the bars were filling with revelers. The Gauntlet, the Eagle, the Cell Block, the Ramrod and others were bursting at the seams as men jammed into them.

Gurney and Kadrovich finally reached the Dome of the Rock. Flags snapped in the wind. The glazed brick sidewalk had been freshly scrubbed.

"Is everything ready for tonight?" Gurney asked.

"Yes, sir," Kadrovich replied.

"Good. I don't want any mistakes."

"There will not be any, sir," was the reply.

"Very good. I'm going back to the compound. You go and join your friends for the afternoon," Gurney told him.

"I'd rather be with YOU, sir," Kadrovich said.

"I don't want you to miss out in the fun," Gurney said as he turned to look back the way they had come.

"May I speak frankly, sir?"

"Certainly, Kadrovich."

"Well, sir. Some of us, myself and a few others, are concerned for your safety," His gaze met Gurney's.

"I see," Gurney replied. "Go on."

"We would all feel more comfortable if one of us was with you at all times, sir."

"Well, since you're chief of security I guess I don't have much choice, do I?" Gurney smiled a little.

"No, sir," Kadrovich replied.

"Very well, then I guess WE'RE going back to the compound."

"Yes, sir," Kadrovich replied, falling into step with Gurney as they headed back the way they had come.

The members of Nimbus that were taking part in the march formed up in the courtyard of the compound. Soon they would head down Market Street to Castro and then to the Dome of the Rock.

Troy had found some Nimbus members with a little musical experience. He had quickly formed a drum and bugle corps. They would lead the way to the Dome.

Gurney stood at the front of the massed men. He would be second in line of the march after the drum and bugle corps.

"Gentlemen," He called out. "Remember who you represent. And, what you represent. Nimbus has always had the highest standards. If you were not the best, you would not be here. Whatever you do tonight, make yourselves proud, make Nimbus proud and make me proud of you."

"YES, SIR!" they all called out in unison.

The drum and bugle corps headed out of the gates at Gurney's signal. The men of Nimbus marched behind Gurney and his personal guards. The sound of their boots echoed off of the buildings.

As they approached the Dome of the Rock, the drum and bugle corps began to play.

The massed members of the other collectives turned and looked in shock. Something like this had never been done before.

Gurney smiled. He knew they had made an impression.

Troy and Kirby were also smiling. They were both glad to see Gurney in a good mood and that they had made an impression on the massed men.

At Gurney's signal his men marched into the Dome for the service. The others followed at a respectful distance.

After the service, Gurney returned to the compound. He didn't feel much like celebrating. He walked down the crowded street slowly. He wasn't looking forward to spending the night alone.

"Good evening, sir," the guard at the compound gate said.

"Thank you, Harrison," Gurney replied.

He entered the main building and slowly walked up the stairs to his apartment.

After he took off his leather Gurney made some tea and took it to the bedroom. He had decided to read for a while.

He woke up during the night. He wasn't alone. He couldn't see who it was in the darkness. Someone gently caressed his body. He moaned when the unknown man lowered himself onto Gurney's lap. Gurney lay there and let the sensations wash over him.

Finally, he reached his peak. He groaned in ecstasy. It had been so very, very long. He felt something splatter onto his chest. His unknown partner disappeared into the night.

Every bar in Lthrtown was packed full of men who partied hard. This was the biggest party of the year. Even the crews of all of Nimbus's ships were in port for the event. The party continued until late in the night.

"I've noticed something in all these reports, Kadrovich," Troy said the next morning at breakfast.

"Sir?" Kadrovich looked up from his plate. His head pounded from the previous night's events.

"Take a look at the physical descriptions. Tell me if you notice anything," Gurney told him.

"Well, let's see," Kadrovich replied. "Oh course, some of this information we got is new, sir."

"Very true, Kadrovich," Gurney continued to eat while Kadrovich scanned the reports.

Kadrovich looked up in surprise. "All early twenties, with dark hair and beards."

"Exactly," Gurney replied.

"But, what does it mean, sir?"

"It means we leave for Labrys today," Gurney told him.

"Yes, sir, I'll make all the arrangements, sir." Kadrovich excused himself and left the dining hall.

Kadrovich appeared at Gurney's office door. "Sir, we sail this afternoon on the Stonewall."

"Very good, Kadrovich," Gurney said. "There are my bags. We'll pickup whatever else we need in Labrys."

"Whatever else, sir?" Kadrovich was puzzled. "We're not staying in Labrys?"

"No, Kadrovich. We're going to the Outlands."

Gurney sat astride his horse on a ridge overlooking the Outlands.

"Well, brother. We're here," M'Lena said, sat on her horse next to him.

"Yes, we are," Gurney replied. "It's just like I remember it." He turned and looked down the slope of the ridge. The rest of the group, led by Kadrovich, was lined up behind them. Everyone was wearing a loose fitting garment, tight at the wrists, ankles and waist. Most wore hats, but some had the hoods that were attached to their suits pulled up.

"Do you think the answer to your question is out here?" M'Lena asked.

"I hope so," Gurney replied.

"What did you tell your men we were looking for?" she asked.

"As little as possible," he replied. "What about your women?"

"Not much, but, they're sure to have questions sooner or later," she said.

"I'll just have to go with the flow," Gurney replied. They started down the slope. Their leather saddles creaked with the movement.

"I sure hope you know what you're doing," M'Lena said.

"So do I," Gurney replied. "So do I."

They rested during the hottest time of the day and did as much traveling at night as possible.

They didn't see another living thing. The few clouds were high and thin. It didn't rain in the Outlands very often.

The second night out Gurney went to answer nature's call.

"Sir," it was Kadrovich.

"Yes, Kadrovich?" Gurney replied.

"What are we looking for, sir?"

"We'll know it when we find it, Kadrovich," Gurney zipped up his suit.

"Yes, sir." He followed Gurney back to camp.

M'Lena sat on the ground by the campfire. "Everything come out all right?"

"Funny," Gurney grinned. "At least I don't have to sit down all the time."

"I like the fire," M'Lena said, quickly changing the subject.

"So do I," Gurney replied. "I still don't know what it is about it that's so comforting."

"Probably something in the ancestral memory," M'Lena replied, the dancing flames lighted her face. "It's security."

"Probably," Gurney replied, as he scratched his new beard.

"You're looking rather scruffy, brother."

"Gee. Thanks for the compliment," Gurney replied.

"In fact all your men are getting scruffy," M'Lena said.

"We can't afford to waste water on shaving. Besides, it's added protection from the sun and wind," Gurney replied.

"I'm sure it is," she said.

They sat there together, yet each was alone with their private thoughts.

M'Lena stood up. "Goodnight, brother."

"Goodnight, sister," he replied. Gurney stared at the dancing flames.

"How long has Gurney been gone?" Spencer asked Pike.

"I'm not sure, sir," he replied.

"Well then, FIND OUT!" Spencer yelled.

Pike hurried out of Spencer's office. "If he didn't pay me so much," he fumed. "I'd tell HIM where to go."

The land began to gradually change as the expedition headed east. Ground cover began to appear. Bushes and finally small trees began to appear.

"Sir," Kadrovich said, "What's that?" He pointed off to the right.

"Let's go see," Gurney replied.

They rode up to the strange object.

"What is it, sir?"

"Well, Kadrovich, it's what the ancients called a bus," Gurney replied.

"A bus?"

"It was a way to transport a large number of people," Gurney told him.

"But, how did it work?" Kadrovich got off of his horse.

"It had what they called an engine."

"I don't understand, sir."

The rest of the expedition rode up to them.

"Well, I guess it's time to tell everyone about the ancients," Gurney said.

M'Lena came and stood next to Gurney. "Gather around, my children," she said. "It's time to learn about the past."

"Let's set up camp," Gurney said. "And, we'll tell you some of what we've been able to learn."

The members of the expedition sat around the fire. Gurney was pleased to see that they were not in two separate groups, but had intermingled. At least they were all getting along together.

"Long ago there was a higher civilization here," Gurney began. "The world was overflowing with people."

"The world was full of a large variety of plants and animals," M'Lena said.

"What happened to it, then, sir?" Kadrovich asked.

"Well, the world was full of conflicting groups. Each fighting the others for control of dwindling resources," Gurney told them.

"Then, something came from out of the sky," M'Lena said.

"Out of the sky," S'haron asked.

"The rings that we see in the sky were once a moon. It was a large body in space."

"Sir, you're using terms we don't understand," Kadrovich said.

Gurney began to draw in the sand. "This is the earth. That's where we are."

"The moon was a smaller body that moved around the earth. It affected tides in the ocean. It stabilized the planet."

"Another massive body came out of space and hit the moon. A lot of the debris hit the earth. The rest formed the rings we see in the sky. The planet was almost destroyed. Civilization was reduced to small, scattered groups," Gurney continued.

"The area we call the Outlands was once a fertile land. Crater Lake was formed by a meteorite hitting the earth."

"I know this is a lot for you all to understand," Gurney told them. "We'll be able to explain things better when we reach our destination."

"Everyone get some rest. We'll leave in a couple of hours," M'Lena said.

The groups split up and went to sleep. Gurney could hear them whispering amongst themselves.

"Gurney's been gone for over a week, sir," Pike told Spencer.

"A week? A whole damn WEEK?" Spencer hollered. "Where the hell did he go?"

"Apparently he went to Labrys. Our sources say he left, but they don't know where he went."

"I know where he went," Spencer said. "Pack your bags. We're going on a trip."

Gurney's expedition came across their first ruins the next morning.

"M'Lena and I were here a long time ago," he told the group. "A lot of what we learned, we discovered here."

"There are the remains of a library here," M'Lena said.

"Farther along the road is where the library is. We'll go there first," Gurney said.

The expedition spent the next few days digging in the ruins. Gurney and M'Lena taught all they could. Dinners around the campfire always had a lively debate of some type.

Spencer and Pike pushed themselves. Spencer wanted to find Gurney's group and the expedition's base.

"What's the rush?" Pike asked.

"Gurney's secrets are going to be mine," Spencer replied.

"Secrets? What are you talking about?"

"Where do you think Gurney gets a lot of his merchandise," Spencer said.

"I guess I never thought about it. He sells it. We buy it."

"Well, you'll see what I mean when we get there," Spencer said.

"Tomorrow we'll break camp and head to our next stop," Gurney told the group at breakfast.

"At dawn, sir," Kadrovich asked.

"Yes. At dawn," he replied.

"Yes, sir, we'll be ready."

"I think we're lost," Spencer told Pike.

"Well, that's just great," he replied.

"Things look different. It's been a long time since I've been out here."

"So now what do we do," Pike asked.

"Just keep looking," Spencer snapped at him.

"Sir, I see something up ahead." Bruno had ridden back to Gurney's position in the line of the march.

"Any idea what it is?"

"I can't be sure, sir," he replied.

"Well, let's go see what's there," Gurney said.

Spencer was trapped under his horse. The path had given way under them. They had slid down the steep incline.

By the time Pike was able to reach him, there wasn't much he could do. "I've got to go get help," Pike said.

"No. NO! Don't leave me alone. Please." Spencer pleaded.

"What do you want me to do?" Pike asked. "I've got to find some help."

"Find Gurney, he's got to be out here somewhere," Spencer gasped.

"But how?"

"I don't know how to find him. Leave the food and canteen I need," Spencer said. "Find him, before it's too late. I, I've got to tell him something."

Pike jumped onto his horse in a frantic attempt to find Gurney and his party.

It's PIKE!" Schmidt called.

"What's he doing out here alone," M'Lena wondered.

"Spencer's got to be here somewhere," Gurney said. "He'd never be here alone."

Pike weakly waved at them as they approached.

Griffith reached Pike first. He jumped off his horse, canteen in hand.

"What are you doing here?" Gurney asked Pike when he got there.

"Spencer. He's back that way," Pike moaned.

"What are you doing here," Gurney said again.

"We, we were looking for you," Pike moaned. "The path gave way. He slid down the slope and he's trapped under his horse."

"As soon as he's capable of moving we'll look for Spencer," Gurney said.

"No. You've got to go, now!" Pike pleaded with them. "He's alone."

"Calm down," M'Lena said. "How do we find him?"

"Just this side of the last ridge,"

"S'haron, take care of him," Gurney said. "Kadrovich, you're with me."

"Yes, sir," S'haron answered.

Gurney and Kadrovich thundered off in the direction of the ridge.

Half an hour later they found Spencer.

"Gurney, Gurney, is that you?" he whispered, as Gurney knelt beside him. Blood trickled from the corner of his mouth.

"I'm here," Gurney replied. "I'm here."

"We've got to get this horse off of him," Kadrovich said.

"No. No time," Spencer coughed, blood splattered onto his goatee.

"We'll get you out of here. Just take it easy," Gurney told him.

"I, I've got to tell you something, Gurney," Spencer gasped.

"Just take it easy," Gurney said. He cradled Spencer's head in his lap.

"I, I'm sorry, Gurney," Spencer whispered. "All the years we lost. I'm so sorry. I was stupid to cheat on you. You were the most important thing in my life, and I screwed it up."

"Rest, save your strength," Gurney told him.

"No. No time," Spencer gasped. "My backs broken, legs and pelvis are crushed. I don't have much time."

"No, you'll be alright," Gurney told him.

"You, you were the one true love of my life and I screwed it up. I'm sorry we wasted all these years," Spencer whispered, repeating himself. "It's all my fault."

"No, no. We'll get you out. You'll be all right. I'll take care of you," Gurney told him as he took Spencer's hand in his.

"I'm so sorry, Gurney, so sorry. I loved you Gurney. I always did. All the wasted time, all those years," Spencer's voice trailed off.

"Spencer? SPENCER!" Gurney yelled. "Don't leave me, Spencer. I love you, too. I need you. Please, Spencer, please! Don't leave me alone!"

"Sir," Kadrovich said. "SIR?"

Gurney hadn't realized that Kadrovich was kneeling next to him.

"Sir, it's too late. He's gone, sir."

Gurney slowly put Spencer's head down. "I, I know." He turned away. His eyes were full of tears. He stood up.

Kadrovich wasn't sure what to do.

Gurney walked away. He was trying to maintain control of his emotions.

"Sir, Sir," Kadrovich came up behind Gurney. He reached for Gurney's shoulder, not sure if he should touch him or not. "Please, sir."

Gurney shook with the effort of trying to maintain control over his feelings.

"Do you need a hug, sir," Kadrovich asked.

Gurney nodded that he did.

Kadrovich gently wrapped his big arms around Gurney.

Gurney turned around and rested his head against the younger man's muscular chest as Kadrovich wrapped his strong arms around Gurney and held him tightly to him.

Gurney lost control. He sobbed uncontrollably. His tears ran down his cheeks into his beard. They left tracks in the dust on his face.

"It's all right, sir," Kadrovich whispered. "Let it out, sir. Let it out. Just let it out, sir." He held Gurney until the sobbing stopped. He was crying himself.

By the time the rest of the group arrived Gurney had regained his composure. But, they could all tell, by his red and swollen eyes, he had been crying.

Kadrovich had put Spencer's body in a sleeping bag. He knew they wouldn't leave the body there.

"Brother? Are you alright," M'Lena asked.

"I will be," Gurney replied.

"What happened," she asked.

"Kadrovich will tell you," Gurney walked away. He wanted to be alone.

A few days later the expedition arrived at the cave Gurney and M'Lena had discovered years ago.

S'haron and Pike had headed back to Labrys with Spencer's body.

"We'll make camp here at the entrance," M'Lena said. "Tomorrow we'll go inside."

Gurney dismounted and walked away. He sat on a large rock and looked up at the night sky. The rings were visible all the time now. He heard the crunch of someone walking on the broken stone.

"Sir?" It was Kadrovich.

"Yes, Kadrovich," Gurney sighed

"Would you like to talk, sir?" Kadrovich stopped about six feet away from where Gurney was sitting.

"Just sit here with me," Gurney said.

"It's a nice night," Kadrovich said.

"Yes. It is," Gurney replied.

"Sir, I know you're unhappy," Kadrovich said.

Gurney didn't answer.

"What happened back there? No one will ever know, sir."

"Thank you, Kadrovich," Gurney replied. "But, I'm sure everyone will know."

"Sir, you're like a father to me, to us all, sir. We all look up to you as an example of how a man should be, do, and act. That's something that will never change. The fact that you let your feelings show doesn't make you any less of a man in my eyes. I'm sure it wasn't easy for you to do what you did."

"Thank you, Kadrovich. I appreciate your understanding," Gurney replied.

"No problem, sir," he replied. "We all try to follow your example, sir. I hope I can be half the man you are." Kadrovich stood up and walked away, leaving Gurney alone in the dark with his thoughts.

"I'm sure this is the right cave," M'Lena. "Why haven't they contacted us?"

"I've got a bad feeling about this," Gurney replied. "Something's wrong."

They entered the main chamber. Garbage covered the floor. Tables and cabinets were overturned. The lights flickered on and off.

"Well, this doesn't look good," M'Lena said.

"As always, the master of the understatement," Gurney replied.

"Let's see if we can find the archives," M'Lena said.

They wandered through the caverns looking for some sign of the former inhabitants.

"Where could they have gone," Gurney said.

"Maybe the sample they got from you didn't work," M'Lena said.

"Or else something went wrong," Gurney said.

They continued their search. They found no one.

"I have a theory," Gurney finally said.

"Which is?"

"I think they may have made a clone of me and something went wrong," Gurney replied.

"Why do you think that?"

"Every one of the men that was assaulted resembled me. Or rather, the me of twenty years ago."

"But, why would he be attacking men who resembled you?"

"That's the part I haven't figured out yet," Gurney said.

"Sir," Kadrovich called, "I've found the archives."

The rest of the team hurried to his location.

"It looks like it's pretty much intact," M'Lena said.

"Let's load up as much as we can on the pack horses," Gurney ordered. "Then we'll go home.

"There's so much, I'm not sure we can take it all," M'Lena said.

"Well, we'll just have to send someone back to get the rest," Gurney said.

As they crested the ridge they could see lights of Labrys glowing in the distance.

"Almost home," Gurney thought.

They slowly made their way through town, down to the docks. The Provincetown was waiting for them. The packhorses were quickly unloaded and their bundles were taken on board and stowed below decks.

"I'll get started on a return trip," M'Lena told Gurney. "I'll get the rest of the material and bring it to you myself.

"OK. When I get done with some business I have to take care of, I'll get started on sorting this all out," he replied.

M'Lena hugged Gurney. "I'm so sorry for your loss, brother."

"Thank you, sister," Gurney struggled to keep his feelings in check. It was already getting easier to do.

She kissed him, gently, on the cheek. "Have a safe trip."

Captain Walker saluted Gurney at the top of the gangplank. "Welcome aboard, sir. Your stateroom is ready for you."

"Thank you, Captain," Gurney replied.

"We'll be in Lthrtown a little after dawn, sir."

"Very good, Captain." Gurney went below to his stateroom.

"Sir," Kadrovich asked, "Would you like something to eat?"

"Just some tea," he replied.

"Yes, sir, I'll go to the galley and get you some." Kadrovich closed the door behind him.

Gurney lay down on the bed.

When Kadrovich came back to the cabin Gurney was asleep. He put the tea on the table, covered Gurney with a blanket and kissed him on the cheek.

Gurney mumbled something Kadrovich couldn't understand.

Kadrovich turned and looked at Gurney's sleeping form. "Goodnight, sir," he whispered.

When the Provincetown pulled into port the flags were at half-mast. A large crowd had gathered on the dock. They silently watched Gurney and his men disembark.

Gurney walked, stone-faced through the crowd, which parted in front of him.

Kadrovich and the rest of Gurney's escort followed Gurney back to the compound.

"Once the crowd has dispersed I want all the material we gathered brought to my office," Gurney said.

"Yes, sir, I'll take care of it myself," he responded.

Gurney slowly walked upstairs to his office. He sat there in the dark.

"Welcome back, sir. Sorry to hear about Spencer," Kirby told Gurney, as he entered the outer office the next morning.

"Thank you, Kirby," Gurney replied.

"Is there anything I can get for you?"

"No, thank you, I don't think so," Gurney replied. He walked into his office and walked to the window. He could see Spencer's compound in the distance.

There was a knock at his office door.

"Come," Gurney called.

"Sir," Troy walked into the office. "Sorry to hear about your loss."

"Thank you, Troy," he replied.

"If there's anything I can do."

"Thank you, no. I just need some time," Gurney replied.

Kirby appeared in the doorway. "Sir, Spencer's lawyer is here."

"Send him in." Gurney sat behind his desk. Nothing was out of place. I t was just as it had been when he had gone to the Outlands.

"Sir, my name is Pallone. I'm executor of Spencer's will," he said. He was stocky, blond and clean-shaven.

"What can I do for you," Gurney asked.

"Spencer's will was very specific on his funeral. Pike is making the preparations right now," he told Gurney. "But, he also had specific stipulations about his property."

"I see. And you're telling me this because?"

"I just wanted to be sure you were there for the reading of his will. That's all, sir," Pallone replied.

"You could have just given the information to my assistant."

"No, sir. The will said I was to contact you personally." He handed Gurney a card. "Here's the information you need."

"Thank you," Gurney said.

"Good day, sir." Pallone nodded and left the office.

The Nimbus drum and bugle corps led the way, playing a funeral march as the procession left the compound. All of Spencer's men walked directly behind the horse drawn wagon. Gurney and his personal guard were right behind them. Those Nimbus members that wanted to participate marched behind Gurney. Other collectives followed them.

The procession marched up hill to the Dome of the Rock. Many men lined the route of the procession. Many more waited at the Dome.

Father Connery waited as they put Spencer's body on the funeral pyre. "My brothers, one of us has passed on to a different plain of existence. He will be missed, but our lives will go on. That is the way it has always been and always will be. Life goes on. As long as we remember those that have moved on they will live in our minds forever. Cherish what you have, friends, family, and lovers. Rejoice in your own lives. Learn from the past and embrace the future."

Gurney stood, stone-faced as Father Connery gave the signal to start the fire.

Troy glanced at Gurney. He could see tears running down Gurney's cheeks into his beard. He made no attempt to hide them. Troy started to reach out to Gurney, but Kirby stopped him with a shake of his head.

The flames quickly engulfed the woodpile. The crowd stood mute.

Gurney stood and stared at the pyre.

The crowd slowly began to drift away.

Finally, Gurney saluted and spun on his heel, and then he marched away, back to the Nimbus compound.

"Tomorrow is the reading of the will, sir," Kirby told Gurney.

"I know, Kirby. I'll be there."

"I think I should probably take DePaul with me.

"Yes, sir, I'll let him know," Kirby replied.

Gurney and DePaul went to Pallone's office in Spencer's compound.

"Well, now that you're here we can get started," Pallone said.

"Where's everyone else?"

"There is no one else, Gurney," Pallone replied. He sat down at his desk.

"Am I to understand that no one else is named in the will?" DePaul asked.

"That's correct," Pallone replied. "He left everything to Gurney."

"But why would he do that?" Gurney asked.

"I couldn't tell you, even if I knew," Pallone replied. "I need you to sign these papers."

DePaul took the sheaf of papers and looked them over. "Everything looks to be in order."

"Well then, I guess I should sign them, eh?" Gurney asked.

"Yes sir," DePaul replied.

"He left everything to you?" Kirby said.

"I don't know what we're going to do with it all," Gurney said.

"We'll have to take an inventory first of all," Kirby said.

"I think we should offer all of the men a choice of working for Nimbus or leaving," Gurney poured a fresh cup of tea.

"From a public relations standpoint that would certainly be a good idea," Kirby said.

"I guess I'll go over there this afternoon."

"Can I have your attention gentlemen?" Kadrovich said.

They stopped talking and lined up in ranks.

"Managing Director Gurney will speak to you now." Kadrovich stepped back and Gurney stepped to the front.

"Gentlemen, this has not been an easy time for any of us. As you may, or may not know, Spencer left all of his estate to me." He paused to see if there was any reaction to this news.

"You will all be offered positions with Nimbus for the remainder of your contracts. If you are so inclined you may leave and you will be given a generous severance package."

"Sir," Pike, Spencer's assistant stepped forward.

"Yes, Pike?"

"Sir, we have already discussed this amongst ourselves. We would all be honored to be part of Nimbus, sir."

"Very good," Gurney said. "Over the next few days we will have new contracts drawn up for everyone."

"Thank you, sir," Pike stepped back in line.

"Also, the name of Nimbus will be changed to Nimbus-Unicorn to reflect our new status."

The men murmured amongst themselves at this news.

"You will find, as members of Nimbus-Unicorn, that the lines of communication are always open. If you wish to discuss any problems or ideas you may do so at any time."

The men still stood at attention.

"Are there any questions at this time?" Gurney asked.

"Sir, no, sir," the men answered in unison.

"Very well, dismissed."

The men hurried back to their jobs.

Gurney, Kadrovich, and Pike went into the main building.

"Would you like to see Spencer's quarters, sir?" Pike asked.

"I think it might be better if you took care of that, Pike," Gurney said.

"Yes, sir," Pike replied.

"We'll have to integrate all Unicorn operations into ours. I'll need to have reports from all your section managers as soon as possible."

"I'll give them their instructions myself, sir," Pike replied.

"Very good, I think I'd just like to look around the grounds and buildings right now."

"Yes, sir, if I may be excused?" Pike asked.

Gurney nodded his consent.

"Thank you, sir." Pike turned to leave.

"Just one more thing, Pike," Gurney said.

"Sir?"

"I'd like you to join us for dinner tonight."

"Yes, sir, I'd be honored, sir."

Dinner was subdued. No one felt much like talking. Gurney sat with Kirby, Troy, Pike, and Kadrovich.

Kirby and Troy watched Gurney. Kadrovich watched Pike. There was tension in the air. Gurney knew it would take some time integrating the former Unicorn members.

He also knew that Kirby and Troy were worried about him.

"Well," Gurney finally said. "I'll be in my office for a while if anyone needs to see me about anything."

"Yes, sir," Kirby replied.

Gurney was going over some of the items they had recovered when there was a knock at his office door. "Come," he called.

"Sir," Pike said. "I found something in Spencer's things I thought you might want to see.

"What would that be?" Gurney asked.

"Some letters that he wrote," Pike replied.

"Letters?"

"Yes, sir, Letters to you," Pike told him.

"I never got any letters from him."

"I know, sir. They're letters he wrote but never mailed to you," he held out a bundle of envelopes to Gurney.

Gurney took them from Pikes hand. "How many are there? It's a big pile."

"As far as I know, sir, he wrote them to you for almost twenty years. But, I wasn't with him all that time."

"I see. Thank you, Pike," Gurney said.

"May I speak frankly, sir?"

"Certainly, Pike," Gurney gestured to a chair.

Pike took a seat. "Spencer talked about you quite a bit, sir."

"I see," Gurney replied. "Why didn't he ever try and reconcile things with me?"

"He felt that you would never take him back after what had happened between the two of you. He often expressed his regrets to me."

"All those wasted years," Gurney said.

"Yes, sir, I understand," Pike stood to go.

"Thank you for bringing them to me," Gurney said.

"You're welcome, sir." Pike left the office.

Gurney sat, staring at the thick pile of letters. He didn't think he could bear to read them.

He picked them up and walked to the fireplace. He hesitated. Should he destroy them without reading them, or should he read them? He couldn't decide. He stood watching the flames for a few minutes.

Finally, he sat down and took the top letter out. He read them all. They were full of regrets and wishes, hopes and fears, sorrows and pains.

Kirby found Gurney asleep by the fire when he came to check on him. He picked up a letter off the floor and looked at it. "Now I understand some of what's been happening." He decided it was best to let Gurney stay where he was. Otherwise, he'd know that his secret was out.

The next morning Rommel took Gurney's breakfast to his suite. Gurney didn't appear all day.

Finally, at dinnertime, Kirby couldn't wait. He rapped on Gurney's door. "Sir, Sir? Are you alright?"

Gurney opened the door. "I'm quite all right."

"You had me worried," Kirby told him.

"Sorry. Didn't mean to cause you a problem," Gurney replied.

"That's OK, sir, just a little concerned."

"I'm alright. I want you, Troy and Kadrovich to join me for dinner tonight."

"Yes, sir, I'll tell the others."

"Gentlemen, The time has come for me to tell you about some events of my past," Gurney told the trio.

"As you wish, sir," Kirby replied.

"When I first came to Lthrtown, Spencer and I were partners. I thought we were committed partners," Gurney began. "I loved him as I had never loved anyone before."

The trio sat silently.

"I came back from a trip to the Outlands and caught Spencer in bed with someone else. I threw him out and didn't see him for quite a while."

"When Nimbus was founded I worked my ass off. Slowly, I built it into the power that it is today."

"But, I never forgot Spencer's betrayal," Gurney paused. His voice choked up. "I felt like he had torn out my heart and stomped on it."

The others watched silently. They knew this was hard for him to talk about.

"I could never forgive him for the pain he had caused me. Or, what he had done to me."

Kirby reached for Gurney's hand.

"Spencer started his own company and became one of Nimbus's biggest customers. That's why whenever we were together we were so hostile to each other. I hated him for what he had done. But, I never really got over him. That's why I was never able to return anyone else's love," Gurney's eyes were full of tears.

"Now that he's gone, I have to deal with it and move on with my life. I hope that you'll excuse the follies of an old man."

"Gurney, you know that we're all here for you. We'll help you in anyway that we can," Kirby said. "We love you. All your men love you and would do anything for you, too."

"Thank you," Gurney looked from one to another. "Thank you, all."

"Whatever you need, sir, we'll be here for you," Kadrovich smiled.

"Me, too," Troy said.

"Thank you, gentlemen," Gurney said. "Right now I think I need to say one final goodbye. And then the healing process can begin."

Gurney stood up and got the pile of letters from the sideboard. He walked to the fireplace, kissed the top of the pile, and threw them all in the crackling fire. "Goodbye my love," he whispered. "I always loved you. I guess I always will. Sleep well."

The others sat and silently watched Gurney.

"Well gentlemen," Gurney said as he turned around to face the others. "It's time to get to work."

For the next week Gurney studied the papers they had brought back from the Outlands. A lot of it was full of scientific terms that he didn't understand. He put that aside for study later. He was looking for something that he could understand. A diary, a journal, something more personal had to be in all the data they had recovered. Everyday M'Lena sent more over on the mail packet.

Looking out his window Gurney could see the site where the new theater was being built.

Troy was busy constantly, not only with the building of the theater, but recruiting men for various projects as well.

The mysterious assaults had stopped, but Gurney was sure that the perpetrator was still out there somewhere, waiting.

Day after day, Gurney went through the mass of papers. He finally had Kadrovich assist him.

"Sir, what's this?" Kadrovich held up a clear plastic rectangle.

"It's what the ancients called a cassette," Gurney replied. "Let me see it."

Kadrovich handed it to Gurney.

"What was it used for?" Kadrovich asked.

"They had a process called recording. It could have music on it or be a voice recording."

"But, how do you know?"

"We need to find a player," Gurney said. "I think we might have something in storage that will work."

After going through crate after crate, Gurney found what he was looking for.

"Is that it, sir?" Kadrovich asked.

"This is a player. All we need is a power source."

"Where do we get that, sir?"

"We need to connect it to the power grid."

Kadrovich looked dubious. "But how, sir?"

"With this," Gurney held up the plug. "Let's go back to my apartment."

Gurney opened a panel on the wall. "Here's our outlet." He plugged in the player and dropped the cassette into it.

The player squeaked and slowly began to turn. All they heard was noise.

"There's nothing on it," Kadrovich said.

"It's very old. Maybe the tape is degraded," Gurney said.

"I don't understand, sir," Kadrovich said.

"Because the tape is so old, it may not be readable. We'll have to see if we can find more of these."

"Yes sir."

M'Lena came to town the next day. "This is something I had to bring to you myself."

"What is it?" Gurney asked.

"It's a handwritten journal," she replied.

"Can you read it?"

"Some of it. A lot of the pages are damaged beyond repair," she replied. "But, from what I can gather, they had started to make clones of you but something went wrong, terribly wrong."

"What do you mean?" Gurney asked, he poured her a cup of tea.

"Something began to happen to the others. I don't know if it was a virus or what," M'Lena took a sip from her cup.

"It's possible we carried some kind of infection in with us," Gurney said.

"Highly possible," she replied. "They hadn't had any contact from outside in a long time."

"But, that still doesn't explain the attacks."

"Well, maybe that's the part of the puzzle we're missing so far," M'Lena replied.

"I guess we'll have to keep sifting through the records until we find something else to go on."

The attacks started again, but in a random pattern for months. The only link was that they were all bearded men with dark hair. There were no more deaths, but the assaults kept getting closer and closer to the main Nimbus-Unicorn compound.

Gurney devoted all his time to trying to make some sense of all the data they had recovered. He progressed very slowly. Gurney let Kirby run the day-to-day operation of the collective.

M'Lena continued to send new data almost everyday. She also poured over the data before she sent it to Gurney, marking notes on things that she thought might be important.

Troy was constantly busy with rehearsals for the theater's various events. The building was nearing completion. Interest was high in all the communities around the lake.

The expected influx of people spurred business owners in Lthrtown to improve their facilities. This resulted in a building boom and so brought even more people to town. The air was full of the smell of freshly cut wood and the constant sound of hammers. Now women were a constant sight on the street as many of them came from Labrys to work. Gurney had even approved the building of a new ship, the Fire Island. She would be slightly bigger than the Provincetown, fitted out mainly as a passenger ship and expected to be the fastest of her type on the lake.

"When's the last time you left your apartment?" Kirby asked Gurney, when he brought him his lunch one day.

"I don't really recall," Gurney replied.

"People are going to talk if you don't make an appearance soon," Kirby sat in the chair across from Gurney.

"I'm sure the answer is somewhere in these papers and tapes," Gurney told him.

"Maybe you should step back and try a different angle," Kirby said as he poured himself a cup of tea.

"Perhaps you're right," Gurney rubbed his eyes. "I know the key to this problem is here. I just don't know what it is, or where to look."

"Well, let me give you a haircut and trim your beard and then you can go out. Frankly, you look like hell," Kirby told him.

"Well, thanks for the compliment," Gurney grinned. "How can I argue with such a persuasive argument?"

"That's what I'm here for," Kirby reminded him.

"Alright, get your equipment and we'll do it," Gurney said.

"I'll be right back." Kirby left the room and returned a few minutes later with his kit.

"OK. Tell me all the latest gossip," Gurney said, as he leaned back in the chair.

"Oh, you know, just the usual. Who's doing who, where, and when they're doing it."

"Hmm, some barber you are. You can't even tell me what's happening," Gurney joked.

"Well, I HAVE been kind of busy," Kirby replied.

"I know," Gurney said. "I guess I've been kind of obsessed with this problem."

"NO! Really? I hadn't noticed," Kirby dryly replied. "Doc's also worried about you. The men all idolize you. They follow your example. And, the merger with Unicorn has opened up a lot of possibilities and brought us a lot of new blood."

"Alright, alright, I'll take a day or two off," Gurney replied.

"Besides the theater will be ready for the gala opening in a few days," Kirby said. "Are you sure you don't want me to dye all these gray hairs in your beard? There's a lot more than I remember."

"I've earned every one of those gray hairs," Gurney replied. "They're like badges of honor, Shows that I'm a survivor."

Kirby silently continued to cut Gurney's hair.

"Our society seems to forget everyone isn't young and pretty," Gurney continued. "Older people ARE still capable of leading productive lives. Besides, you're not that much younger than I am."

"I know, Gurney. I think you show everyday that older people can still contribute to society," Kirby replied. "Do you want me to shave your head?"

"No. I don't think so," Gurney answered.

"Well, you're the boss."

"How's business been?" Gurney asked.

"Profits are up. Market share is up. Everyone's happy."

"Good. Everyone likes to make money."

"There are a lot more women and breeders in town. Most are just visiting, but some are moving here."

"Any problems?" Gurney asked.

"None at all," Kirby replied. "I'm kind of surprised. I don't know of anyone who moved here and then changed their minds and moved out."

"Do you have any ideas as to what Troy's first production is going to be?" Gurney asked.

"Something called Phantom of the Opera, I think." Kirby moved to the side. "All done sir."

"I'd like to see him, if you can get him away from rehearsals," Gurney said, standing up behind his desk.

"I'll get the message to him," Kirby said, as he gathered up his barber kit.

"I'm going to take a shower," Gurney told Kirby as he got up and walked into his apartment.

"Need any help?" Kirby grinned.

"You're a wicked, wicked man," Gurney laughed.

"I learned it all from you, sir," Kirby replied.

"And, as I recall, you were one of my more willing pupils," Gurney laughed.

"But, not this time."

"No problem, sir. I'll find Troy and get him up here."

Gurney stood on his veranda in his robe and looked out at the lake. All around him he could hear the sounds of men working on various construction projects. He had decided to introduce telephones earlier than he had planned on doing. The first wires were going up. There was a lot of technology that he had recovered from digs in the Outlands that he was planning on introducing. He heard a knock on his door. "Come," he called.

"You wanted to see me, sir?" Troy asked.

"Yes, Troy, I do," Gurney replied.

"Did you want a progress report?" Troy asked.

"No. Kirby told me what's happening."

"Oh. Well, if I may be so bold as to ask, what did you want?"

"This isn't easy for me to say to you, Troy. But, I wanted to apologize for the way I acted before."

"Before?" Troy queried.

"When I found out you had been a drag queen."

"Oh, that. That's all right. I got over it a long time ago. I had a talk with Kirby. He explained things to me."

"Yeah, Kirby's a good man. He's been with me a long time."

Troy stood and listened to Gurney.

"Gurney, nothing will ever change the way I feel about you. I know you've been to hell and back, what with Spencer and all. I'll always be here for you."

"Thanks," Gurney reached out to Troy.

Troy moved into Gurney's embrace. He rubbed his red beard against Gurney's salt and pepper beard.

"I've missed you, Troy," Gurney whispered. "How can I ever make it up to you?"

"You don't have to make anything up to me. I understand what you've been through. It's not easy to be in love with someone who either can't or won't return that love to you."

"Sometimes it just takes a long time to get over," Gurney said. "All those wasted years. You can never make them up once they're gone."

"The past is the past." Troy replied. "It can't be changed."

"Yeah. And, I've been living in the past for far too long," Gurney said. "Sometimes I just feel so old and alone."

"You'll never be alone as long as I'm here." Troy wrapped his arms around Gurney. "Never."

Gurney returned the hug. "I know, Troy. I appreciate all the help and support you've given me."

Troy looked Gurney in the eye. "You know I love you."

"Yes, I know," Gurney replied. "I love you, too. At least as much as I can love someone."

"Kirby does, too," Troy told him.

"Yeah, I know that, too. The problem is I don't know if I can return that love to the two of you. I've been in pain for so, so long."

"We'll work on it. There's plenty of time," Troy said as he hugged Gurney again.

"I've got to find the solution to all these assaults. Then, we'll have plenty of time to get reacquainted," Gurney told him.

"OK. I'll let you get some rest." Troy gently kissed Gurney.

"You'd better go before I change my mind," Gurney said. He felt a stirring in his groin.

"Yeah, I can see that," Troy said. He nuzzled Gurney's neck.

"Oh, Troy," Gurney whispered.

"Come on," Troy pulled on Gurney's arm. They tumbled onto the bed.

"Oh, Troy," Gurney whispered again. "Don't leave. I've got to have someone to hold on to tonight."

"I'm here. I'm not going anywhere without you, Gurney." He slowly worked his way down Gurney's body.

Gurney walked the street alone. It was well past midnight, but there were still plenty of activity on the streets. He turned down an alleyway.

"Father," he heard a raspy voice.

"Who's there? Show yourself," Gurney called.

"Father, why did you leave me?" the voice rasped. "Why, father?"

"Who are you? Show yourself," Gurney called.

"I need you, father."

Gurney couldn't tell where the voice was coming from. "Come out! Show yourself," Gurney called out again.

There was no reply to his calls.

"You have no idea who it was?" Troy asked.

"I've never heard the voice, yet it was somehow familiar," Gurney said.

"Why didn't you use your link and call someone?" Kirby asked.

"I don't know. I was a little surprised, I guess," Gurney replied.

"Well, I don't think you should go out alone anymore," M'Lena told him.

"I didn't find anything unusual in the alley, either," Kadrovich put in. "And no one's ever mentioned hearing anything, either."

"Well, I'm sure I wasn't dreaming. So who was it calling out?"

No one had an answer to his question.

"Have there been any assaults in that general area?" M'Lena asked.

"There have been a few in the general area. But, none in the alley way," Kadrovich replied. "Or, at least none reported."

"Well, check around again and keep me informed," Gurney said.

"Yes, sir," Kadrovich said.

Kirby followed Kadrovich out the door.

"I didn't want to talk about this in front of the others," M'Lena said.

"Why not? You know that we don't have any secrets about the assaults," Gurney replied.

"Well, in a way it's kind of personal, for you," she told him.

"Personal?" he questioned.

"I've been trying to piece together the journal I found," she paused and took a sip from her cup.

"And?"

"I'm seeing references to instabilities in the new clones. The ones they made from your sample."

"But, what does that mean? Physical or mental?"

"I haven't found that part referenced yet."

"So, until we find some reference point we're still shooting in the dark," Gurney said.

"Unfortunately, that's right."

"The one thing I don't understand is, if these clones look like me, why haven't we had any reports about sightings?"

"One constant in all the reports is that all of the attacks have been at night," M'Lena said. She drained her cup. "The only other factor is that all the men resemble the you of twenty years ago."

"True," Gurney agreed.

"I'll be in my apartment going through more data. Somewhere there has to be a clue of some kind."

"OK. If I'm out, have Kirby contact me."

"We'll get to the bottom of this yet, brother." M'Lena stood up.

"I know we will, sister," Gurney replied as M'Lena left his office.

"Well, tonight's the night," Troy said.

"Nervous?" Gurney asked.

"Of course, I've never done anything this big before," Troy replied.

"I've heard THAT before," Gurney chuckled.

"I meant a show this big," Troy replied.

"I KNOW what you meant," Gurney chuckled again.

"You're such a pig. That's why I love you so much," Troy said.

"I love you, too, buddy," Gurney replied.

"I'll see you later. I've got a million things to take care of today before the show," Troy kissed Gurney's cheek and hurried out the office door.

When Gurney and his escort arrived at the Hudson Theater most of the seats were already full. This was a very special event. No one had seen a building so big or grand. It rivaled the Dome of the Rock. Gurney and Troy had decorated the lobby in what Gurney called "Art Deco." The lobby was full of colored marble and thick carpeting. Troy didn't know what the style had been called, but he certainly liked it. The auditorium was also decorated in the same style. The curtains were decorated with gold tassels.

As Gurney walked down the center aisle the crowd erupted into thunderous applause. It made him feel good. The theater was something he had wanted to build for quite a while. Now it was finished.

As Gurney and his party reached their seats, he acknowledged the applause. He motioned for the crowd to stop, but instead, many rose to their feet. The rest followed suit.

Now, Gurney was embarrassed. This had gone on for far too long.

"Maybe you should say something," Kirby shouted in his ear.

Gurney went to the end of the stage and went up the steps.

The crowd was now yelling and whistling.

Once again Gurney motioned for them to stop.

Slowly, the noise dropped and many took their seats.

Gurney was not prepared to make a speech, but he knew he had to say something. "My brothers and sisters," he began. "First, let me thank you for all your enthusiasm and support. This theater is the culmination of a longtime dream of mine. Now, it is a reality. Tonight we begin a new chapter in the history of Lthrtown, Labrys, Chiffon and Breederstown. A new chapter that I hope will see all of us working together to make all our lives better. I hope that we will all embrace our differences and that will make us all stronger," Gurney paused.

"And now, let us all take our seats and enjoy the very first performance in the Hudson Theater," Gurney waved one more time and then walked back to the steps.

The crowd applauded wildly.

"Very good, sir," Kirby said.

"Especially when I was not expecting to have to make a speech," Gurney replied.

The curtain opened and the production began. The audience sat, enthralled. They had never seen a performance so lavish and polished and grand. Troy had spent a lot of time on getting everything done properly and it showed.

The performers had been picked with no regard where they were from. So, all four communities were represented in the production.

The same was true throughout the creative people behind the scenes.

No one left their seats for the entire performance. They didn't want to miss a thing.

When the production was done, the applause continued to go on and on.

Gurney finally got up and he and his party left the auditorium.

The audience saw this and took it as their cue and the applause slowly died down.

Even Kirby and the others were awestruck with the response.

Gurney worked his way backstage to find Troy.

"This is fantastic," Troy's face was flushed with excitement. He gave Gurney a big hug.

"It's amazing," Gurney said as he kissed Troy.

The cast and crew crowded around them. Everyone was talking at once.

"I'm sure everyone knows the cast and crew party is at Como's," Troy called out. "Let's go and celebrate our success!"

Slowly, the group drifted away. Gurney and Troy still hugged each other backstage.

"Well, come on," Gurney said. "Let's get going."

They walked through the streets hand in hand. People rushed up to tell them how they had enjoyed the show.

"Let's go this way," Gurney said. "It's a shortcut." They walked down the dark alley.

"Alright."

"Father, why did you leave me?" a voice called out in the dark.

"What, what was that?" Troy whispered.

"It's the voice I heard the other night," Gurney replied.

"Father, why did you leave me? I need you, father," the raspy voice said.

"This is weird," Troy said.

"Come out! Show yourself!" Gurney called out. "I'm here."

There was no answer.

"Well, at least you know I wasn't dreaming it," Gurney said.

"I never doubted you for a minute," Troy said.

"Let's get out of here," Gurney said. "We'd better not mention this until we're with the others."

"Well, it took you long enough to get here," Kirby joked.

"We took a shortcut," Gurney replied.

"We heard the voice," Troy whispered.

"Again," Kirby said.

"It's the first time we've had a pattern of any kind," Kadrovich said.

"I think that tomorrow night I'll go down the same alley," Gurney said.

"But, it's too dangerous!" Troy protested.

"Troy's right," Kirby put in.

"I'll be wired," Gurney said.

"Wired?" Troy questioned.

"I'll have a wireless microphone," Gurney said. "It will transmit anything I hear."

"We could be right there. Then, we could grab him," Kadrovich said.

"NO!' Gurney said. "I've got to try and get him to talk to me. If he can tell that anyone else is there he may not talk."

"But, sir," Kadrovich protested.

"No," Gurney cut him off. "It's my call." He stood up and stormed out of the dining room.

"Gurney knows what he's doing," M'Lena told the others.

"Troy," Kirby said. "Go to him. I'm sure he'll need someone he loves close to him tonight."

"Thanks, Kirby," Troy kissed Kirby on the cheek and followed Gurney.

"Gurney," Troy whispered.

"Troy," Gurney replied. "What are you doing here?"

"Kirby thought you might need some company," he replied.

"Always thinking of my welfare," Gurney said.

"I'm here if you need me, Gurney. I just want to help you in any way I can."

"Come to bed," Gurney said.

Troy quickly shed his clothing and got under the sheets with Gurney. H e gently kissed Gurney's cheek.

"Hold me, Troy," Gurney murmured. "Just hold me."

Troy laid his head on Gurney's hairy chest.

"I love you, Troy," Gurney whispered.

"I love you, too, Gurney."

Gurney made no reply. He was already asleep.

"Test your microphone, sir," Kadrovich said.

"Test, test, one, two, three."

"Loud and clear, sir," Kadrovich said.

"Very well," Gurney said. "I'm heading for the alley now." He walked through the compounds main gate.

"Good luck, sir," Gurney heard Kadrovich's voice in his ear.

"Thank you, Kadrovich," Gurney replied.

Gurney walked the empty streets. It had rained earlier and the air was fresh and clean. The pavement was slippery. Gurney skirted the puddles.

"I'm at the alley way," he whispered in to his microphone."

"We're reading you loud and clear, sir," Kadrovich said.

"I'm going in," Gurney slowly walked down the alley. He had his side arm in his hand.

The alley was quiet. Gurney could hear water dripping somewhere.

"Father, Why did you leave me, father," the raspy voice said.

"I'm here," Gurney replied. "Come to me."

"We hear him," Kadrovich's voice said in Gurney's ear.

"Show yourself. Come to me," Gurney called out.

"I'm afraid, father."

"No one will hurt you. I'll protect you," Gurney said. "I promise. No one will hurt you. Come to me, son."

"I'm afraid, father."

"I can't help you if you won't come out," Gurney said.

"Help me, father," the voice sobbed.

"Come to me, my son," Gurney took a step forward.

"I'm afraid."

"Everything will be all right," Gurney said. "I promise you. Come to me. Please."

There was no reply.

"Where are you, son?" Gurney called out.

"I'm afraid," was the reply.

"No one will hurt you. I promise. Please come out where I can see you."

"I can't. Not here."

"Where then," Gurney asked.

"In the big building, father."

"The dome," Gurney questioned.

"No, father, the new building."

"The theater? You'll show yourself to me in the theater?"

"Yes, father."

"When son?" Gurney asked. "Tonight?'

"Tomorrow, Father. Tomorrow night," the voice faded away.

Gurney walked out of the alley. "Did you hear all that?" he said into his link.

"Yes, sir," Kadrovich replied. "We'll put some guards at the theater."

"No. If you do that, he'll never show," Gurney said.

"Then what are you going to do, sir?"

"I'm going to meet him," Gurney replied. "Alone."

"I wish you wouldn't do this," Troy said.

"I have to. It's the only way to try and get him to stop what he's doing," Gurney replied. "Besides I've got my side arm."

"The whole thing makes me nervous," Troy snuggled against Gurney.

"I know it does," Gurney replied. "Everything will be alright though. Trust me."

"He's the one I don't trust," Troy replied.

"After you've gone into the theater, we'll surround it with security men," Kadrovich said. "That way no one can get in or out without us seeing them."

"Very well," Gurney replied. He was pleased that Kadrovich was gaining confidence in his abilities as he matured.

"Be careful," M'Lena said.

"I will," Gurney answered.

Gurney entered the lobby of the theater and went into the auditorium. The lights were turned down. The stage was in shadow. "Hello," he called out. "I'm here. Where are you?"

"Father? Is that you?"

"Yes. It's me. Where are you?"

"I'm back here, father."

"Come out so I can see you," Gurney said. "Show yourself."

"I'm afraid, father."

"No one will hurt you, I promise," Gurney walked down the aisle towards the stage.

"You promise, father?"

"Yes, I promise. No one will hurt you," Gurney reached the stage.

There was no reply.

"Are you still here?" Gurney called out. He walked up the steps to the stage.

"Yes, father."

Gurney jumped and spun around. "You startled me."

"I'm sorry, father. I didn't mean to scare you."

Gurney peered into the deep shadows in the wings. Finally, he could dimly make out the figure of a man. But, something didn't seem quite right. "Come into the light so I can see you."

There was a shuffling of feet. Gurney now could see what looked like a parody of himself. Not only was he taller but the features were all distorted, like they had melted. "Where did you come from?"

"Where, father?"

"Yes. Where did you come from?" Gurney asked again.

"I came from you, father."

"From me," Gurney questioned. "I never had any children."

"I came from the desert, father," he replied. "I was created in your image. I'm part of you, father"

"The desert?" Gurney had now gotten conformation of what he had been suspecting for a while.

"Hold it right there!" someone yelled.

"No! Stay back," Gurney yelled.

It was too late. The grotesque parody ran to the back of the stage and started climbing a ladder to the overhead catwalk.

"You lied, father. You lied," he bellowed.

"No, I didn't. Come down here."

"No. No, you lied," he ran across the catwalk.

"Hold it right there," Bruno said, from the other end of the catwalk. Schmidt was now at the other end of the walkway.

"No! NO! Stay back!"

"We're not going to hurt you. Come down. We want to help you," Kadrovich called.

The man/creature sat on the catwalk. "I, I'll jump. Stay back."

"KEEP BACK!" Gurney hollered.

Bruno and Schmidt stopped their advance.

"Please come down," Gurney called. "No one will hurt you."

"No. You lied. YOU LIED!"

"STOP!" Gurney yelled.

The man/creature slipped off the catwalk. He landed on the stage with a loud cracking noise.

Gurney ran over to where he had landed. "Why did you do that?"

"I, I just wanted to be with you, father."

"You're with me now," Gurney lifted the man/creatures head.

"I'm sorry, father. I just wanted to see you, to be with you."

"Don't talk. The doctor will be here soon."

"No. No father. I am the last of your sons. All the others are gone," he gasped.

"Gone? Where?" Gurney asked.

"They are all gone. I'm the last of my kind, father."

"Hold on. Hold on. The doctor is coming."

"No. I've only got a few moments left."

The others surrounded Gurney. They watched silently.

"I'm sorry, sir," Kadrovich said. "We didn't think he'd jump."

"It's alright. It's alright," Gurney said.

"Goodbye, father." The man/creatures breath rattled in his chest.

Gurney gently laid his head on the stage.

The others stood and watched.

"Let me through," Doc said.

"You're, you're too late," Gurney choked up.

Troy knelt next to Gurney. "I'm sorry, Gurney."

Once again the flags of Lthrtown flew a half-mast.

This time Gurney lit the funeral pyre himself.

Troy stood hand in hand with Gurney.

"I have to go," Gurney said.

"Go? Go where?" Kirby asked.

"I have to know if there are anymore clones out there." Gurney replied. "You're in charge until we come back."

"Who's going with you?" Kirby asked.

"Bruno, Smith, Anderson, Black, and Jones. We'll go to Labrys and head to the Outlands from there."

"Well, I'd ask you if you've thought this out, but I'm sure you have."

"Yes, I have. We'll leave tomorrow."

"Well, good luck, Gurney. I hope you find your answer."

"I hope you understand, Kirby," he replied. "I mean about Troy and everything."

"I do. Take as long as you need. We'll be here waiting for you to come back."

The next day Gurney and his party sailed on the Provincetown to Labrys.

"Do you want me to come with you, brother?" M'Lena asked.

"No, sister, I don't know when we'll be back. Someone has to continue the research."

"You're right, of course," she replied. "Just be careful."

A few days later, Gurney and the rest of his expedition rode off into the Outlands and disappeared.

THE OUTLANDS

Rain was not a common occurrence in the Outlands. Little plant life grew there. Even fewer animals lived there. Temperatures were often boiling hot in the day, freezing at night. Those few people that attempted to cross it usually failed. They either died in the attempt or turned back.

Gurney's party continued across the desert. All the terrain they went through was unexplored. As far as they knew no one had ever reached the other side. For all they knew there WAS no other side. Every night they put up a solar powered relay station for the radios that they now carried.

They had finished building a relay station at the highest point of the pass. Gurney stood up in the stirrups on his gelding as they paused on the top of the ridge. Spread out before them was the last thing he had really expected to find. Ahead was a lush and green range of hills, spread out before them as far as the eye could see. Wild flowers of all colors grew in profusion. Trees were in groupings that suggested they had been planted according to a plan. Perhaps as wind breaks.

"I think I see what could be a road, sir," Bruno called out.

"Where," Gurney replied.

"Off to the south, sir," Bruno said. He wiped his face with his bandana.

They slowly made their way down the hillside.

"I hope there's some water nearby," Smith said. He was a strapping blond. "I could sure use a bath."

"You're telling me," Gurney grinned. Bruno and the others laughed.

"I can't remember the last time we had enough water to do that," Smith said, ignoring the laughter of the others. "Seems like weeks."

"Yeah," Gurney said. "I guess we are a little ripe."

Finally, they reached the bottom of the hill. Gurney could hear birds singing somewhere.

"Well, this is definitely a roadway," Anderson said. Geology and archeology were his specialties. He pushed his black hair out of his eyes. "Difficult to say if there's been any traffic lately."

"I don't see any signs of habitation," Gurney said. "Let's check out the nearest grove of trees and see if there's a creek or something."

They dismounted when they reached the trees. "Keep your eyes open. You never know who or what could be around."

"I hear water," Bruno said.

"I hear it, too!" Black exclaimed. He untied the lacing that held his red hair in a ponytail. "Let's find it."

"You guys watch your step," Gurney cautioned them.

"This way," Jones called. He also released his long brown hair.

Soon the six of them were standing beside a babbling brook. The water looked fresh and clean.

"Let's set up camp. Then we can get cleaned up," Gurney said.

"Sir, why don't you go get cleaned up and we'll set up camp," Bruno suggested.

"OK. I think I'll see if there's a little pool just downstream." Gurney got a bar of soap and some shampoo out of his kit.

"OK, sir. We'll take care of everything," Smith said.

Gurney stripped down and walked into the water. "Damn, this waters cold!" he thought. He untied his hair and ducked under the surface. He washed his hair and scrubbed the accumulated dust and dirt of weeks on the trail off his muscular body. The cold water was invigorating. His muscles ached from long hours in the saddle. He was in the best shape he'd ever been in his life. If it weren't for the abundance of gray in his hair it would be hard to believe that he was at least twice the age of the others. Muscle for muscle, pound for pound, his body was as developed as the younger men he traveled with.

Bruno had always been one of Gurney's favorites. The others were all young and eager to explore and gain experience in the field. Kadrovich had suggested them as the best men for the job when Gurney had informed him of his plan to search for more of the mutated clones.

He walked out of the water and dried himself off.

"How's the water?" Bruno asked, as he walked out of the woods.

"Cold, but invigorating," Gurney replied.

"I can see that," Bruno said, he glanced at Gurney's crotch. He tossed him a bundle. "I brought you a change of clothes."

"Thanks. If the area seems secure, I think we'll stay here for a few days and rest," Gurney said, as he slipped into his shirt.

"Sounds like a good idea. Give us a chance to recharge our batteries," Bruno replied. "Damn, this water's cold!"

"That's what I said," Gurney laughed.

"Nobody likes an I told you so," Bruno responded.

"Get a move on. You know how Smith is if we aren't there when the food's ready," Gurney told him.

"I'll be right out," Bruno said.

"Hey you two," Smith called. He was the group's biologist. "Food's ready. Come and get it before I throw it all away."

Gurney and Bruno both laughed at the remark. Smith had become the chief cook and always made the same threat with every meal. He was an expert at combining what little native food that they could find with the rations they had brought with them.

"Well. It's about time, you two," Smith pretended to be mad.

"Sorry," Bruno grinned.

"Yeah, sure," Smith grumbled.

"Where's Jones?" Gurney asked. Jones was the group's botanist.

"Downstream, digging a latrine," Schmidt replied.

Finally the six of them sat around the campfire.

"What do you make of this place, sir?" Bruno asked.

"I'm not sure yet. I'm kind of surprised at the rapid change from the desert to this type of landscape," he paused as he swallowed a mouthful of food. "But, I guess it's not impossible. The mountain ridges might be high enough to affect the weather pattern."

"I saw animal tracks in the woods," Bruno said. "So, there must be some kind of wildlife here."

"Sure. There are birds and insects. Probably fish in the stream, too," Smith put in.

"It would be nice to have some fresh meat instead of this canned and dried stuff," Bruno said.

"Well, sir," Black, the zoologist, looked at Gurney, "If we're going to stay here for a few days I can do some hunting. I can make some snares, too. See what I can find."

"Just be careful," Gurney replied. "I don't want us to get separated."

"And I can look for roots or something. Mushrooms, berries, nuts, maybe," Anderson said

"Check them first with Smith. You don't want to kill us all," Gurney cautioned him.

"Think we should keep a lookout tonight?" Bruno asked.

"I think so. At least until we know that it's safe," Gurney answered.

"I'll take the first watch," Smith volunteered.

"Six hour shifts," Gurney said.

"Yes, sir."

"I hadn't realized it was so late," Bruno said.

"Well, the tarps are up. We can just spread our bedrolls out there," Gurney said.

"It'll be nice to have something besides rocks to sleep on," Bruno said. "I always seem to get a rock in just the wrong place."

The others all laughed.

Gurney thought back to the last time he and Troy had made love. It had been a long intense session. They both knew it might be a long time before they were together again. He smiled to himself and felt a stirring in his groin as he thought about it.

"I've got the barber kit out. Anyone want a haircut?" Bruno asked.

"Yeah, I do," Gurney replied. "This long hair is making me crazy."

"Well, get your butt over here," Bruno laughed. Gurney had let strict protocol go for the time being. He thought everyone would be more comfortable if there were no labels. Even so, the others often called him "sir" and they pretty much took care of setting up camp and grooming the horses.

"Probably should do everyone's hair while we've got time," Gurney sat on a large rock. "I think you should shave my head."

"If you say so," Bruno agreed. He worked silently on Gurney's scalp with a straight razor. There seemed to be a lot grayer then he remembered. He knew better than to make any comment on it. The last thing Gurney wanted to be reminded of was his advancing age.

"That's much better," Gurney said, running his hand over his scalp.

Bruno didn't tell Gurney, but he thought it made him look younger.

Black and Anderson returned from their foraging. Black had snared some rabbits. Anderson had found some wild raspberries.

"I saved the pelts. I thought they might come in handy," Black said, as they sat around the campfire eating their rabbit stew.

"Good idea," Gurney said. "You never know who or what we may find out here. They could be valuable."

"How so, sir," Jones asked.

"If we find someone here, possibly from a lower culture, we might be able to trade them," Gurney replied.

"The area seems clear, sir," Bruno said. "Are we still going to keep sentry duty?"

"Yeah, I think it's a good idea."

For the next few days, they followed the ancient roadway. They saw no sign of life. No buildings, no signs. It seemed like there was no one left in the world except the six men on horseback

"The countryside is beautiful," Bruno said.

"I wonder if there's anyone here, though," Gurney replied. "Either the population is so small they can easily evade us or there might have been a plague or something that killed everyone."

"But, that would mean we might get sick ourselves or carry it back home," Bruno responded.

"Anything is possible," Gurney replied. "We'll just have to keep an eye on each other."

"Well. Doc gave us all the protection he could," Bruno said. "I just hope it was enough."

The others were silent.

They rode along, taking in the splendor of the countryside. The air was fresh and clean. Bright flowers dotted the fields. Birds flew overhead. It seemed that the farther they rode the more wildlife they saw.

"Looks like a storm brewing off to the west," Gurney said. They could see the rain angling down from the flat bottom of a towering thunderhead. The lightning flashed, but it was so far away they heard no thunder. "We'd better find some shelter. And soon."

They rode into a cluster of trees. The rain came at them like a wall. They could see it advancing across the landscape towards them. It was on them so quickly they didn't have time to put up any shelter. The wind whipped the trees.

"Be sure and tie up the horses good," Gurney hollered, trying to be heard over the howling winds. They each had three packhorses besides their regular mount.

Thunder crashed around them. The horse's eyes were big and wild. They were clearly terrified. They pulled against their reins. They wanted to run, to get away from the storm.

The rain lashed at them in waves. It would peak and drop off. Then it would increase again. The thunder rolled and rumbled around them. Lightning hit a tree and split it down the middle.

The men were soaked. It had gotten so dark they were having a hard time even seeing where they were going. Lightning flashed again. The noise of the thunder deafened them. It exploded again and again.

Gurney looked at his chrono. It seemed like the storm had gone on for hours, but it reality, it had only been ten minutes.

Then, as quickly as it had engulfed them, the storm passed. The rain tapered off into a drizzle and finally stopped altogether.

"Man that was some storm!" Bruno exclaimed.

"Sure was," Gurney replied. "I've never seen one that bad before myself."

"We'd better get out of these wet clothes before we get sick," Jones said.

"Yeah, that's the last thing we need right now," Gurney agreed. "Then we'll have to set up camp."

"What about a fire?" Black asked.

"I've got some wood on one of my packhorses," Smith said. "I just hope it's still dry." He went to his packhorse and lifted the flap on one of the packs.

"Well?" Bruno queried.

"We're in luck," Smith smiled. "Some of it is damp, but most of it seems to be dry enough to get a fire started."

"Get the fire going while we get changed," Gurney said.

"Yes, sir," Smith replied. "Then I'll get dinner started."

"Yeah, I'm starving," Bruno said.

"Then get your butt over here and help me," Smith mumbled. The others laughed.

In short order they changed their clothes, got the fire started, and set up camp.

"How much longer are we going to follow the road, sir?" Bruno asked as they huddled around the fire to get warm.

"Probably just another day or two," Gurney replies. It doesn't seem we're going to find anything going this way."

"Do you really think there could be anymore clones of you out here, sir?" Smith asked.

"I think it's possible. Unfortunately, the only one we saw died before I could get any answers to any questions," Gurney replied.

"But, I heard him say he was the last, sir," Bruno commented.

"Yes. But did that mean that he was the last at the outpost and the other's had gone elsewhere? Or, did it mean the others were dead?" Gurney replied. "That's what we're out here to find out."

"But, there's no way we can possibly go everywhere," Black said.

"True enough," Gurney replied. "For some unknown reason one of them was driven to find me. But why not all of them?"

"Something in the way he was put together, maybe," Bruno said.

"That's a possibility," Gurney replied. "Maybe he had some kind of programming to find me at a certain time. Unfortunately, he sought out men who resembled me. I don't think he meant to kill Rogers, either."

"Doesn't a clone usually behave like the original person?" Smith asked.

"Well, the problem is, it's all pretty theoretical. I haven't found much in the old writings about it," Gurney replied. "Maybe M'Lena will find something while we're out here. And, as you said, there is the possibility of some kind of programming. Maybe it was genetic. When he found someone who resembled the me of twenty years ago, and then discovered that they were not his genetic match, he was frustrated."

"And so he hurt them out of anger, not malice," Bruno said.

"Right," Gurney replied. "Or rage."

"Obviously a complicated set of circumstances," Smith said.

"Yeah, and it's something we may never have an answer to," Gurney said.

"Well, we'd better get to sleep," Bruno said.

"Same sentry duty as before," Black asked.

"Yes," Bruno replied.

Smith and Anderson put their sleeping bags together. Gurney could hear them in the dark.

Gurney had a hard time sleeping. He was suddenly wide-awake. He thought he heard Spencer calling his name. He went down to the brook and splashed his face with the cold, fresh water.

"Sir?" It was Bruno.

"Over here, Bruno," replied Gurney.

"Are you alright, sir?"

"I'm fine. I just had a bad dream," Gurney replied.

"Did you want to talk about it?"

"I just thought I heard Spencer calling my name," Gurney replied. "That's all."

"You must have really loved him, sir," Bruno murmured.

"Yeah, I did. I eventually forgave him, but I could never forget the pain he caused me."

Bruno sat, listening to Gurney.

"There was so much I wanted to do and I expected him to be by my side when I did it. I guess it's unfortunately that he refused every attempt I made to patch things up. And, he wasn't man enough to admit that he was wrong and try to patch things ups between us himself," Gurney said.

"Why didn't he make the first move, if I may ask, sir?"

"I guess his pride," Gurney replied from the shadows. "And, after a while, I couldn't take the rejection." He heard an owl hooting somewhere in the distance.

"So you never found Mr. Right," Bruno said. "Never had a family."

"No. Nimbus and all of you are like the family I never had," Bruno couldn't see Gurney smiling in the darkness. "You're all my sons in a way. I care about all of you."

Bruno was quiet.

"Someday, I'll retire or die. You'll have to carry on without me."

"I'm sure you'll be around for a long time, sir," Bruno said.

"No one lives forever," Gurney replied. "Someday, I'll pass the torch to some-one else.

"I'm proud to serve you, sir," Bruno said. I'll always be here for you, if you need me."

"Thanks, Bruno," Gurney said.

"Looks like the sun's coming up," Bruno said.

"Time to wake the other's up," Gurney said.

"Thanks for talking to me, sir."

"Thank you for listening, my boy," Gurney replied.

"Has there been any communication from Gurney?" M'Lena asked.

"Nothing recently," K'Ren, one of her assistants, answered.

"Be sure someone is by the radio at all times," M'Lena told her.

"We have two people here at all times."

"Everyone has been instructed to contact me if we hear anything?"

"Yes, M'Lena," she replied. "We'll keep you informed."

"Look at that!" Bruno exclaimed.

"By the Rock, what is it?" Smith said.

"It's the remains of an ancient city," Gurney said.

Laid out on the plain below them was a pile of rubble. There were a few tow-ers canted at strange angles, leaning against other buildings.

"It's amazing that this is here," Gurney said. "Perhaps it was underwater dur-ing the bombardment."

"Do you think anyone lives here?" Jones said.

"I'm curious as to the name of the place," Gurney said. "I have some old maps. It would give me an idea where Lthrtown is located, in relation to the rest of the world. If we're going to reclaim the planet, we need to map it out and that will take a very long time to do."

Slowly, they began to ride down the slope towards the ruins.

"Keep alert," Gurney told them. "You never know what kind of reception we might get."

"Yes, sir," Bruno said. He held his horse's reins in one hand. The other rest-ed on his right thigh holster. The others were all alert, ready for action, and in similar posture.

They stopped about three hundred yards from the edge of the rubble.

"What do you think we should do?" Bruno asked Gurney.

"It's getting late. We should probably withdraw to the last ridge and set up camp. We can come back in the morning."

They entered a nearby grove of trees and set up camp quickly. The night was warm and there was no need for a fire.

Gurney removed the saddle from his gelding and brushed him down. He gave him an apple and patted his neck. Then he tied him so he could graze.

The men sat in a circle, relaxing after the evening meal. Each was quiet with his thoughts. They had bonded as a unit a long time ago and instinctively knew how the others would react.

"Another beautiful sunset," Smith said. The western sky was a vibrant yellow and orange. As the sun slid below the horizon the sky turned red and then quickly black. The rings dominated the night sky, but the stars were bright.

"Listen," Black said.

They heard a howling in the distance.

"Dogs?" Jones queried.

"Hmm. It's hard to say. Could be," Smith said.

They sat quietly listening to the howls.

"Seems like they're getting closer," Black said.

"Definitely more than one," Smith added.

"I think we should start a fire," Bruno said. "Bring the horses closer, too. If they're wild dogs the fire should probably keep them away."

"There seems to be a pattern to the howls," Black said.

"They're communicating?" Anderson asked.

"Certainly, Lots of animals communicate, especially pack animals," Smith replied.

"Keep alert," Bruno said. "Check your weapons."

The howls were coming from all around them now. The volume was getting louder and louder.

Suddenly, the noise stopped.

"What the," Smith began, as something came out of the woods.

"Is that a man?" Jones said.

"I don't think so," Gurney said.

"What do you want here, monsters?" the creature snarled. His mouth was full of large teeth.

"We are travelers," Gurney called out. "We mean you no harm."

"We have heard that before from others like you," the creature snarled, his black fur glistened in the firelight.

"Others like us?" Gurney said.

"They killed many of us and took our bitches and pups away," he growled.

"We are not your enemies. We are strangers here," Gurney said. "We come from a distant land."

"How do I know you're telling the truth?" the creature asked.

Gurney put his pistol back in its holster and walked towards the creature.

"GURNEY!" Bruno exclaimed.

"I know what I'm doing," Gurney whispered.

"I sure hope so," Bruno replied.

Gurney slowly approached the creature, his open hands in front of him.

The creature's nostrils flared as he sniffed the air. "Your scent is strange to me. Perhaps you are telling the truth."

Gurney's men stood ready for action.

Gurney stepped closer.

The creature leaned forward and sniffed Gurney's hand. His wet nose touched Gurneys palm. 'No. No, you are not the one who did this." His tongue licked Gurneys hand.

Gurney held out his right hand. "I'm Gurney."

"I am Spike. This is my pack," he took Gurneys hand in his.

Gurney could feel the pads, like a dogs paw, but the hand was very human like. The creature's body was lean and muscular. His colors reminded Gurney of a black and brown Doberman.

"You are the pack leader?" Spike asked.

"In a way, yes. I am the oldest."

"We saw you earlier when you came to the edge of the lair."

"The lair? Oh, the ruins."

"Your pack members are still aiming their weapons at me," Spike observed.

"Lower your weapons," Gurney called out. "Where are your pack members?"

Spike signaled and the pack members came out of the woods. No two of them had the same coloration.

Bruno and the others approached.

The two groups stood there, eyeing each other.

"We don't know where they came from," Spike said, as they sat around the campfire. "They killed many of us. Took our bitches and pups with them."

"But why?" Gurney asked.

"We don't know," Spike said. "We had never seen them before. They came from the south"

"And they were men like us?"

"They all looked like they were from the same litter," Spike replied.

"How do you mean?"

"They all had a very similar look. Their scent was even very similar. But, it was different from yours."

"Did you notice anything else?"

"They all seemed to be males," Spike answered.

"Interesting," Gurney said.

"Where did you come from?" Spike asked.

"The west," Gurney said.

"But, there is only the Land of Death that way."

"None of our people who have try to cross it ever came back," Bandit, another of the Canis said.

"We had some experience with the terrain. We came equipped for a long trip," Gurney told them.

"Does this place have a name?" Bruno asked.

"A name?"

"What do you call this place?"

"It is the Lair. That is what we have always called it," Spike replied.

"It's the remains of a city built by the Ancients," Gurney said. "They would have had a name for it."

"We will return in the morning. Perhaps we can help you find what you are looking for," Spike said. "You will be under our protection. No one will bother you."

"Do you think we can trust them?" Bruno asked Gurney.

"They outnumber us, and with those teeth and claws? No contest. They'd tear us to shreds."

"Yeah, I guess you're right," Bruno replied.

"Where is your pack Leader?" Spike asked Black the next morning.

"He's washing himself in the creek," Black motioned with his thumb in the direction Gurney had gone.

Gurney stood knee deep in the creek washing himself. He ducked underwater and rinsed off. When he came up, Spike was standing on the bank.

"Morning, Spike," Gurney said, as he walked to shore.

"Greetings, Gurney," Spike replied. He looked Gurney up and down, his eyes taking in the details of Gurney's body.

"Something on your mind," Gurney asked.

"You are like us, but different," Spike said, in way of reply.

"Well, we're all mammals, if that's what you mean," Gurney said. He quickly dried off and got dressed.

"I am here to take you to the Lair," Spike carefully watched Gurney's movements.

"Very well," Gurney replied.

"May I ask you a question?" Spike said.

"Sure," Gurney replied.

"You are the leader of your pack, correct?"

"Yes, I am," Gurney said, as he gathered up his soiled clothing and wet towel.

"Yet, you have no scars of battle," Spike said. "You are much older than your pack mates."

"Yes, that's true. We do not choose our leaders by combat. I am the leader because of my experience. Leaders must also show the ability to take charge and handle problems."

"I became pack leader by besting Shadow in combat."

"What happened to Shadow? Is he still here?"

"No. When you are no longer pack leader you are banished from the pack."

"Kind of severe, I'd say." They began to walk back to camp.

"We can only support a small number of us here. It is always possible Shadow joined another pack," Spike said. "Or, he could have gone off and lived alone."

"Are there a lot of other packs?"

"Yes. They are scattered all over the woods north of here."

"Interesting, When you were attacked they didn't come to help you?"

"It happened so fast, even if they were so inclined, it would have been over before they got here," Spike replied. "We usually only see the other packs at our annual counsel gathering. We trade some with the other packs that are nearby. Sometimes members leave one pack to join another for some reason."

"So that is why your pack is not all the same?"

"Yes," Spike answered. "Sometimes we might mate with a bitch from another pack. If she doesn't join our pack, we get pick of the litter."

"A very interesting situation," Gurney said.

"It is what works for us, pack leader Gurney," Spike replied.

Spike and Bandit led Gurney and Bruno into the ruins.

"There's no way we can search the entire area," Bruno said. "It's way too big." The ruins looked like they stretched for miles.

"What are you looking for?" Bandit asked.

"A library," Gurney replied.

"What is a library?" Bandit asked.

"A library is a building full of records," Gurney relied.

"Tell us what to look for and we will find it," Spike said.

"A library is a building where books are kept. But, after all this time, they have probably disintegrated," Gurney said. "So, what we're looking for would probably be on compact disc or tape."

"RANGER," Spike called.

Another of the pack members came and joined them. He looked like pictures Gurney had seen of an ancient breed called a Jack Russell. Gurney liked him right away.

"Yes, pack leader?"

"Ranger knows the area better than any other pack member," Spike told Gurney. "Tell him what you seek and he will find it for you."

Gurney showed Ranger examples of what they were looking for.

"I think I know the place, pack leader," Ranger said.

"Is it very far from here?" Gurney asked.

"No, pack leader Gurney," Ranger replied. "It is very close by."

The group walked along a path through the crumbling piles of ruins.

"I think this is the place you are looking for, pack leader Gurney," Ranger said. "If not, there are many others like it."

Gurney and Bruno walked up a slight incline towards a large pile of rubble. Spike and Ranger followed them.

"By the Rock," Bruno said, as they surveyed the site.

"Looks promising," Gurney said. He squatted down and moved a few small-er blocks of stone revealing what appeared to be the remains of books.   " I f this is what we're looking for I'll contact M'Lena and have here send a team out to excavate the site."

"Gurney," Bruno called. "Look at this." He held up some square, flat, cases.

"Let me see those," Gurney said.

Bruno gave them to Gurney. "What are they?"

"They're called compact discs," Gurney replied. There could be music or data of some kind on them."

"On this?" Bruno took a disc out of its box and looked at it. The sun reflect-ed off of the silver surface.

"Is this what you were seeking, pack leader Gurney?" Spike asked.

"It seems to be," Gurney replied. "But, I'd like to get more of our people here to work on it."

"But what about our bitches and pups? You said you would help us," Ranger said.

"We will," Gurney told him. "I'll get in contact with my people and they'll bring us more equipment and reinforcements. The six of us would not make much of a difference."

"M'LENA! Gurney's on the radio," K'Ren called.

M'Lena hurried into the communications room. "Gurney, is everything OK?"

"Yes, sister, everything is fine," Gurney replied.

"Your signal is very weak," M'Lena said. "Have you found something?"

"Yes. I think we've found the remains of a big library," Gurney replied. "We've even met some of the locals."

"Locals?"

"It's complicated. I'll give you a list of what we need," Gurney said. "Then you can just follow the relay pylons to our location. We'll be waiting for you."

"Hurry and give me your list. The signal is fading," M'Lena said.

Gurney quickly gave her his list of supplies and equipment.

"I'll contact Kirby and we'll be on our way as soon as possible," M'Lena said.

Gurney replied, but she couldn't hear his answer.

"The Provincetown is leaving first thing in the morning," Kirby told Troy. He had called him as soon as he had heard from M'Lena.

"I want to go along," Troy told him.

"Don't you have a new show coming up?"

"My staff can take care of it. We're just in the planning stages," Troy replied.

"It's not going to be an easy trip," Kirby said. "Kadrovich will be in charge. Pike will be going along, too."

"You're not going?"

"As much as I want to, no, I can't. Besides, someone has to mind the store."

"I'd better get down to the dock," Troy said.

"Be careful," Kirby said.

"I will. Thanks."

At dawn the Provincetown sailed for Labrys. Troy slept fitfully on deck. He wondered what kind of reception he would get from Gurney.

M'Lena met the Provincetown at the dock. "Troy, I didn't know you were part of the second team."

"Well, officially, I'm not. I just want to be with Gurney."

"Don't expect any special treatment. It's going to be rough. Everyone has to pull their own weight," she told him.

"I don't expect any special treatment," he replied.

"Good. Now that we understand each other, let's get the ship unloaded. Gurney's waiting."

"Can we expect any help from any of the other packs?" Gurney asked.

"I doubt it," Spike replied.

"You said the raiders were like us?"

"Yes, some were. But, there were also Felis with them," Ranger said.

"Felis?" Gurney said.

"Our sworn enemies," Spike said. "They also live to the south of us."

"What are Felis?" Bruno said.

"They are our traditional enemies," Spike replied. "For as long as anyone can remember."

"How many days will it take to get to Gurney's location?" Troy asked M'Lena.

"A couple more days," she replied. "All we have to do is follow the relay pylons. They'll lead us right to him."

"Well, I hope we get there soon."

Gurney and Bruno wandered through the ruins. Ranger was somewhere nearby. He had become their unofficial escort and guide.

"There's got to be something that tells us the name of this city," Gurney said. "The remains of a famous building or something else recognizable."

Bruno stopped to look at something. Gurney kept walking.

Bruno looked up. "Ranger, where's Gurney?"

"I thought he was with you," Ranger replied.

"He was. I stopped to look at something, but he must have kept going."

"It's getting dark. We'd better find him," Ranger said.

They called to the others and organized search parties to look for Gurney.

Gurney climbed to the top of the nearest pile of rubble, looking for some sign of Ranger or Bruno. He called out, but the only noise he heard was some rubble falling somewhere.

Someone lurked in the shadows nearby.

As Gurney returned to the pathway, he heard more rubble falling. He took his pistol from its holster. He was wary.

Gurney's watcher was now his pursuer. It crept closer and closer.

Gurney paused at a fork in the path and the creature jumped onto his back. He pistol disappeared into the dark somewhere, knocked from his hand.

The creature's claws raked Gurney's back. He cried out in pain, he struggled to dislodge his attacker.

Again and again the creature's claws slashed his back.

Gurney managed to get his knife out of its sheath. He could feel his blood soaking his shirt.

Summoning all his strength, Gurney managed to get to his feet and shake his attacker off.

The creature snarled and charged at him.

Gurney lashed out wildly. Blood from a head wound half blinded him and he had to try and rely on his hearing to tell him where his attacker was.

The creature knocked Gurney down and tried to claw his throat.

Gurney could feel the creature's hot breath on his face.

Its jaws neared Gurney's throat.

Gurney continued to stab blindly, hoping to land a lucky blow. He could feel the creature's claws digging into his neck. As he made a few more thrusts he could feel resistance around the knife.

"GURNEY!" Bruno hollered.

Gurney thought he heard a Canis snarl and a shot rang out. The creature suddenly went limp and collapsed on top of him.

Gurney passed out.

"I'm not equipped for wounds this severe," Smith said. The head injury is just a cut. The blood makes it look worse that it really is."

"But," Bruno said. "There must be something you can do for him."

"Some of the clawing on his back is pretty bad. They may even need to be stitched."

"M'Lena has a doctor with her, but it'll be a few days before they get here," Bruno said. "Can he last that long?"

"I really don't know. He's lost a lot of blood," Smith replied.

"Damn. I should have kept a closer eye on him."

"It's not your fault, Bruno," Ranger said. "The Felis are very good at concealing themselves."

Bruno looked over at the body of the Felis. It had definite feline features. He remembered how much dogs and cats usually disliked each other. That might explain much.

"Bruno," Spike said. "Let our healer look at pack leader Gurney. Perhaps he can be of some assistance. We have many natural remedies."

"Very well," Bruno agreed. "We have to keep him stabilized until M'Lena and the doctor get here."

M'Lena rode down the line of march to Troy. "Gurney has been hurt."

"What happened?" Troy asked, immediately concerned for Gurney

"He was attacked by some kind of animal or something," she said. "They don't have a doctor with them."

"What are we going to do?"

"Our doctor and his assistant will ride ahead, all day and night to get there."

"I want to go along," Troy said.

"Are you sure? It's going to be rough going."

"I've GOT to be there with him. Please. Let me go along," Troy pleaded. "Please. If something happens to him, I don't know what I'll do."

"Alright, be ready to go in five minutes."

The Canis erected a shelter for Gurney. Their healer Snoopy, or Ranger, stayed with him all the time. Snoopy carefully cleaned Gurney's wounds and put a healing salve on them.

Bruno and Black sat with Gurney, Watching.

"Did you get to examine the Felis?" Bruno asked.

"Yes, I did," Black replied. "It had retractable claws in both the hands and feet. Eyes better suited to night vision. The palms and soles of the hands and feet are heavily padded. Definite feline features."

"So do you think Canis and Felis are advanced ancestors of dogs and cats?"

"It's possible," Black said. "But, I think it might have been done in the laboratory, genetic research perhaps, or mutants. Of course I have no data to go on so it's all speculation at this point."

"So when the disaster happened, some of them survived and bred," Bruno said. "Of course, that could all be some kind of genetic accident, too."

Black shrugged. "Anything is highly possible."

"I hope the doctor gets here soon," Bruno said.

"We'll just have to keep him as comfortable as possible."

"There's not a whole lot we can do at this point," Bruno replied.

"Gurney wants to talk to you," Ranger told Bruno later in the day.

Bruno hurried to the shelter where Gurney lay.

"Bruno," Gurney croaked, "What happened? I feel like hell."

"You were attacked by a Felis," Bruno told him.

"What, what does it look like?"

"A cat, though certainly much bigger. Definite feline features though," Bruno replied.

"That fits in with my theory," Gurney said.

"What's that?"

"Someone did some genetic modifications," Gurney replied. "Mutants, something like that."

"How are you feeling?"

"Very weak," Gurney replied. "How bad is it?"

"It's hard to say," Bruno said. "The Canis are doing all they can. I radioed M'Lena. They have a doctor with them. They should be here soon."

"Is everyone else all right?"

"Everyone's fine," Bruno assured him. Someone is always nearby in case you need anything."

"I've never killed anyone or anything before," Gurney whispered.

"You didn't have a choice. It was you or him. You had no choice."

Ranger came into the shelter. "Bruno, Gurney needs to rest now."

"Okay," Bruno said.

"Drink this, Gurney," Ranger said. "It will help you sleep."

Laboriously, Gurney sucked the fluid through a reed straw. "Thank you, Ranger."

"Snoopy and I will be right outside. If you need anything just call."

Gurney had already fallen asleep.

Snoopy came in and changed the dressings on Gurney's wounds.

The sun was just disappearing behind the western ridge when a howl was heard in the distance.

"Bruno," Spike said. "Your people have cleared the pass."

Going over to his saddlebags, Bruno got a flare gun.

"What is that?"

"Something to attract their attention," Bruno replied. He raised the gun and shot it into the air.

When the flare ignited, some of the Canis barked or whimpered.

"It's nothing to worry about," Bruno said, to no one in particular.

"LOOK!" Troy exclaimed. "A signal flare!"

"How could they know we were here?" the doctor said.

"What does it matter? They know." They hurried down the trail to the camp.

Bruno met Troy and the others before they reached camp. He quickly explained what happen as they rode to camp.

"So, the Canis and Felis are intelligent dogs and cats?" Troy asked.

"Basically, yes," Bruno said. "They've been very helpful. Well, the Canis have been anyway. We haven't seen a live Felis, yet."

"Where's Gurney?"

"This way," Bruno led them to the shelter. "This is Spike, the pack leader, Ranger, he's our liaison, and Snoopy. Snoopy is the packs healer."

"I'm Troy and this is Doctor Gunnar."

"I'd like to examine Gurney if I could," Gunnar said.

"Certainly," Snoopy led the way. Gently he took the dressings off Gurney's back.

"When did this happen?" Gunnar asked.

"Two days ago," Bruno replied. "Why?"

"He's already started to heal," Gunnar said.

"How is that possible?" Troy asked.

"I put a healing salve on his wounds," Snoopy said. "I was unsure if they would help Gurney."

"I'd like to learn more about this salve," Gunnar said to Snoopy.

"Certainly," Snoopy replied. "I'll give you some, if you'd like."

"Is there anything you can do for Gurney?" Troy asked Gunnar.

"Well, at the rate he's healing, I don't think he's going to need stitches. There may be some scarring, though," Gunnar replied. He took Gurney's pulse and blood pressure.

"I gave Gurney something to help him sleep," Snoopy said. He redressed Gurney's wounds.

"Well, Gurney seems to be in good hands," Gunnar said. "I'll just examine him in the morning."

"Is it alright if I stay with him?" Troy asked.

Gunnar looked at Snoopy.

"He will sleep all night, but it should be alright," Snoopy said.

"Do you require anything?" Ranger asked.

"I have my kit on my horse," Troy replied. "It has all I need."

"We will be right outside," Ranger said. "If you need anything, just call."

"Thanks," Troy replied.

"I don't know what they're using, but Gurney's healing at an unbelievable rate," Gunnar told Bruno. "If there's scarring there isn't really anything I can do about it."

"How can that be?"

"I'm sure it's something they've developed over time. Folk medicine often works as well as our so called advanced methods."

"So you expect a full recovery," Bruno said.

"I expect so. I saw no sign of infection," Gunnar responded. "He did lose a lot of blood, so I expect he'll be weak for a few days though."

"Well, that's a relief," Bruno said. "I'm not sure we'd know what do to without him to lead us."

Two days later Bruno met M'Lena at the edge of camp. "How's Gurney?"

"You're not going to believe this," Bruno said as he led her to the shelter.

Gurney was sitting up. "Hello, sister."

"How are you feeling?"

"All things considered, not to bad," Gurney replied. "I'm just a little weak."

"Turn around, sir," Gurney said. "Let's take a look."

Except for some angry red marks, Gurney was healed. "They tell me it was pretty bad," Gurney said. "I don't remember too much about the attack. Bruno told me, though."

"It's amazing," M'Lena said.

"You'll be on your feet tomorrow," Gunnar said.

"Yes, Gurney," Ranger replied. "We have had some dealing with a few Felis."

"But, do you have any way to contact them?"

"The encounters have always been in the forest. We have never been in any of their settlements."

"So, they do band together," M'Lena said.

"They call them prides."

"I do not understand what they would want with our bitches and pups," Spike said.

"You said there were others. Men like us," Gurney said.

"Yes," Spike said.

"Perhaps the Felis were assisting them," Bruno said.

"But for what purpose?" M'Lena asked.

"Slaves, maybe?" Bruno speculated.

"What other use would they have?"

"I think we need to make a little scouting trip to the south," Gurney said.

"I will lead you there, Gurney," Ranger said.

"All right, Ranger," Gurney replied.

"Where's the dig site?" M'Lena asked.

"Someone can show it to you," Gurney said.

"Do you require our assistance?" Spike asked her.

"Sure," she replied. "We can use all the help we can get."

"We'll let your team get some rest and start in the morning," Gurney said.

Ranger trotted alongside Gurney's horse as they headed for the area where the Felis were known to gather.

Gurney was amazed at the seemingly endless stamina of Ranger and Scout. He had suggested they ride horseback, but they had refused. The horses seemed to be a little skittish around the Canis. Gurney figured the Canis felt the same.

"How far is it?" Gurney asked.

"Not much farther," Scout replied.

"Do you think we should approach on foot?" Gurney asked.

"It would probably be advisable if you and your people were to keep out of sight for the moment," Scout said.

"Right," Gurney agreed.

A simple camp was set up quickly.

"Pike, you stay with the horses," Gurney said. "Everyone stay sharp. We don't know if they have any kind of security or not."

Ranger and Scout led the way as they headed into the forest.

Gurney and the others were in camouflage clothing as they went deeper and deeper into the silent forest. The thick ground cover of pine needles muffled their footsteps. Occasionally a shaft of golden sunlight would penetrate the dim light. They silently followed Ranger's lead, rifles at the ready.

Ranger stopped his advance. "I detect the scent of a Felis."

"Can you tell how many?" Gurney asked.

"No. Not at this distance. But, we are downwind of their location," Ranger replied.

"So," Bruno said. "What's our next move?"

"I will go alone and check out the situation," Ranger told them. "I will return after I get an accurate count."

Gurney and the others squatted down to wait. There was no telling how long Ranger would be gone. The silence in the woods was a little disconcerting.

"I need to pee," Jones said.

"Don't go too far," Gurney told him.

"Yes, sir," Jones nodded. He disappeared into the underbrush.

The others sat and waited patiently.

"Sir," Jones reappeared. "There's something here I think you should see."

"What is it?"

"I think it would be better if you just take a look, sir," Jones led Gurney through the underbrush.

"Where are we going, Jones?"

"Right here, sir," Jones said, pointing at the ground.

"What the," Gurney began. He stopped when he realized what he was looking at. In a shallow grave, lay the body of a Canis.

"I didn't look to close, but I think it's a female, sir," Jones said.

"The Felis must have done this," Gurney said. "I doubt the Canis would bury someone this far from their territory."

"Should I get a body bag, sir?"

"Ask Scout to come here and take a look. We'll do whatever he says," Gurney said.

Jones disappeared into the underbrush.

A few minutes later he reappeared with Scout.

"You wanted me to see something, Gurney?"

"Yes, Scout. Jones discovered something I thought you should see."

Scout knelt down and looked at the body.

"Do you know who it is?"

"Yes, I do," Scout replied. It is Sassy, Spike's mate."

"I'm not familiar with your customs," Gurney said. "Should we take the body back to the Lair?"

"Yes. We should take her back."

"I'll have Jones and Black take care of it."

"Thank you, Gurney."

Jones withdrew again. Scout followed him back to camp.

"Take a quick look and see if you can determine the cause of death," Gurney told Jones and Black when they returned.

"Yes sir."

"I saw few Felis," Ranger said. "The main camp must be further south."

"Well, we'll so back to the Lair," Gurney said. "We've got bad news for Spike."

"Scout told me."

"Let's get out of here. I don't think it's a good idea for us to be here after dark," Gurney ordered.

Pike already had the horses ready to go when they rejoined him.

Gurney reached down to Scout. "I think we'll make better time if you ride with us."

Scout took Gurney's hand and pulled himself up behind him. Ranger was with Jones.

"Sir," Black rode up to Gurney. "It looks to me like the females' neck was broken. If it was an accident or homicide, I have no way to tell. Gunnar should be able to tell, though."

"Thank you, Black, Gurney said.

"Yes sir. No problem, sir," Black fell back in line.

"If it will help us against the Felis, you may examine Sassy's body," Spike told

Gunnar.

"As soon as I know anything, I'll let you know," Gunnar said.

"I'm sorry about your mate, Spike," Gurney said, after Gunnar left.

"Thank you, Gurney."

"If there's anything I can do," Gurney paused.

"I thank you, Gurney," Spike said. "But, that is not our way."

Gurney and Spike stood by a rain-swollen creek.

"I had a loss recently myself," Gurney said.

"I know that you are different than we are, Gurney," Spike said.

"Oh? And, how do you mean, Spike?"

"I know that many of you are in bonded couples. Male to male, bitch to, sorry, female to female."

"Well, yes. That is the way for many of us. But, there are also traditional male-female couples, too. I'm not bonded to anyone, anymore."

Spike silently regarded Gurney.

"If this is a problem," Gurney said.

"It is not a problem with us, Gurney. We know that there are many different ways to do many things. If that is what makes your people happy, then who are we to say that it is wrong?"

"I'm glad of that, Spike."

Spiked turned to face Gurney and held out his right hand. "I would be honored to call you brother, Gurney."

Gurney clasped Spike's hand. "And I you, too."

"The pack has already discussed it. We would like to make you all members of our pack."

"We would be honored, Spike."

"Where isss Pantera?" Tiger asked.

"I do not know," Boots replied.

"He ssshould have been back a long time ago," Tiger paced back and forth, his tail lashed around.

"Maybe the Canisss caught him, sssomehow," Boots replied.

"Perhapsss," Tiger said.

"I am having sssecond thoughtsss about our alliance with the outlandersss," Boots said.

"Ssso am I, Tiger replied. "Ssso am I."

"We've put up surveillance cameras on the main trails," M'Lena said. " I f anyone heads this way we'll know about it"

"How will that help us?" Spike asked.

"If the Felis are coming to raid, it will give us time to prepare a defense," Gurney said.

"We have sent messengers to the other packs asking them to join us against the Felis," Ranger said. "So far there has been no response."

"Well, more of my men will be arriving soon," Gurney said.

"Do you have a plan, Gurney?" Spike asked.

"The short term goal is the release of the Canis prisoners," Gurney replied. "The long term goal is to be sure this doesn't happen again."

Two days later, a train of packhorses arrived with Kadrovich in the lead. "You're a site for sore eyes, sir," he said to Gurney.

"It's good to see you, too," Gurney grinned, as they hugged.

"I think we've got everything you wanted."

"Unload now and get some rest," Gurney said. "In the morning I want you to head back with a load of material for analysis in Labrys."

"Yes, sir," Kadrovich replied. He headed for the packhorses, barking out orders to the crew.

"Spike, there is something we would like to do with your permission," Gurney said.

"What is that, Gurney?"

"We'd like to establish an outpost here for our studies. But, if you object, we will not do it."

"I see no problem with that, Gurney."

"If there is anyplace you do not want us to go, let us know," Gurney said.

"As pack members you may go anywhere," Spike replied.

"So far most of the printed material is damaged beyond repair," M'Lena told Gurney. "But, I hope that as we get deeper we'll find some usable materials."

"So, do you think this was a library?"

"Yes," she replied. "But the Canis know what we're looking for and they've shown us some other promising sites."

"Other libraries?"

"Possibly, but I think some may have been retail outlets," she replied. "There appear to be many copies of each item. And, there's not very much printed material."

"Are the Canis being helpful?"

"The pups are quite interested," she replied. "Just like kids everywhere they like to dig." She sat on a fallen tree by the stream.

"We've been doing some cross training," Gurney said. "They're teaching us tracking, trapping, foraging, and hand to hand combat. We've been showing them some weapons use." He sat down next to her.

The sat together in silence for a while, enjoying the mild weather.

"Lthrtown has changed a lot in the short time you've been gone," she said, finally breaking the silence.

"What's been happening?"

"There has been a population explosion like you wouldn't believe. People from the west and north, mostly, and the other towns are growing, too," she said.

"Well, I guess it's a good thing," he replied.

"When are you planning on coming home?"

"I've been a bit busy with things here," Gurney replied. "Besides, you know the reason I'm here."

"I know, but people are starting to ask questions."

"Once things are under control here, I'll resume my search."

"Well," she said. "There are even some people who are talking about you running for mayor, maybe president, if all the communities can band together."

"Me? President?" Gurney snorted.

"That's what they're saying."

"I was thinking of retiring," he laughed. "My outside business interests would keep my living at a comfortable level. And besides, there's still of lot of the world to explore."

"I don't think I can see you retiring, brother," she said.

"I think I could put together a good team. Kadrovich, Bruno, a few others."

"What about Troy?"

"I can't ask him to wait, even if I wanted to," Gurney replied, standing up. "Besides, he has the theater to keep him busy."

"But, I though you loved him?"

"As much as it's possible for someone like me to love anyone," he replied. "And, besides, I'm twice his age anyway."

"I understand," M'Lena said.

"I hope he does."

"I'm sure he will."

They walked slowly back to camp.

"A night raid would not be to our advantage. The Felis have better night vision," Spike said. "We rely more on sight and scent."

"We can have some night vision scopes sent in," Gurney said.

"How does that work?"

"Infrared sensors," Gurney said. "All bodies put out heat radiation that the sensors can detect."

"Also, the Felis will probably never expect us to attack at night," Kadrovich added.

"I think we need to ssstop thisss before it goesss any further," Tiger said.

"There is a report that the Canisss are having a large gathering," Boots put in.

"The outlandersss have disssappeared," Tiger said. "We may not get along with the Canisss, but I sssee no reassson to continue with thisss courssse of action."

"What do you think we ssshould we do?" Boots asked.

"Return the Canisss captivesss to the edge of the foresssst and releassse them," Ling said. "Otherwissse there maybe blood ssspilled for no reassson."

"Sir," Kadrovich rushed to Gurney's tent. "The cameras have detected activity in the forest."

"What's happening?"

"There is a group of Canis being escorted by some Felis," he replied. " I t looks to me like they are being released."

"Well," Gurney said. "Let's go and meet them."

"Yes, sir, I'll go get Spike."

The two groups stood looking at each other across the clearing. The crickets were silent, but fireflies flitted between the trees.

Finally, a white Felis turned to the Canis that were standing in the rear. "You are free to go."

The Canis rushed into the waiting arms of their pack mates.

The white Felis approached. "I am Sssnowball," she said. "We have decided it would be in everyone'sss bessst interessst to releassse the prisssonersss."

Gurney and his group remained hidden in the background.

"We were ill advisssed by human outlandersss that taking your pack member'sss hossstage would get you to give usss concessions in the foressst," Snowball continued. "All Felisss do not consssider Canisss to be enemiesss. Many of usss would prefer to be your friendsss."

"We have allies, too," Spike said, as Gurney stepped into view.

Snowball hissed and moved back a few steps. "Human alliesss? Here?"

"They have just joined us," Spike said.

"I sssupossse it isss only fair that you would ssseek alliesss asss well," Snowball said.

"Snowball," Gurney said. "What did these allies of yours look like?"

"They were very tall and all of them looked very sssimilar," she replied.

"Do you speak for all Felis?" Spike asked.

"Not for all, but for many," Snowball replied.

"We will do what we must to protect ourselves and our young," Spike said.

"Asss will we," Snowball said.

"If I might make a suggestion," Gurney said. Establish a neutral zone where no one goes, Perhaps this forest."

"But, we both hunt in the forest," Spike said. "If we are to continue to live here, we need to hunt here."

"Well, I leave it to you, then," Gurney said.

"Let usss meet and talk together about thisss," Snowball said.

"Very well," Spike replied. "You are welcome to come to our lair, if you wish."

"We thank you," Snowball said.

"When do we leave, Gurney?" Kadrovich asked.

"I'm heading south," Gurney replied. "I want you to coordinate the flow of material back to Labrys and Lthrtown."

"You're not coming back with us?" Troy asked.

"I still don't have my answers. I'm relying on you all do to your jobs while I'm gone."

"I'll be here until the next pack train gets here," M'Lena said. "I'll leave with that one."

"Pike," Gurney called.

"Yes, sir?"

"You'll be in charge of the dig crew," Gurney told him.

"Yes, sir. Thank you, sir," Pike excitedly replied. "I'll handle everything, sir."

Gurney was saddling his gelding the next morning, when Troy walked up to him. "I don't understand why you need to do this," Troy said.

"It's something I have to do," Gurney replied.

"Why can't I go with you?"

"For the same reason Kirby isn't," Gurney replied as he slipped the bit in the gelding's mouth. "Someone has to mind the store."

"But,"

"NO! Please, Troy. Don't make this harder than it has to be," Gurney said.

"I, I," Troy stopped. He turned and walked away.

"Gurney," Spike called. "Did you think you could sneak out of here?"

"I didn't want you to make a fuss," Gurney replied.

"I just wanted to thank you and your people for all your help," Spike said. "Don't forget about us. And, don't forget that you are all our pack brothers now."

"Thanks, Spike," Gurney replied, as Scout and Ranger joined the group.

"We are ready to go," Scout said.

"Ready to go?" Gurney questioned.

"You are headed for unexplored territory," Spike said. "You may need assistance that only our different abilities can help with."

"Besides, we volunteered to go along," Scout said.

"And," Ranger said. "As pack members it is our right and duty to accompany you."

"Surely there will be many new dangers lurking in the south that we will be able to help you with," Scout added.

"Well," Gurney said to Bruno. "I guess we don't have much to say about it, eh?"

"Looks that way," Bruno replied.

"Safe trip, brother," M'Lena said.

"Come back soon," Troy said, as M'Lena put her arm around his shoulders.

"We'll be back as soon as we can," Gurney answered.

The expedition headed south. The forest was on their left, grasslands to the right.

Suddenly a pair of Felis appeared out of the forest.

"Greetingsss, friendsss," one of them said.

"Greetings," Gurney replied.

"In the sssspirit of cooperation, we have been sssent to accompany you," the first Felis said.

"Tiger wissshsss to ssshow hisss good intentionsss," the second Felis added. "We are to follow your inssstructionsss and help in any way we can."

"I am Ling," the first Felis introduced herself. "This is my mate, Yang."

"We welcome you in the spirit of cooperation," Gurney replied.

They continued their journey south.

"There isss freasssh water thisss way," Yang said, pointing to the west. "No doubt there will be an area to ssspend the night."

Camp went up quickly. The Canis were on the north side, the Felis on the south. Gurney and his men were in the middle.

The group sat silently around the campfire as they ate dinner.

Finally, Gurney broke the silence. "Ling, tell us about the humans that you were helping."

"They were all very tall," Ling replied. "There were no females among them."

"They jussst ssseemed very ssstrange," Yang added.

"And then, they jussst disssappeared," Ling said. "One morning they were all gone. They sssaid nothing, they jussst left."

"Yes," Gurney said. "That does seem very strange."

For the next week the expedition continued south. The landscape changed. It became lusher. No sign of a settlement was seen.

They mapped the terrain as they went and put up radio relays every night.

"This is beautiful country," Gurney said.

"Yes, it is," Bruno replied.

As the Canis and Felis got used to each other they began to interact with each other more.

Soon, Gurney was sure they would all see each other just as people. Not as Human, Canis, or Felis.

Gurney often dreamed of Spencer or Troy. He knew that Spencer had loved him and that Troy still did. He also knew that Kirby was in love with him, too. But, even though he desperately wanted a partner, he was afraid of being hurt again. The trauma was more than he could stand. Besides, what kind of life would it be? He wanted to see and touch and smell everything the world had to offer. How could he ask someone to give up everything to roam all over? No home, no roots, never in any one place for very long. Perhaps it was better to be alone. No strings, no attachments. Nimbus-Unicorn could take care of itself. Kirby was well suited to run the organization. Troy had his theater. They'd be fine without him there.

On the eighth day out, they heard a shriek that made their blood run cold.

"What was that?" Bruno said.

"There is an old saying, 'Something evil, this way comes'," Gurney replied. "I'm sure we'll know very soon."

"Keep alert!" Bruno called out. Everyone took out their rifles. The Canis and Felis took out their knives.

Everyone looked around nervously.

Once again the shriek chattered the air.

"What IS that?" Bruno said, not really expecting an answer.

Gurney took out his binoculars and began to scan the area.

"What's that? A bird?" Jones said, pointing into the distance.

Gurney tried to focus on the object. "I'm not sure what it is, but I don't think it's a bird," he said.

The object approached with alarming speed.

"Quick," Gurney urged. "Everyone into the woods."

They heard the flap of wings behind them. The shriek shattered the air again.

"It IS some kind of bird," Smith said. "It's got to be."

The creature made a few more passes and then left in the direction it had come from.

"We'd better have some bigger firepower," Bruno said. The men quickly unpacked and assembled some machineguns.

"Let's set up camp, but everyone stay alert," Gurney said. "I have a feeling we'll be having a return visit."

Smith applied the salve to Gurney's back. "I'm amazed at how quickly you're healed."

"I'm still a little stiff, but I'm sure the will go away in time," Gurney said. "What about scarring?"

"There may be some, but I don't think there will be much."

"I sure the Canis would look at them as badges of honor," Gurney said.

"I'm sure they would."

"They will probably fade in time."

"That's OK. I guess they would add to my rugged appearance." Gurney laughed.

"GURNEY," Bruno called. "The bird, or whatever it is, is coming back and he's got company."

They peered out from behind cover.

Ranger and Scout growled, the hair on the back of their necks stood up.

Ling and Yang hissed and spit, their tails lashed around in a frenzy.

"By the rock," Anderson whispered. "What are they?"

The creatures grew in size as Gurney and the others watched.

"We'd better get the heavy artillery," Bruno said. "I think we're going to need em."

"Be sure the horses are secure," Gurney said.

They could hear the birds shrieking in the distance.

Bruno tossed Gurney a machine gun and kept a grenade launcher for himself.

The birds climbed higher and then began a steep dive, claws outstretched. They shrieked again.

"Wait and pick your shots," Bruno called.

The brightly plumed birds screamed again as they drew closer.

"NOW!" Bruno hollered. The guns erupted in a cacophony of noise.

A couple of the smaller birds plunged to the ground. Others cried out in rage and surprise and wheeled away.

"Everyone OK," Gurney called.

Everyone replied that they were fine.

"They're coming back. Be sure you've got enough ammunition," Bruno called. "Keep on your toes."

The birds climbed higher and split into smaller groups of twos and threes.

"Looks like they're going to come at us from different directions," Gurney said to Bruno.

"Watch yourselves," Bruno said.

The birds screamed again as they dove at the group.

Explosions and gunfire shattered the air as the birds drew close.

Gurney picked up the flamethrower he gotten earlier and had kept nearby.

The largest bird focused his attention on Gurney. Its red eyes were filled with hate and blood lust. Its yellow beak was hooked on the end.

The rest of the flock scattered. But, the biggest bird was still intent on Gurney.

Gurney waited until the last possible moment before he pulled the trigger. The flames shot out, engulfing the bird. It screamed out in pain and rage as it crumpled at Gurney's feet. The stench of burning flesh filled the air.

The few surviving birds shrieked in rage and flew off in the direction they had come from.

The flames slowly consumed the fallen bird's bright plumage.

"Gurney, you alright," Bruno asked.

"Yeah, I'm fine," Gurney replied.

"Everyone," Bruno called out, "Be sure they're dead before you approach them."

"Scales and feathers," Gurney said. "It's like something from a fairy tale or a legend."

"Gurney," Ranger said. "It might be a good idea for us to leave the area. If there are scavengers in the area, surely they will be drawn here by the smell of the burning flesh. It would be dangerous for us to be here. They might attack us, too. You never know."

Gurney looked at Bruno.

"Everyone saddle up," Bruno said. "We're outta here."

They quickly gathered their equipment and hurried further south.

Ling and Yang led the way, while Ranger and Scout walked on the left side, closest to the forest. Smith and Black rode on the right side, near the desert, followed by Anderson and Jones in the rear. Gurney and Bruno rode in the middle of the formation.

"Things are getting stranger and stranger," Bruno said to Gurney.

"I think that's an understatement," Gurney replied.

"Talking dogs and cats, flying creatures that are half bird, half dragons. What's next?"

"I'm sure we'll find out soon," Gurney replied.

The mountains slowly receded and finally disappeared over the western horizon. The desert gradually turned into a broad green plain. Tall trees grew in clumps. Gurney was reminded of pictures of a place called the veldt in old Africa.

Ranger and Scout sniffed the air. "We smell water," Ranger said.

"There is a lot of it, too," Scout added.

They crested a hill.

Before them was a beautiful, blue body of water. Waves lapped gently against a broad, white sand beach. Small birds ran up and down the sand in rhythm with the waves.

"It's an ocean," Gurney said. "Salt water. It's got to be."

"It's beautiful," Jones said. "I've never seen so much water."

"That's an understatement," Anderson replied.

Seabirds wheeled overhead, crying out. The arc of the rings seemed to disappear into the water.

"Now what," Bruno said.

"Well, in theory, if we go to the west we should eventually reach the mouth of the River Styx," Gurney said.

"And if we go east."

"Unknown territory," Gurney replied.

"Well, let's set up camp here and rest," Bruno said. "Tomorrow we can decide what to do."

A roaring fire of driftwood made an oasis of light on the beach. Sparks flew up into the cool night air. With the sky full of stars and the bright rings, it wasn't all that dark.

Gurney stood on the beach, just beyond the reach of the waves.

"It isss an amazing sssight, isss it not?" Ling asked.

"Yes, it certainly is. The world is full of many beautiful sights," Gurney replied.

"I am curiousss, Gurney," Ling paused. "May I asssk a quessstion?"

"Ask away," Gurney said.

"What isss the purpossse of your journey?"

"Many years ago, I was taken captive by a group of men living in what we call the Outlands. The Dead Lands, to you. They took cells from my body and grew copies, called clones, of me."

"For what purposse?"

"That was the way they did things. There were no women for them to mate with."

"But, they were much taller than you."

"Yes. They made some changes to the copies."

"It isss sssomething I do not undersssstand. Perhapsss I will in time."

"What did they offer the Felis?"

"Domination over the Canisss," Ling replied. "But, not all Felisss hate the Canisss."

"And, the Outlanders simply left?"

"Yesss, The day you arrived they sssimply left. It wasss almossst asss if they knew something wasss going to happen. We did not even know they were gone. They had a camp a ssshort dissstance away from usss."

"And when they left, you needed to find a way out that would preserve your honor."

Ling paused. "Yesss, we did."

The pair stood in silence for a few minutes.

"I return to camp, Gurney."

"Sleep well, Ling." Gurney stood and watched the ocean late into the night.

"I think we should go west, find the river and head home," Jones said.

"You forget yourself, mister," Bruno said sharply. "It's not your decision to make."

"Sorry sir, I meant no disrespect."

"I know you're all tired," Bruno said. "We can stay here for a few days and refresh ourselves."

"We could supplement our supplies with local items," Scout said.

"Let's relax for a few days," Gurney said, looking at Bruno. "I think we've earned it."

"I think you're right," Bruno replied.

"I'd like to try and see if I can catch some fish," Black said.

"I'll help you," Anderson announced.

"We will help, too," Ling said. "We naturally enjoy fish, alssso."

"I bet we'll catch some real whoppers, too," Black said.

"M'Lena, we've lost contact with Gurney," K'Ren said.

"When's the last time we heard from them?"

"They've missed their last couple of check in times."

"Well, it's possible there's a failure in the system," M'Lena said. "Keep me informed."

"Gurney, something's wrong with the radio," Bruno said.

"What's wrong?"

"I'm sending, but I'm not receiving an answer."

"Something may have happened to one of the relay stations," Gurney said.

"I'm sure I checked out the instillations," Bruno said.

"I'm sure you did. I'm just thinking out loud," Gurney said.

"Without going back the way we came, there's no way to check the system."

"We'll just have to hope it's a temporary problem."

"Changing the subject, what do you think we should do next?"

"We could go east for a few days. Then, if we find nothing, we can come back this way and continue on to the west."

"What about the Canis and Felis?" Bruno said, as he continued to work on the radio.

"They may want to return home. I'm not sure they'd want to go home with us."

"Why not?"

"Many people fear the new and unknown. Just because we except them as equals, doesn't mean everyone else will," Gurney replied.

"That's too bad," Bruno said. "I was hoping they'd come with us."

"I've been doing some reading of the writings of the Ancients," Gurney told Bruno. "It the ancient past, the majority of people were like those in Breederstown. People like us were in the minority. People were often killed just for that reason."

"But, why?"

"Many were threatened because they were insecure in their own sexuality."

"But, why should they care? It's a private matter. Why would they feel threatened?"

"It was called homophobia," Gurney replied.

"I've never heard the term before."

"People couldn't accept the fact that people were born with that preference."

Bruno made no comment.

"Then, I found some references to a plague of some kind. Even though no one was immune, people like us were blamed for the spread of the disease."

"What happened then?"

"Eventually a cure was found, but those with the disease were still considered outcasts. Even children, who had been born with the disease or gotten it from blood transfusions, were given the same treatment."

Bruno shook his head in disbelief.

"Even organized religion, which claimed there was a god who loved everyone, equally, mistreated our people. The so-called Moral Majority. They considered themselves good Christians, but they hated our ancestors just for being who they were."

"Unbelievable," Bruno said.

"But true, unfortunately," Gurney replied. "And, there were even different definitions of god to different people."

"How could people justify doing things like that?"

"People can justify anything in their own minds."

"Is there anything we can do?"

"We just have to do our best to make sure it doesn't happen again."

"And, that's why you're hesitant to take the Canis and the Felis back to Lthrtown with us," Bruno said.

"Yes. I'm afraid of the reception they'd get," Gurney said. "People fear the unknown, as I said before."

"Sooner or later we'll have to tell people about them."

"I know we will. I just think we may need to ease into it. I don't want there to be any problems."

"Problems?"

"More people have been killed in the name of gods, the churches, and religions than in wars," Gurney said. "I don't want our new friends to get hurt out of ignorance on someone else's part."

"I'd hate to see them get hurt."

"Well, as long as I have something to say about it, they won't be," Gurney said.

A few days later the group headed east along the coast. The Canis and Felis had replenished the food supplies.

"Gurney," Yang called, as they headed out the next day.

"Yes, Yang? What can I do for you?"

"I wanted to thank you. We have found many new varietiesss of medicinal plantsss. They will help all our peoplesss."

"Are you going to return home now?"

"Oh, no, Gurney, Not yet at any rate. If we return thisss way we will head north asss you head farther wessst."

"Good. We would hate to see you go. We would miss you."

"We would misss you, too, Gurney," Yang replied.

The group had once again camped overlooking the ocean. They had still seen no sign of intelligent life.

Gurney had spent many hours with his binoculars scanning the horizon. He had hoped he might see a sail. But, he saw nothing except the broad expanse of the blue ocean.

He knew it was time to return home. They had been out of radio contact for far to long.

"Hey, Gurney," he turned at the sound of Bruno's voice.

"Hey, yourself," Gurney replied.

"Everything OK?"

"Oh, yeah," Gurney replied. "Just thinking about a course of action."

"Well, we haven't found anything going this way."

"When we return, the Felis and Canis will leave us and return home."

"I know. Ranger told me yesterday," Bruno said.

"We'll head back tomorrow. I think they're eager to return home."

"I wish we had found something," Bruno said.

"But, we did," Gurney said.

"We did?"

"Knowledge," Gurney told him. "And, knowledge is power."

"Well," Smith said. "You're finally back. I wasn't going to be able to hold dinner much longer."

Gurney and Bruno took the plates Smith offered to them.

"Your usual wonderful meal," Gurney said when he was finished.

"Thanks," Smith replied. "Fresh food really makes a difference."

"We'll start the return trip tomorrow," Gurney announced. "I'm sure everyone is eager to return home."

"We will all profit greatly from the knowledge we have gained," Yang said.

"When we part company, we will give you radios. They will be on my private channel," Gurney said. "If you need us all you have to do it call."

They had returned to the point on the beach where they had first camped at the side of the ocean.

"Well," Gurney said. "This is our last meal together."

"We will miss you, Gurney," Scout said.

"We'll miss you, too," Gurney replied. "I hope the Felis and the Canis will continue to work together."

"I am sssure we will," Yang said.

The next morning, Gurney and the others waved back at the Felis and Canis as they disappeared over the brow of the hill.

"Now what, Gurney?"

"Well, Bruno, I think that the river must be to the west. We can go there and follow it back home."

A few days later, on the top of a ridge, Bruno said, "I think I see a town down there, but I'm not sure. We don't have anyone out this way."

Gurney got out his binoculars. "We're to far away to make out much. But, I think I see a ships mast."

"It'll probably be nightfall before we get there," Bruno said.

"We'll observe things when we get there," Gurney replied.

The bright sunlight danced on the placid water of the harbor, but the town was dull and drab. The buildings were low and painted in shades of dark browns and greens. No banners waved in the breeze and few people were on the streets.

It didn't appear to Gurney to be a place that would welcome travelers.

They approached the settlement after the sun had set. Dressed completely in black they merged into the darkness. Few lights showed in the windows. No one seemed to be out on the streets.

"Bruno," Gurney said. "Go and see if you can find anything. We'll wait here."

"Yes sir."

"Alone?" Smith said.

"One person has less chance of being caught," Bruno said.

The others watched, as Bruno ran in a crouch, to the nearest building. They were all low one and two story buildings. The walls were plain and unadorned. Gurney and the others waited silently in the shadows of the woods.

Bruno disappeared as he worked his way to the river. He wanted to see if there was a ship there.

Nothing moved on the dimly lit streets except Bruno.

He turned a corner and saw the ship tied to a dock. He saw no guard on the gangplank. The ship had a single mast, with a high stern, and a bow that seemed to be designed for ramming. Round shields of differing designs and dark colors lined the sides and oars lay against the side of the hull.

Slowly, Bruno made his way to the gangplank. He crept on board and looked down into an open hatch. "By the Rock," he muttered.

Inside the compartment were Canis, Felis, Humans, and others he didn't recognize. They were chained to their rowing stations "What kind of place is this?"

The captives looked up.

"Who are you?" one of the men said.

"What is this place? Why are you in chains?" Bruno whispered.

"This is a war galley of the Krocks. We are prisoners," the captive replied.

"War galley? Krocks?"

"You must go. If the Krocks catch you, you'll be put in chains, too."

"What are Krocks?"

"I can't answer your questions. You must go!"

Suddenly a door that Bruno had not noticed was flung open.

Bruno dropped between the rowers.

"What's all this noise?"

"I had a bad dream and woke the others. I'm sorry master," the slave said.

"Don't let it happen again, or you'll be having more than a bad dream. Understand?" A whip cracked against the slaves back. The speaker came into view.

"Sorry, master," the man whimpered.

The creature stomped back to the cabin.

Bruno recoiled, he was repulsed and surprised by what he had seen. Quickly and silently, he went back the way he had come.

"What did you find?" Gurney asked.

"You're not going to believe it," Bruno replied. "Let's get away from here."

At his urging they hurried away from the settlement.

"Now," Gurney said. "What's going on?"

"Slaves, Human, Canis, Felis, others I didn't recognize." Bruno replied. "They were chained to oars. The man I talked to said it was a war galley of the Krocks."

"I've never heard of Krocks," Gurney said. "Has anyone else?"

The others shook their heads.

"Who or what are Krocks?" Gurney asked.

"They appear to be intelligent crocodiles," Bruno replied. "Of course they can walk upright and talk."

"Well, let's make camp and we can investigate more tomorrow," Gurney said.

"And, if we find they are slaves?" Black said.

"No one should be a slave to another," Gurney replied.

"I think we'd better get some sleep," Bruno said. "I have a feeling tomorrow will be a busy day."

"Man, if it's not one thing it's another," Jones said.

"That's for sure," Anderson replied.

"Still no word?" Kirby asked M'Lena.

"No. Nothing," she replied.

"Well," he said. "What are we going to do?"

"I'm going to the Canis settlement," she said. "Maybe they've heard some-thing."

"OK."

"I'll be in touch as soon as I find out anything," M'Lena said.

"Do you want me to send more men to help?"

"No. We'll handle it," she replied, breaking the connection.

Scout, Ranger, Ling, and Yang traveled north, following the relay towers. They inspected them to be sure they were in proper working order.

"This unit is not working properly," Ranger said.

"Do you think we can fix it?" Ling asked.

"We watched them install the equipment," Scout said.

"Then I think that we ssshould try and repair it," Ling said. If one tower isss out, the whole sssysssstem isss usssslessss."

"Then we owe it to our friends to get the system to work," Ranger said.

"I wish our Canis and Felis friends were still here," Bruno said. "Their spe-cial abilities would be very useful."

"Don't you remember? We gave them radios," Jones said.

"Oops. Yeah. That's right. I forgot," Bruno replied.

"I suggest we withdraw over the ridge and see if we can raise them," Gurney said.

"Sorry I screwed up," Bruno said.

"You've got a lot to think about. Besides, everyone makes mistakes," Gurney said. "That's what we're here for anyway."

"I don't understand."

"For you and the others to learn how to handle situations in the field," Gurney replied. "And, to try and profit from my experience. Besides, no ones perfect."

"I understand now."

"Ranger, Scout, Ling, Yang. Can anyone hear me?" Gurney said into the microphone.

"We hear you, Gurney. This is Ranger. We hear you."

"Ranger, Good. How far north are you?"

"Only one day," Ranger replied. "We had to repair a relay station."

Coming right to the point, Gurney said, "We need you and the Felis."

"Where are you?"

"Head back to the beach and then head west," Gurney said. "We'll meet you."

"I will tell the others. As soon as we do a final check on the relay, we will head out."

"Very good. We'll meet you along the beach," Gurney said, breaking the connection.

"But what about the captives?" Smith said.

"I don't think another day or two is going to make all that much of a difference," Bruno replied.

"Let's set up camp," Gurney said. "We've got a lot of work to do."

As they waited for the Canis and Felis to arrive they cleaned their weapons and made sure they were fully loaded. Fortunately, they didn't need a fire. The weather was warm and balmy. The breeze was mild and they had plenty of prepared food to eat.

The next afternoon the Felis and Canis arrived.

Gurney and Bruno explained what they had discovered.

"We have never heard of the Krocks," Ranger said.

"Neither have we," Ling said.

"I suggest that Smith, Jones, Black, and Anderson withdraw with the pack horses," Gurney said. "The fewer of us there are the less chance of being discovered."

"I agree," Ranger said.

"At nightfall, we will be able to ssscout out the sssettlement, if you wisssh," Ling said.

"Yes," Bruno said. "That might be a good idea."

The next morning the packhorse train headed back to the east.

"We'd better getting moving," Bruno said.

"Do you have a plan of action?" Ranger asked.

"Well, if the galley is still there if would probably be easier for one of you or a Felis to get on board."

"And, when we get on board?" Ling asked.

"Release the prisoners and get out of there."

"I have a feeling that we'll find a lot of people who disappeared into the Outlands," Gurney said.

"I think you are right, Gurney," Scout said.

It was drizzling when they returned to the settlement. The clouds were low and heavy with rain.

It had been decided that Ranger and Yang would go into the settlement while the others waited in the woods.

The street was dimly lit and as deserted as it had been the previous night.

Ranger and Yang silently crept up the gangplank of the galley.

"Who are you? What are you doing here?" the man Bruno had talked to the previous night asked.

"We have come to release you," Ranger replied.

Yang signaled everyone to keep quiet. "We will get you all out of here. Be patient."

They easily broke the locks that held the chains.

"Go down the gangplank and straight into the woods. Our companions are waiting for you," Ranger said.

Scout and Ling waited across the street to guide the former captives towards Gurney and Bruno.

They were almost done when the door to the rear cabin open. "What's going on here? Who are you? Where are the slaves?" the Krock said, as it advanced on Ranger and Yang, a wickedly curved cutlass in hand. He reached for a whip that hung from his belt.

Ranger growled and sprang forward, taking the Krock by surprise. They fell to the deck, a tangle of fur and scales.

Ranger clamped onto the Krocks neck and bit down.

The Krock screamed in pain, but it was cut short as Ranger broke the Krocks neck. The body hung, limply, in Rangers mouth.

"That isss all of them," Yang said. "Let usss get out of here."

Ranger dropped the body to the deck and looked around. "I want to check the cabin. There may be something Gurney can use."

They went into the cabin and took a quick look around.

"Look here," Yang said.

"A map, Gurney would be glad to have that, I am sure," Ranger said. "Let us grab what we can and get out of here."

Yang found a sack and stuffed papers into it.

"We need a diversion," Ranger said, looking around. He spotted a heater in the corner. "There we are."

"I am heading topsssside," Yang said.

"Go ahead," Ranger said. "I'll be right behind you." He kicked over the heater and knocked over an oil lamp. The flames spread and grew as he watched.

Yang waited for him at the foot of the gangplank.

"Quickly, run," Yang said. The pair disappeared into the woods.

"The others are already on their way back over the ridge," Gurney said. "What took so long?"

"Thisss." Yang handed Gurney the papers they had picked up.

"Gurney took a quick look. "This looks promising."

"We thought it might," Ranger said.

"Are you hurt?" Bruno asked. "You're covered in blood."

"I had to kill a Krock," Ranger said, without any remorse.

The settlement was in an uproar. Krocks ran down to the burning galley, but it was too late. It was already engulfed in flames and was sinking at the dock.

"Let's get going," Bruno said. "We don't want to be here when they discover the slaves are gone."

They hurried through the woods and over the ridge.

"Gurney," Yang said. "Many of thessse people need medical treatment. We need to ssstop ssso we can treat them."

"Very well," Gurney replied. "Treat the most serious first. We want to put some distance between us and the settlement."

Looking back they could see the glow from the burning galley reflected off the low rain clouds.

Half an hour later Yang came back to Gurney. "We are ready to go. Once thessse people get sssome decent food and sssome rest, they will be fine."

"Good," Gurney said. "Get them ready to travel."

Bruno came up to Gurney as Yang left. "There were about forty people, but some of them slipped away."

"Slipped away?"

"The types we didn't recognize," Bruno replied.

"Well, let's just hope they went home and not back to the Krocks."

"Just to make sure, let's get as far away as we can tonight," Gurney said. "I suggest we get back to the Lair as soon as possible."

"We should be able to make good time. No one is unable to move under his own power," Bruno replied.

"Good. Perhaps some of those in better shape can be the rear guard, just in case the Krocks track us somehow."

"The relay system is back up," S'Haron told M'Lena.

"How long ago?"

"Just a few minutes ago," S'Haron replied. "I could just barely hear them though."

"What did it sound like?"

"Something about the Lair, I think."

"Maybe they want us to meet them there," M'Lena said.

"Could be," S'Haron replied.

"The next time they make contact, tell them I'm on my way."

"Yes, I will," S'Haron replied.

"I'll be leaving within the hour."

The weather had begun to cool when they returned to the Lair. One of the former captives told Gurney that the Krocks couldn't stand cool weather or to be away from the water for long.

Scout had run ahead with the news. When they reached the Lair there were representatives from many other packs looking for lost members.   There were many joyful reunions as long lost kin returned to their homes.

M'Lena arrived the next day.

"I wasn't expecting to see you, sister."

"Your message was garbled. I thought it best to meet you here. Besides we had updated components for the system. They're all working better."

"Good. I have a feeling they will be getting a lot of use. Bruno can bring you up to speed on our current situation. I need to get some rest."

"I can see you're tired, brother."

"Why it that when I think everything is going to work out, something else happens?"

"I guess that is just the nature of the universe, brother," M'Lena said. "Get some rest. I'll see you at dinner."

Gurney went to the shelter the Canis had built for him, but he couldn't sleep. He sat at the table and began to look through the papers they had gotten from the Krock galley.

"If all the Canis packs and Felis prides will join together, I don't think you would have anything to fear from the Krocks," Gurney told the assembled leaders.

"Will your people join with usss in resssisssting the Krocksss?" a Felis asked.

"I'm sure they will," Gurney replied. "This threatens us, too. But, they also seem to have a limited range that they can cover, from what the former captives have told us."

"How do we know we can trust YOU?" A Canis from a pack to the far north woods asked.

"Gurney and his men have always been truthful with us in the past," Spike said. "We have no reason not to trust him now."

"Asss they have between with usss," Yang added.

Spike got up and went to stand with Gurney and Bruno. "We will join them in this battle."

"Ssso will we," Yang said. He joined Gurney, Bruno, and Spike.

One by one, all the other leaders stood to show their support.

"Very well," Gurney said. "We have a lot of planning to do."

A contingent of Canis and Felis went with Gurney and the others across the Outlands. They were amazed as they thought the land impassable and unending.

A base of operations was chosen on the eastern bank of the River Styx a few miles south of Labrys. From that location they would do recognizance of the Krock town and yet still be close to the resources of Lthrtown and the other lake communities.

Gurney would provide technical assistance and weaponry. The Felis and Canis would teach Gurneys men stealth techniques, various forms of hand-to-hand combat, and living off the land.

"Gurney," Kirby said, "There are all kinds of rumors about what we're doing. Perhaps you should have a meeting. Besides, Nimbus-Unicorn can't afford all this. It's going to cut into our cash reserves."

"OK. Set up the meeting," Gurney replied. "I'll have to get representatives from the Canis and Felis to attend, too."

"I'll start right away," Kirby said. "Also, the phone lines should all be working later today, according to the status reports."

"Just keep me informed. I'll keep the Canis and Felis in reserve. I'm leery of the reception they may get."

"Troy, I'm sorry we haven't had much time together since I've been back," Gurney said.

"I know," Troy replied. "I've kept myself busy with the new show."

"Maybe it would be better…"

"Not to see each other?" Troy finished.

"I've just got so much to do," Gurney replied. "I just don't want you to feel neglected."

"You don't have to worry about me, Gurney. I can take care of myself."

"It's up to you," Gurney said. They sat and stared at each other for a moment.

Finally, Troy stood up and walked over to Gurney. "I'll wait as long as I have to. If you want me, you know where to find me." He kissed Gurney's cheek and left the office.

Kirby came into the office a few minutes later. "The phone lines are working now. But, to make sure everyone got the message, I had security hand deliver copies."

""What about the officals in Breederstown?"

"The mayor and police chief will be here for the meeting as well as representatives from Labrys and Chiffon."

"And what time is the meeting schedules for?"

"Tomorrow night. We'll roll out the red carpet. I've arranged a buffet that even includes items for the Canis and Felis."

"Spike and Yang will arrive tonight."

"I've arranged quarters for them and their aids."

"You're so efficient, Kirby. I don't know what I'd do without you."

"I know," Kirby replied.

They sat in silence for a moment.

"Can I ask you a personal question?"

"You can ask," Gurney said. "I may not answer though."

"What's happened between you and Troy?"

"Well, that's a hard one."

"You know how I feel about you, Gurney."

"Yes, I know how you feel. I'm just so afraid of being hurt again. I still hear Spencer calling my name in my dreams."

Kirby sat and listened.

"I want to explore more, once we've come to grips with the current situation. Somewhere out there is the big cache. I want to be the one to find it."

"But, you've done so much already."

"There's always something new. You've got to keep performing. If you don't, someone else will. You're only as good as your last success. When I go, I want people to know that I was here and that I made a difference."

"But,"

"NO," Gurney interrupted him. "There's a lot more to me then what's in my pants. I know I'm not the best looking man around. But, if you've got a big dick they don't care. When I was younger, I felt like a piece of meat."

Kirby didn't try to interrupt Gurney. He knew there was no point to even try.

"Do you have any idea what that's like? To know the man you're sleeping with is only there for one reason? Of course they don't tell you that. But, you can never manage to hook up with him again. He's always busy, always has some reason to blow you off."

"Men are pigs," Kirby grinned.

"Yeah, well I even seem to be losing interest in sex. I still enjoy it, don't get me wrong, but it's not the driving force it once was," Gurney said.

"I understand, Gurney. Believe me. I understand."

"Troy is still young. He deserves to be with someone who can take care of his needs."

"And, you don't think you can meet those needs."

"No," Gurney shook his head. "I don't think I can. Not anymore."

"Have you told him yet?"

"We've decided not to see each other anymore." Gurney leaned back and closed his eyes.

Kirby got up and paused in the doorway. "I'm here for you if you need me."

Gurney didn't reply. He had fallen asleep already, sitting up in his chair.

Kirby came back a few minutes later and covered Gurney with a blanket. He kissed his forehead, turned out the lights, and went to his own apartment.

Gurney stood on the veranda in the cool morning air, facing north in his robe with a steaming cup of tea in his hand. The early morning sun flashed off the copper barrel roof of his house, far to the north side of town. Soon, he knew, it would have a green patina to it. If and when he retired, it was where he planned on living. He owned a lot of acreage around it so he wouldn't have to worry about neighbors. With one last look of longing, he turned away from the view.

He couldn't believe how Lthrtown had grown. It sprawled northward along the western side of the Russian River and along the northern shore of Crater Lake towards Cruiseville. The population grew everyday. All the communities around the lake were experiencing similar growth. The economy was robust. People were happy. Looking southward, he could see the masts of their newest ship, the Saugatuck. She was even bigger than the Provincetown or the Fire Island.

Gurney hoped the Krocks weren't the problem he though they were. Slavery wasn't something he condoned.

That night was the meeting with the community leaders and heads of the collectives. He still hadn't decided if, or how, he would introduce the Canis and Felis.

Kadrovich had debriefed the former human captives. None of them were local. They had all come from somewhere to the west. They had been shipwrecked. When they found the Krocks, instead of being helped, they had been imprisoned as galley slaves.

Information from the Canis and Felis was that their captives had all gotten lost attempting to cross the Outlands or on hunting trips.

They also reported that the Krocks were fierce fighters. Their heavy scales made them impervious to any of the weapons the Canis or Felis had at their disposal. There were other Krock settlements, but the prisoners didn't know where they were. From their observations they saw that the Krocks advanced in the ranks through duels or murder. The Krocks used knifes and swords as well as their claws and teeth in battle. It was easy for them to gut an opponent with a swipe of their razor sharp claws, or bite an opponent's hand off with their equally sharp teeth.

"Everything is in place, Gurney," Kirby said.

"Good. As soon as the last person is here let me know and I'll come down," he replied.

"Yes, sir."

Gurney looked across the lake towards Labrys. He could see the glow of the lights reflecting off of the clouds.

Fifteen minutes later the phone rang. "They're all here."

"I'm on my way," Gurney replied. He took one last look in the mirror and headed downstairs.

Gurney opened the door. Kadrovich and Bruno waited for him. "Ready to go, sir?"

"Yes, Kadrovich."

Bruno and Kadrovich led the way to the top of the grand staircase where Schmidt and Griffith waited.

"Well," Gurney said. "It's show time."

Kadrovich and Bruno led the way. Gurney was a few steps behind. Schmidt and Griffith followed.

The crowd applauded as they waited at the foot of the staircase. They followed Gurney and his escort into the banquet room.

Gurney went to the podium and waited for everyone to find their seats. He looked out at the faces of the expectant people.

"Good evening," he started. "I know you're all wondering why you have been asked here tonight."

He paused. "I have recently returned from an expedition to the Outlands."

A murmur went through the crowd.

"You all know that I built my business on Outland salvage. I won't bore you with all the details, you'll get written reports if you are interested later."

"When we crossed the Outlands, we discovered other cultures."

Another murmur went through the crowd.

"We made new friends who have much to contribute, but we also discovered an insidious foe that either kills or enslaves their enemies."

"But first, let me introduce our new friends and allies." Spike and Yang came from backstage and walked over to flank Gurney.

The crowd gave a collective gasp. Someone dropped a glass.

"This is Spike, of the Canis, and Yang, of the Felis."

It took longer for the noise level to drop this time.

"Spike and Yang would like to address you all," Gurney said.

"Good evening," Spike began. He had to wait for the noise level to drop again. "We hope that all our people will work together and make a better future for us and our descendants."

Yang took Spike's place. "Greetingsss people of Lthrtown, Labrysss, Chiffon, and Breedersssstown. We are happy to meet the leadersss of our new alliesss. I am sssure that working together there isss nothing we cannot accomplisssh."

Gurney stepped back behind the podium. "I know this is a lot to take in at one time. As I said earlier, we have prepared reports for all of you."

"When will we get a chance to ask questions?" someone called out.

"Everyone will get a briefing later. Please call my office to get your appointment time," Gurney said.

The next days were full of meeting after meeting. Gurney didn't get much sleep, but then neither did any of his staff either.

Recon reports from the outpost came in everyday. The galley that had burned was still sunk at the dock.

They had also discovered that the Krock settlement was on both sides of the mouth of the river.

"Since we were there at night, with the fog on the river, we were unable to see the other side," Bruno said. "It's almost a mile across."

"They ssseem to be attempting to sssalvage the galley," Yang said.

"Is it possible they think it was an accident?" Gurney asked Spike.

"Hard to say," Spike replied. "They do not seem to be in any great hurry, according to the reports."

"But, by now, they should know there are no bodies on board," Bruno said.

"True," Gurney replied. "But, you would think if they do know there would be more activity."

"Yesss," Yang said. "I concur."

"We'll just have to keep up the surveillance and see if anything happens," Gurney said.

"There's going to be hell to pay if we get caught," Simons said.

"IF is the operative word," Clinton said. "We just don't get caught that's all."

"I've got a bad feeling about this," Simons replied. They were heading south from Breederstown on horseback.

"If freaking dogs and cats can talk, what do you think a live, walking, talking, Krock would be worth?"

"I don't have any idea," Simons said, nervously.

Two days later they reached the seacoast and headed east.

The pair reached marshland. Slowly, they worked their way across it. Simons looked around constantly. He was terrified that they would get caught. The humidity was high. Small insects buzzed around them.

"Will you calm down?" Clinton said. "You're getting on my nerves."

"Sorry," Simon's eyes constantly moved, never resting on any spot for longer than a second or two.

"I don't know how you talked me into this," Simons said to Clinton.

"You're as curious as I am," Clinton replied.

"Yeah, but it's freaking me out."

The pair began to ford a sluggish backwater. They were unable to find another way around. They advanced slowly with Simons following Clinton.

Dragonflies and other insects buzzed around constantly. The brackish water smelled.

Suddenly, the water erupted. A Krock lunged at Clinton as Simons tried to get back to solid ground.

Clinton's scream of terror was suddenly cut short as the Krock slashed at him with its claws. Clinton tried to shove his intestines back into his body with one hand and fight off the Krock with the other.

The Krock lunged again and bit Clinton's head off. The body slumped into the brackish water.

Simons finally reached shore and fled north along the edge of the swamp. He thought if he could find the river he could follow it back home. He didn't know that another Krock was stalking him. But, this Krock had more patience that the first one had.

Simons fled, dropping pieces of equipment in his wake.

The Krock followed, picking up everything Simons dropped.

An outpost had been built at a narrow part of the river, on both sides, at a point where it was felt it would be easy to defend. The fortifications were designed to blend in with the landscape. Observers constantly scanned downstream in case the Krocks headed north up the river.

"I think I see someone coming upstream on the western bank," Rover said.

"It'sss a man," Tiger said.

"Better sound the alarm," Rover said. He picked up the phone and called the situation room.

Immediately more observers looked downriver.

Simons splashed through the shallow water next to shore. The plants grew right up to the edge of the water; there were no paths in the woods.

He stumbled on the gravel riverbed.

"Come on, man," Rover muttered to himself.

A squad headed south along the western bank of the river.

Simons stumbled again and fell into the water.

The Krock that had been following him had had enough. It burst from the water behind him and pulled him down before he could even cry out.

"Can we get a shot at that thing?" Sport asked.

"Too far," was the reply.

"Damn!"

They watched helplessly as the Krock tore Simons to shreds.

By the time the squad got there, there wasn't much of Simons left, just some scraps of material and a boot. Simon's foot was still in the boot.

"Look here," Bear said, picking up something.

"What is it?"

"A wallet," Baffa said, "With identification papers."

Boots asked, "Where wasss he from?"

"Breederstown," Bear replied.

"Stupid breeder," one of the men said.

"We had better get this information back as soon as possible," Bear said.

They didn't see the Krock lurking in the shadows a little ways downstream. After watching them for a while, it floated lazily away.

"Gurney is NOT going to be happy about this," M'Lena said, picking up the phone. "We'll have to keep a tight security lockdown on this. We don't need a panic."

"I'll take care of it," K'Ren replied.

"Gurney," Kirby called. "M'Lena is on the phone. Priority call."

Gurney picked up the phone and M'Lena gave him a quick report.

"Contact Breederstown and tell them what's happened," he said. "Be sure to remind them to keep a lid on it. Someone else could be missing, too. Someone he hangs out with."

"Anything else?"

"Go to a level two alert."

"Right away," she said.

"Keep me informed." Gurney broke the connection.

Kirby came into the office. "What was that about?"

Gurney quickly told him what had happened.

"Damn. What a mess."

"Yes, it is. I want that road along the river done as soon as possible. We may need to move a lot of men and equipment in a hurry."

"So the Krocks know where we are."

"I think we have to go on that assumption."

"Anything else?"

"Set up a picket line a couple of miles in a line east and west of our fortifications. I don't want anything getting past them."

"I'll see to it right away," Kirby said, leaving Gurney's office.

"I'm only telling you what I saw," Ktang said.

"I find it hard to believe. Canis, Felis and Humans working together, it doesn't sound possible," Croton said.

"I know what I saw," Ktang replied. "The one I got in the river was delicious, too."

"Perhaps we'll have to go upstream and check things out," Croton said.

Ktang grinned a toothy smile.

"I just hope they're not tough and stringy like those giants were," Croton added. "We did eat them though, and they did have a nice flavor."

"Apparently, the Krocks will eat anything," Kadrovich said. "Except for other Krocks."

"So they're cannibals," Gurney said.

"That's what the reports say. Debriefing of the former captives supports this, too."

"This is going from bad to worse," Gurney replied.

"We also have a report from Breederstown about the two casualties."

"Two?" Kirby said.

"And, what is that?"

Clinton and Simons, both mid-twenties, single. Disappeared a couple of days ago. No criminal records of any kind."

"So, they were curious, and it caused their deaths."

"What's that?"

"I think it's a mast," was the reply.

"Well, then it hasss got to be a Krock galley," Ling said. "No ssshipsss have passsed usss."

Bear looked downstream again. "Better sound the alarm."

"Yesss, I think ssso," Ling sssaid. "Then, I will call headquartersss."

"Deploy the blockade measures on the river," Bear said.

"Gurney," Kadrovich called out. "A Krock galley has been sighted approaching the river outposts."

"Current alert status?"

"Red."

"I'm going there," Gurney said.

"Wait a minute. I'm coming, too."

"The galleys stopped moving," Bear told Gurney. "Patrols are close by the galley. It's under constant observation."

"Any activity?"

"Nothing unusual so far."

"Very well, keep me informed."

"Yes sir."

"What kind of heavy caliber weapons do we have at the outposts?"

"Heavy machine guns, grenade launchers," Bruno said.

"I think we'd better move some heavier equipment in," Gurney said.

"I'll see what's available and have in brought down," Kadrovich said.

"The Labrys militia is on guard along the upper river and Labrys harbor," Bruno added.

"Let's hope all our efforts aren't for nothing," Gurney said.

"The Human outpost is just around the bend," Washow said. "It looks like they have been expecting us."

"Well, I don't think they'll be much of a problem," Ahab said. "The others certainly weren't any trouble."

"I'm looking forward to some tasty meals."

"So am I."

"I've been told these Humans are very tender."

"I've heard that, too."

Sport looked downstream through his binoculars. He scanned the river looking for telltale signs. "I know they are out there somewhere."

"We are doing all we can," Buddy said. "Reinforcements are on the way."

"I know. But, this waiting is making me crazy," Sport replied. "I am sure they will make a move sooner or later."

"Everyone is ready. They will not get past us," Buddy said.

"I hope you are right."

"We can't go further than a mile or two inland," Washow said.

"I don't know if we should attack or wait for them to make a move," Ahab said.

"These Humans are new to us. I think they are controlling the Canis and Felis and keeping them from attacking us."

"I think you're right. Let's wait a little longer and see if anything happens."

"Perhaps they do not have the courage to attack us."

"That seems unlikely. If these are the Humans that we suspect sunk the galley, I don't think they would have a problem attacking us."

"Do you really think so?"

"I think this is a different, more aggressive Human than we have never been in contact with before."

"I think you are right."

"Still no reports of any movement. The galley is still in the same place. No sign of any recent activity," Sport said.

"Thisss worriess me," Ling said. "Why would they leave it there?"

"Since it is a total loss, they may just leave it there."

"It doesss not ssseem like sssomething they would do," Ling replied. "Gurney sssent me sssome information. In the old daysss, Krocks were predatorsss. Usssually, they were patient. But, if they got hungry enough, they would attack."

"So you expect them to attack soon?"

"Yesss, I do."

"I'm tired of waiting. Besides, I'm getting hungry," Ahab said."

"Very well, send a patrol upstream," Washow replied.

"Good," I am eager to kill these Humans," Ahab said.

"You will have your chance very soon," Washow replied, as they left the room and went to find the others.

"I sssee sssomething," Ling said.

Bear looked downstream. "I see them. Looks to small to be an attack though."

"A ssscouting party, then."

"I agree. Pass the word not to attack unless the Krocks make a hostile move."

"I will get word to headquartersss."

"Gurney, the Krocks are on the move," Kirby called. They were halfway across Crater Lake on the Provincetown. They would be in Labrys by nightfall.

"What's going on?"

"They seem to be sending a scouting part upstream. No hostile moves so far."

"Contact M'Lena, have horses for us. I want to get to the command post as soon as possible."

"Yes sir."

Gurney went back to contemplating the passing scenery. The lake was full of traffic. There was a constant flow of men and equipment heading for the expected front.

Even though he had not really wanted it, the collective leadership of the Crater Lake communities had pressed him to oversee the war effort. He had to devote himself to the seemingly endless details. As soon as one problem was solved there were two more to deal with. He wasn't getting much sleep.

"Gurney, don't you think you should try and get some sleep?"

"I'll lie down for a while, but I'm not sure if I'll get any sleep," Gurney replied. He went to his cabin.

A few minutes later, Kirby knocked on Gurney's cabin door. There was no answer.

As he opened the door, he heard Gurney snoring. "Sleep well, Gurney," he whispered, as he covered Gurney with an afghan and slipped out the door.

Kirby stood at the stern of the Provincetown, watching Lthrtown fade into the distance. He wondered, not for the first time, where Gurney got his energy. He knew Gurney really didn't want the responsibility, but there was no one else capable of doing the job. Gurney had forgotten more than HE would ever know.

Irv had gotten separated from his patrol. He had stopped to pee, but the patrol had kept going, not realizing he had stopped.

Under the heavy canopy of trees it was strangely quiet. Not a bird or an insect made a noise.

Irv tried to get his bearings. He thought he heard the noise of the river and headed towards it.

After a few minutes he found himself on the rocky riverbank. He could see the defensive positions upstream. He hurried to reach it. He thought he could see people waving at him.

Suddenly a Krock reared up in front of him.

Irv scrambled to get away but the Krock blocked his way.

The Krock lunged at Irv but somehow it missed him.

Irv got past the Krock somehow. He splashed through the shallow water.

The Krock appeared in front of him again.

Irv could hear gunfire and men yelling encouragement.

The Krocks claws grazed Irv.

He gasped in pain, but somehow managed to keep going. "If I can get close enough, the others can put down some cover fire," Irv thought.

The Krock appeared again and took another swipe at him.

Irv stood dumbfounded as his intestines spilled out of the gashes in his body.

"He's done for," someone yelled. "Get those fucking Krocks!"

As Irv collapsed to his knees the bullets flew. He knew he would be dead soon.

More Krocks appeared around him. Their claws slashed at him, cutting him to pieces.

Irv slowly slumped forward. He was dead before he finally fell face first into the shallow water. His blood turned the water red.

One of the Krocks dragged Irv's remains away.

Gurney was just preparing to leave Labrys when the report came in about the attack on Irv.

"Well, that tears it," Gurney said. "I'd say that shows their intentions towards us."

"Unfortunately, I have to agree," M'Lena said.

"That was delicious," Ahab said, wiping his mouth with his hand.

"Yes, it was," Washow replied.

"We need to get more of this," Ahab belched.

"Soon, we'll have all we want."

"We should have some heavy equipment soon," Scout said.

"Thessse creaturesss are monssstersss," Sheik said.

"I agree," Scout replied.

"Gurney will be here sssoon," Sheik said. "He will want a sssituation report."

"I'll make it personally," Scout said. He got his reports together and went to the command center.

"Full alert sssatisss," Sheik said.

"I'll sound the alert," Buddy replied. He followed Scout to the command center.

Hundreds of eyes looked downstream, straining to see some sign, some indication that the Krocks were on the move.

A second Krock galley had joined the first.

A raft was constructed and sent downstream with a message, telling the Krocks to withdraw or face the consequences"

"Do you think they can read?"

"I hope so," Gurney replied to M'Lena.

They waited for a response.

An hour later they got it.

Fireballs arched out from the galleys. But, they fell short and landed in the river.

"Well," Gurney said. "I guess we have our answer."

Kadrovich asked, "Orders, Gurney?"

"I want those galleys captured or sunk for starters."

"Consider it done," Kadrovich replied.

Squads followed both sides of the river. Few of the men had been in combat situations, but for the Canis and Felis it was a way of life.

The Krocks lurked in the shallow water. Only their eyes and nostrils were above the surface.

The squads began to set up their weapons on the narrow areas between the forest and the river.

The Krocks watched the proceedings with interest.

The riverbank gave way under one of the men in a patrol and he slid towards the water.

The Krocks took that as their cue. They burst from the water armed with crossbows.

Coalition troops were not expecting a surprise attack. Numerous troops were injured or killed in the initial volley.

The Krocks dragged away some of the bodies.

The Coalition troops regained their balance quickly. Their heavy machine guns cut through the ranks of the Krocks. Once again the river ran red with blood and bodies floated downstream.

The Krock galleys continued to lob fireballs at the defenses, but they never found the range.

Troops on the west bank prepared their mortars. They knew they were not the focus of the Krock catapults. They wanted to sink the galleys and avenge their fallen comrades.

They found the range quickly. The second galley drifted downstream in flames.

Some Krocks returned to the first galley. They seemed to be preparing to leave when the galley exploded. Debris floated away down the river.

The Coalition troops cheered.

The few surviving Krocks floated downstream. They had never fought a battle like this before. They knew the Humans they now faced were more dangerous that any previous foe.

Gurney and M'Lena had arrived at the west bank outpost after the battle had ended.

"Sir, I have an early report," Scout said.

"Very well."

"The first galley exploded and sank. The second drifted downstream in flames."

"What about our causalities?"

"It's too early to tell yet. I'm afraid they may be higher than we expected."

"Well, bring me a detailed report as soon as possible."

"Yes sir."

"I want to take a look around. We'll be back later."

"I will have the information you want when you return, sir," Scout said.

"By the Rock," Bruno gasped. "Look at that!"

The two halves of the exploded galley had settled on the river bottom. Burning debris still floated on the water and lay on the riverbank. They could see scattered fires in the woods, too.

Suddenly there was a distant explosion.

"What the…" Kadrovich started to say.

"I'd say the second galley exploded," Gurney said.

"I'll get the situation reports and bring them to you," Kadrovich said.

"I'm going to get something to eat," Gurney said.

"I'll find you."

"These Humans are very formidable foes," Washow said.

"Perhaps we should send for reinforcements," Ahab said.

"With what? We have no galley to send and none expected for weeks."

"Send someone by foot, overland."

"We could always leave ourselves."

"But, what about the slaves? What do we do with them?"

"They're only slaves. They have no future anyway. Just take care of them."

"Our casualties were fairly high," Scout told Gurney. "We were not expecting a surprise attack."

"Are there any Krock survivors?"

"None so far."

"Keep looking. I'm eager to talk to one of them."

Gurney stood on an observation deck and looked up at the night sky. The rings were high in the northern sky. The stars blazed with cold light. "How can the world be so full of beauty, yet be such a cruel place," he thought. He longed for some peace and quiet. Every time he thought he had achieved his goal something happened the shattered the illusion. No peace.   No quiet. No rest. He sighed and went back inside.

Gurney and M'Lena sat at a small table in the spartan quarters he was using.

"What's troubling you, brother?"

"I'm getting too old for this sort of thing."

"I know what you mean," she replied.

"There must be more Krocks that the ones were dealing with right now."

"No doubt about that," she replied, as she poured them both fresh cups of tea.

"I think this may be a long, bloody, fight."

"I'm afraid you're right."

"We have found no Krock survivors," Scout reported to Kadrovich.

"How far south did the patrols go?"

"Within sight of the settlement."

"And, there was no opposition?"

"No sir. None at all, no sign of patrols or sentries."

"Something's wrong here."

"What do you mean, sir?"

"Why would they leave the town open to attack? It doesn't make sense."

"Perhapsss they are waiting in hiding for usss to enter the town," Ling said.

"That could be," Kadrovich answered. "And, I've got just the unit to send in to check it out."

The Amazons marched south along the new road on the western bank of the river. Their armor flashed in the early morning sun.

"They're ready for anything," M'Lena said.

"I'm sure they are," Gurney replied. "Just as my Spartans are."

"Care to review the troops?"

"Yes. I'd like that very much," Gurney said. He had never seen them before, but he knew that M'Lena had been working on the unit with Canis and Felis advisors, just as he had with the Spartans.

As Gurney and M'Lena care out of the command post, the last of the Amazon units entered the area. They all snapped to attention.

Kadrovich, Bruno, and Scout walked behind Gurney.

Kadrovich was impressed. The women looked like they could handle anything the Krocks threw at them. They were all tall and muscular. He could see many had shaved heads.

Gurney had to look up to see most of the women's faces. They were all his height or more. They were all tall and muscular.

The Amazons all stared straight ahead, their jaws set.

When they reached the Amazon commander she saluted them. "Sir."

"You have a very formidable unit here," Gurney said.

"Yes sir. Thank you, sir," she replied, looking him in the eye. "We are eager to do our part for the Coalition, sir."

"I'm sure you are," he replied. "I'm sure you know the mission objectives."

"Yes sir. Secure the eastern part of the town. Capture a Krock, alive, if possible."

"Very good, commander," Gurney said. "You may release your troops until it is time to head out."

"Yes sir. Thank you, sir." She gave a hand signal and the women relaxed. Many of them drifted away to find a spot in the shade, something to drink, or a latrine. They knew they would be in battle soon. They also knew that not all of them would return. It was their job after all.

"Very impressive," Gurney said to M'Lena as they walked away.

"No more so than the Spartans are," she replied.

The Spartan commander, Remus, and the Amazon commander, Diana, met to discuss tactics for the attack.

"I would agree that a building by building search would be best," Diana said.

"There are no galleys to worry about, so the waterfront may not be a priority," Remus said.

One of the Felis scouts returned. "I sssaw no one on the ssstreet."

"No one at all?"

"No, sssir."

"I think they must all be in hiding," Remus said.

"I agree," Diana replied.

The eastern bank settlement was very small and the Spartans had no problems as they went building to building.

But, the same could not be said for the western side.

Everything went well until the Amazons reached the waterfront.

"I don't understand why there has been no opposition," Pamela said.

"Can they have evacuated the town?"

"It doesn't seem likely," Diana said.

"Do you smell something?"

"Over here," someone called.

They went to a low warehouse like building. The doors were locked. A pair of Amazons kicked the door in. An overpowering stench came out.

They slowly went inside.

"By the Goddess!" Diana exclaimed.

"What is it?" A voice in the back asked.

"The Krocks are monsters. They've killed all the slaves," Diana said.

"I can't believe the Krocks would do something like this," M'Lena said.

"I can," Gurney said. "They're monsters."

"They must have decided that they couldn't manage to take them along when they evacuated the town. But, I don't think they've really evacuated the town."

"Probably more like they were a liability."

"What do you plan to do?"

"I was thinking of complete and utter destruction. But, that would make us no better than they are."

"True," M'Lena said.

"Now, I think we should give those poor devils a decent burial and secure the town."

"And then?"

"We find the Krocks and punish them for their crimes."

The Lthrtown shipyards worked around the clock. Gurney had designed a new class of ship. He called it a cutter. It was smaller and lighter than the Provincetown, but heavily armed. He felt they would be able to easily defeat the Krock galleys.

A road had been constructed across the Outlands. There was a constant flow of Canis and Felis on it.

Recovery teams had spread across the few ruined cities. Everything recovered was first taken to Labrys and then on to Lthrtown for analysis. After that it was taken to Gurney's new headquarters in Libertyville, the name he had given to the liberated town.

Gurney and his staff constantly worked on battle plans. The troops played war games, where one team would attack and the other would defend to hone their fighting skills.

"Excuse me Gurney, but you need some rest," Kadrovich said.

"I know. I just can't take the time," Gurney replied, as he leafed through an old book the Canis had found in the Lair and brought to him.

"It won't do you or anyone else any good if you're worn out."

"I know," Gurney replied, rubbing his eyes. "But..."

"Don't make me call Doc and make it an order."

"Alright, alright, I'll get some rest," Gurney finally replied. He turned out the lights and went to bed.

"How long has he been asleep?"

"Twelve hours," Kadrovich told M'Lena, as he glanced at his chronograph.

"You're sure he's still there?"

"I stayed with him until he fell asleep, which didn't take to long. And, I check on him every once in a while."

"Good. Someone needs to be with him. He drives himself so hard, I'm afraid he's going to burn himself out."

"I know. But, you know he doesn't listen."

Gurney tossed and turned. He dreamt about Spencer and Troy, Canis and Felis, giant birds, mutant giants, lunging Krocks, and explosions.

He woke up, drenched in sweat.

Immediately the door opened. "Are you alright?" Kadrovich asked.

"I just had a bad dream," Gurney replied.

Kadrovich disappeared for a moment. "Here," he said, handing Gurney a mug. "This will help you sleep."

Gurney drank it quickly and lay back down. "It's hell getting old. And, I think I've slept enough."

"Why do you say that?"

"It just is," Gurney replied. "I expect impossibly high levels of performance of myself that I can't match myself. It's like I'm setting myself up to fail."

"But, you've seen and done so much. And, you've succeeded at everything you've ever done."

"You're only as good as your last success. And someone is always waiting for you to fall flat on your face," Gurney laughed.

Kadrovich sat on the edge of the bed. "Well, you know that we always do our best for you. Even if you do feel they are unreasonably high standards of performance. You've made us what we are. I, we, have all learned so much from you. You've always said experience is the best teacher. You've had us do things we're uncomfortable with. Remember the first time I went with you to Labrys? But, I survived it. We don't want to fail you and so we do all we can for you. We even try to think like you do."

"There's an old saying that which does not kill us, makes us stronger."

Kadrovich laughed.

"Stay with me tonight," Gurney said.

"I don't think..."

"Just sleep with me, that's all. It's been a long time since I've shared a bed with another warm body. Maybe I'll sleep a little better."

"Well, alright."

Within minutes, Gurney was again sound asleep.

Kadrovich watched Gurney for a few minutes. He leaned over and kissed Gurney's cheek before finally falling asleep himself.

When Gurney came out of the shower his breakfast was on the table. "What's this?"

"Doc's orders, you've been losing weight."

Silently, Gurney sat down and ate his eggs and sausage.

"Did you sleep well, Gurney?"

"Yes, I did. Thanks for staying."

"You're welcome."

"Any other surprises for me?"

"There's someone here to see you."

"And, who might that be?"

Kadrovich went to the door and Spike came into the room with another Canis.

"Gurney, this is Scruffy, one of my pups. I would be honored if you would add him to your staff. It would be a way for our people to get to know each other better."

"I see. Well, I'm sure we can find something for him to do."

"Thank you, Gurney. I will let you get back to your morning meal," Spike said.

Gurney didn't see the look that passed between Kadrovich and Spike as they passed.

"Kadrovich, please find Scruffy some quarters," Gurney said.

"Right away."

"Did Spike explain this assignment to you?" Kadrovich asked.

"Yes sir," Scruffy replied. I'm to be assistant and bodyguard to Gurney. Keep him out of trouble, be sure he gets enough to eat and enough rest."

"That pretty much sums it up.'

"I will do my best, sir."

"That's all we can ask for."

"We have sent a few teams west along the coast. We hope to find where the Krocks have gone," Spike said. "They have instructions to contact us twice a day at a minimum."

"The first of the cutters is done and will be here tomorrow," Kadrovich reported. "We've also been working on improving the waterfront and the docks."

"Actually," M'Lena said. "A lot of the buildings are in pretty good condition. We've been converting some of them to barracks and support facilities for the troops and the navy."

"I want to wrap this up as soon as possible," Gurney said. "I need some rest. I have a house north of Lthrtown that I've never even been in. There are just so many better ways we could use our resources."

"Well, we've already been able to do a lot, Even if it is all because of the Krocks." M'Lena said.

"We have two options," Gurney said. "We can either contain the Krocks or destroy them. But, as I've said before, if we destroy them, we're no better than they are."

"So we have to force a settlement from them," Spike said.

"One way or another," Gurney replied.

"Unfortunately we have no way to contact them. We send anyone to talk to them and they could end up as dinner," M'Lena said.

"That's why we need to capture one of them. They can take a message back with them," Gurney said.

Somehow, that's what we have to do, then," Kadrovich said.

"How is the question," Gurney said.

"Are you not curious about these Humans?"

"Well, sure," the other young Krock said. "I just don't know if we should be doing this."

"I'm going to take a look. With or without you."

"Alright, when do you want to leave?"

"Tomorrow morning."

A few miles from Western Libertyville a picket line had been set up. They started at the beach and went north a few miles.

"I sssee sssomeone coming east along the beach," the Felis sentry said to his Canis companion.

"I see them, too. They look pretty young to me."

"Good. They might not put up much of a fight."

"Right, besides, our orders are to capture one if possible. Two would be even better."

"The wind isss from the wessst. They probably have no idea we are here."

"I will pass the word," the Canis said, picking up his field phone.

"So, where are they?"

"Maybe they're in the town."

"I'm still not sure this is the right thing to do. What do we do when we find them?"

"I just want to see what they look like," the young Krock told his companion. "It shouldn't be much further."

"I hope it's not. I'm getting hungry and we didn't bring anything to eat or drink."

"Trapsss ready?"

"All set."

They watched the Krocks approach.

"They are much very younger."

"Good. Maybe thisss will be easssier than we hoped."

The young Krocks struggled, but couldn't get out of the trap.

"We mean you no harm," the Canis said.

"I knew this was a bad idea,"

"Oh, shut up."

"We have just gotten word, Gurney," Scruffy said excitedly said. "They have captured two young Krocks on the coast."

"Very good," Gurney replied. "When will they be able to bring them here?"

"They are already on the way back," Scruffy reported.

"Good. Maybe we'll get some answers to our questions."

A squad, with the captives in tow, returned to Libertyville. The young Krocks had not put up much of a fight, once they realized that their captors meant them no harm.

"What so you want from us?"

"We want you to take a message back to your leaders," Kadrovich told the young Krocks.

"What is your message?"

"They must stop capturing others to be used as food and slaves."

"And if they refuse to listen to us?"

"We will do whatever we feel is necessary to stop them," Spike said.   "Up to, and including, genocide, if necessary."

"You would kill us all?"

"We would rather have you as friends and allies, but if you leave us no choice, yes. You are either with us or against us."

"I doubt you can stand against our weapons," Kadrovich said.

"We will deliver your message. I'm just not sure our leaders will believe us."

"That's all we can ask. We have written down our terms. You can take it back with you," Kadrovich said.

"What? We are free to go?"

"Certainly, whenever you want to."

The Krocks walked out the door and headed to the west.

"Do you think they believed our bluff?"

"I hope so," Spike said to Kadrovich.

"We would be no better than they are, if we lower ourssselvesss to their level," Ling said.

The older Krock asked, "You expect us to believe you?"

"How else could we have gotten this information? Do you think we made it up?"

"Bah. Forget this. I say we attack them and retake our town," an old bull said. "Humans have never been a problem before. These will be no different."

"I agree. We will show them what happens to someone who makes threats against us."

Gurney looked out his office window, which gave him a view of the waterfront. Four of the new cutters were in port after their sea trials. The Swift, the Falcon, the Sparrow Hawk, and the Shrike.

There had been no answer from the Krocks. Gurney knew that they would soon be in a full-scale war. He wasn't looking forward to it, but knew it was inevitable. The Krocks were ruthless. He knew it would be a long, bloody campaign.

The waterfront bustled with activity. The cutters were being ready for their next voyages, fresh crews were reporting. The dockside was piled high with boxes, bundles, and crates. People were everywhere, laughing, talking, and attending to their affairs.

"Morning, Gurney," Scruffy said, as he walked into the office. He put the tray he was carrying on the desk. "Here is your breakfast and the morning reports."

"Thank you, Scruffy," Gurney replied. He knew what Kadrovich and Spike were up to. He went along with it because he knew they were only doing it out of their concern for him. Besides he was very fond of Scruffy and liked having him around.

Scruffy came back a little while later and took the dirty dishes away. "Anything else I can get you?"

"No, thank you, Scruffy, I'm just going to go over the reports."

"Just call if you need anything," Scruffy said. He left the door to the outer office open.

"We'll be heading out tomorrow," the old bull said.

"We'll rip those Humans to pieces."

"Lots of good eating."

"Yeah, and I'm real hungry, too," they all laughed.

Gurney and Scruffy walked along the waterfront.

"I expect things will pickup soon," Gurney said.

"Why do you say that?"

"The Krocks are not pushovers. They're going to fight us to the bitter end."

"Do you really think so?"

"Yes. Fanatics are always the most dangerous enemies. Their way, to their way of thinking, is the only way. No one should be a slave to anyone."

"My sire tells me that we almost went down the same path. He said you showed us and the Felis the right way."

"Do you know any of the Felis personally?"

"A few, it takes time to heal wounds that have existed for generations."

"That's very true," Gurney said, looking to the west. "I have a feeling something will happen very, very soon."

"Many will die, but more will live."

"I like you Scruffy," Gurney said. When this is over I'd like you to stay with me."

"It would be a great honor for me," Scruffy replied.

"When we've won and this is over, I have one more task to accomplish," Gurney said.

"What is that?"

"The ultimate cache of ancient technology," Gurney replied. "I know it's our there somewhere."

Suddenly the alarm sounded.

"The Krocks have been sighted," someone said.

"Let's get to the situation room," Gurney said to Scruffy.

"Sir," Bruno said. "A fleet of Krock galleys had been sighted. No land troops sighted yet."

"Full alert," Gurney ordered. "Defensive positions."

Ground troops rushed to their positions. The cutters prepared to cast off.

Gurney and his staff went to an observation deck that had been built on the roof of the building.

"I can see the galleys," Kadrovich said, looking through his binoculars.

"I see them, too," Gurney said.

"A few ground troops have been sighted," Spike reported.

"Let them make the first move," Gurney ordered.

"Gunnery crews report ready."

"This will be a good test for the new metal hulls," Kadrovich said.

"Yes, it will," Gurney replied. He could see the cutters in a line waiting for the galleys to approach.

The galleys approached, sis by side, catapults in the bows.

"Ground troopsss approaching the city limitsss."

The galleys fired their first volley, which went long.

"Wait for it," Gurney said.

The next volley was short.

"They've got the range," Gurney said. "Prepare to return fire."

The Krocks next volley bounced off the cutters metal hulls.

"Return fire when ready," Gurney ordered.

The Krock galleys made the mistake of turning parallel to the cutters.

The cutters guns ripped through the wooden hulls of the galleys. One of the galleys exploded.

The remaining galleys sheared off and retreated to the west.

Faint gunfire could be heard from the west.

Suddenly, there were shouts from the waterfront.

Krocks had come in underwater and were attempting to establish a beach-head.

Amazons waited on shore for them. The front line had interlocked shields. The second line was armed with high-powered crossbows.

The Krocks rushed the docks only to be met by a hail of crossbow bolts. Many fell, wounded, dead, or dying.

"The surviving galleys are headed back to the west." Bruno said. "Should we follow them?"

"No. Let them go. Maybe they'll learn from their first loss," Gurney said.

The Krocks that had attempted to make the landing retreated back into the water. They left their dead and dying behind.

"Let's go down to the waterfront," Gurney said. "I want to see one of these Krocks up close."

As they walked along the waterfront, Kadrovich said, "Very preliminary reports say we have very light casualties."

"Good," Gurney replied. He walked a few steps ahead of the others.

One of the fallen Krocks stirred.

"GURNEY!" Scruffy called out. He jumped and pushed Gurney, taking the blow from the Krocks slashing claws.

Gurney rolled and came up on his feet, pistol in hand.

Kadrovich and Bruno pulled their pistols and emptied the clips into the Krock. Blood spurted everywhere.

Gurney rushed back to Scruffy.

"You're bleeding," Scruffy said.

"MEDIC! MEDIC!" Kadrovich called.

"I do not think I will be with you when you make that final find, Gurney," Scruffy gasped."

"No. No, you'll be OK," Gurney said. "We have a lot to do together."

The medic pushed his way into the circle.

"It is too late," Scruffy murmured. "I'll miss you, Gurney."

"I love you as if you were my own son, Scruffy," Gurney whispered.

"I love you too, Gurney. Don't forget me."

"I won't, Scruffy. I won't."

The medic looked Gurney in the eye and shook his head.

"It was an honor to know you and serve you, Gurney," Scruffy murmured. He exhaled and stopped breathing.

Gurney felt a hand on his shoulder. He looked up to see Spike standing there. Gurney's uniform was soaked with Scruffy's blood.

Spike helped Gurney standup. "He was correct, Gurney. Do not morn for him. His life was a good trade for yours. Among my people there is no greater honor than to give your life for the life of your leader."

Gurney stood, he hurt so bad he wasn't sure if he should cry or run or both.

"Gurney?" Bruno said.

Slowly, Gurney walked back to his quarters.

"Leave him alone," Kadrovich said. "He needs to be alone."

"I guess you're right," Bruno replied.

The others got busy cleaning things up.

Gurney sat in his dark quarters, still wearing the uniform soaked with Scruffy's blood.

Someone knocked on the door.

"Come."

"Gurney? Spike wants to see you," it was Kadrovich.

"I really don't feel like see anyone right now."

"He's very insistent."

"All right," Gurney sighed. "Let him in."

Spike came in and sat across from Gurney. "Do not blame yourself, Gurney. Scruffy knew the risks of the assignment when he took it."

"That doesn't make it easier for me. Or for you."

"No it does not. But, dying is part of living."

"I want this war over as soon as possible."

"We will do everything we can to do that," Spike replied.

"I think I'm going home."

"Home? To Lthrtown?"

"To the house I built on the north side of town. I've never even been there, you know."

"But, what will you do there?"

"Think. Rest. Wonder if anything is worth all the pain I've gone through."

"Is there anything I can do for you?"

"No," Gurney shook his head. "I just need, want, to be alone for a while."

"I understand. If there is anything you need let me know."

"If there's anything I can do for YOU let me know," Gurney replied.

"Count on it," Spike said, as he left.

Gurney sat in the dark for a long time and softly cried.

"I don't want us to arrive in port until late tonight," Gurney told Captain Walker. "I want to attract as little attention as possible."

"Very well, sir," Walker replied.

"Thank you, captain."

When the Provincetown arrived in Lthrtown, Kirby was waiting dockside. "Rommel has gone ahead to air out the house."

"Good," Gurney replied. He stood with Bruno at the bottom of the gangplank.

"If there's anything..." Kirby began.

"I'll let you know."

Bruno loaded the horses as Gurney said good-by.

The pair rode through the nearly deserted streets. The clop of the horse's hoofs echoed off the buildings in the narrow streets of the old town. Few people were on the streets. Those who were didn't give Gurney and Bruno a second look. They were just two men on the street. It wasn't uncommon for people to be on horseback in town. It was the main way to travel. The night was clear, but the rings and the stars were washed out by the streetlights.

Bruno knew that when Gurney wanted to talk, he would. He would wait until he was ready.

"Gurney will still be advising us from Lthrtown," Kadrovich told Ling and Spike.

"Will he be alright?"

"Well, Spike, I think Scruffy's death was very hard on him. It's the second time someone he's care about has died in his arms."

"No wonder he isss upssset," Ling said.

"It might take some time, but I know Gurney. He'll be OK," Kadrovich said. "He's a survivor."

"The daily reports are on your desk."

"Thanks, Bruno," Gurney replied. He hated looking at the daily reports. There always seemed to be a name on them he recognized. He stood on the deck that surrounded the house. The breakfast Rommel had brought him was cold on the plate.

"You need to eat something," Bruno said. They had been at the house a week now and Gurney seemed to be living on tea. He never ate breakfast, but Rommel made it everyday.

"I just don't feel like eating," Gurney sighed.

"Bruno," Rommel called.
"What's wrong?"
"Something's happened to Gurney. He's unconscious."
Bruno hurried to Gurney's room. He lay face down on the desk.
"Call Doc. Tell him we have an emergency," Bruno said.

"Has he been eating?" Doc asked.
"Not unless he's been doing it late at night," Rommel replied.
"Well. He's exhausted for starters. Looks like he's lost weight, too."
"So, what do we do?" Bruno asked.
"We'll have to get someone here fulltime to keep an eye on him."
"I doubt he'll go along with that," Bruno said.
"He'll have to," Doc said. "If he doesn't cooperate, I'll confine him to bed and feed him with IV's, even if I have to have him tied down."

For the next week, Gurney rejected everyone Doc sent. He used every excuse he could come up with.

Ling visited one day, Spike the next, Kadrovich followed.
"He rejects everyone," Bruno said. "What are we going to do?"
"There's got to be someone he'll accept," Kadrovich said.
"Well, we'd better find someone soon," Bruno replied.

"Gurney, there's someone here to see you," Bruno said.
"Another nursemaid you mean?"
"Well, I have a feeling this one might to more to your liking." Bruno stepped out of the way.
"Hello, sir," the young Canis said.
"And, who are you?"
"I'm Rufus, sir. Scruffy was my brother."
Gurney looked at him for a moment. "Let's go out onto the deck and talk."

"Kadrovich," Bruno said into the phone. "It looks good so far. They've been talking for some time now."
"Well, it's a start. Keep me informed."
"I will, as soon as there is a change on any kind."

"Scruffy talked about you all the time. I already feel as if I know you."

"Really now."

"He was honored to be part of your staff and to be your friend. He was devoted to you."

"I was very fond of him, too," Gurney replied.

"He told me one time, that given the chance, he would gladly sacrifice himself for you."

"I never knew that."

"You have to understand, Gurney. Like our more primitive kin, we mature much faster than humans. Our lives are shorter than yours."

"No one ever explained that to me, Although, I'd wondered about it."

"Also, sacrificing yourself for your pack leader is the greatest honor a Canis can achieve. It is often a reflex action, done without thinking."

Gurney watched some hummingbirds flit about the garden from one colorful flower to another.

"You should not blame yourself for Scruffy's death. We would not want you to do that. It would be as if you were punishing yourself for something you could not control."

"I see."

"The best way to honor his memory is to think of the good times you had together," Rufus said.

"We have a saying," Gurney said. "As long as we remember someone and think of them, they are still alive in our minds."

"As do we," Rufus replied. "That is the best thing to do. Honor his memory. Do not morn for him anymore."

Gurney sat and thought for a few moments. "Care to join me for lunch?"

"I would be honored, sir."

"Gurney seems to be getting better. Sending Rufus was a good idea."

"I'm glad it worked. He needed some help working through his problem," Kadrovich said.

"I'm not sure if he wants to come back. You know he's talked about retiring a few times."

"Whatever he wants, we'll be here."

"I think it might take a little time before he's ready to make a final decision."

Gurney and Rufus walked through the woods surrounding the house. Gurney had over one hundred acres insulating his house from the ever-growing Lthrtown. There were a number of paths through the woods and one down to the river.

"I think Scruffy would have liked it here. I never got the chance to bring him though."

"It is very beautiful," Rufus said. It was spring and the flowers were in bloom. Honeybees, dragonflies, and hummingbirds buzzed around them as they walked along the pathway. The river could be heard in the distance. Their boots crunched in the gravel.

"A lot of the plants came from other places."

"I thought I recognized some of them," Rufus said.

"It's very quiet and tranquil here.'

"What do you do all day?"

"Well," Gurney laughed. "When I'm not feeling sorry for myself, I just walk and think."

"What do you think about?"

"The decisions I've made, good or bad. If there's a reason for all this, or, is it just someone's idea of a bad joke."

"I know what you mean."

"Sometimes it just seems to be so pointless."

"Well then, I guess the challenge is we have to find a point to it all."

"Let's get going," Gurney said.

"Going? Where?"

"We've got a war to win," Gurney replied, as he headed back to the house.

Gurney stood on the deck of the Swift, Rufus at his side. The squadron had arrived at a second Krock town during the night. Now, they were blockading the harbor.

"Sir," Bruno said. "A small boat is approaching."

"Very well, keep a close watch on them."

As the boat approached, Gurney could see that the young Krocks they had captured and released were on board along with a couple of others.

"Keep alert," Bruno called out to the crew.

"May we come aboard?"

A ladder was put over the side.

The Krocks climbed up to the deck. "We would like to meet with your leaders."

"I'm in charge," Gurney said, stepping out of the knot of crewmen.

"Is there somewhere we can talk in private?"

"Certainly," Gurney said. "Bruno, please show our quests to the conference room. I'll be there directly."

"Yes, sir. If you'll follow me?" Bruno led the way followed by a large contingent of security men.

"We gave our leaders your message."

"And their reply?"

"What are your terms?"

"The terms are complete surrender," Gurney replied, sitting down behind his desk. "No more slaves, release the ones you have. No galleys outside the harbor."

"And, if they refuse?"

"Our weaponry is far superior to yours. We could easily lay waste to your town, sink all your galleys and wipe out your people."

"That does not leave us much room to maneuver," the larger of the two Krocks said.

"No, it doesn't."

"Very well, we will deliver your terms to our leaders."

"My assistant will see you to your boat."

"We will return when we have an answer."

"I have been studying their weapons. Unfortunately, aside from a suicide attack I see no other options, as hard as it is for me to admit," the old bull Krock said.

"I vote to attack. If we are going to die, let's take some of these accursed Humans with us."

The galleys slowly approached the blockade in the early morning light.

"What's this?" the officer of the deck said.

"I'm not sure, but I don't like it."

"Get the Captain and Gurney."

Minutes later the Captain and Gurney stood, looking at the still approaching line of galleys.

"I think I saw a flicker of fire," Gurney said.

"BATTLE STATIONS!" the captain yelled. "All hands to battle stations." Alarms went off on the Swift, followed by the other cutters in the blockade.

"All guns report ready."

"Prepare to fire."

A volley of fireballs came from the galleys.

"Fire! All guns, FIRE!"

Something impacted the hull of the Swift.

"What the hell was that?"

"We'll check later. Let's just worry about those galleys."

"I don't think there's much to worry about," Gurney said.

The cutters fired again and again.

The galleys had all been reduced to debris. Krock bodies floated on the water amid the burning debris.

"There seems to be a mass exodus in progress," Rufus said.

"Hmmm. I don't see any Krocks in the crowd," Gurney said. "Maybe that means they plan to make a fight of it."

As they watched, most of the people headed east, away from town.

"Someone is waving at us from the waterfront," Bruno said.

Gurney shifted his focus to the waterfront, as did the others.

"Who or what is that?" Bruno said.

"It kind of looks like a bird," Rufus exclaimed.

Gurney asked, "Have you ever seen anything like that?"

"I think I saw someone like that in the first galley," Bruno said.

"Send a boat to pick him up," Gurney said.

"Yes, sir," Kadrovich said. He went to the main deck and dispatched a launch with a heavily armed security team onboard.

Gurney could see the officer in charge talking to the being. After a short exchange, the being was helped into the launch and it returned to the Swift.

"Looks like we have a guest coming to visit," Gurney said.

As the launch approached, Gurney was able to get a better look at the passenger. It appeared to be around five feet tall and covered in black feathers. Large yellow eyes dominated its face and it had a large, multicolored bill with a downward hook at the end.

The creature climbed up the gangway that had been lowered over the side. It stood on the deck and looked from person to person, its gaze finally stopping on Gurney. "You are in charge," he said, it was a statement not a question.

"Yes, I am," Gurney replied.

"I am Pele of Avian," he said, bowing to Gurney.

"Welcome, Pele of Avian," Gurney replied.

"I have been sent as a representative by the former slaves of the Krocks," Pele said. "We would ask your plans for us."

"My plans for you?"

"Surely, as our new lord, you must have plans for us."

"I have no plans," Gurney replied. "You are all free to go."

"I don't understand."

"We do not condone slavery. You may all return to your homelands."

"But, I see Canis and Felis here."

"They are our friends and allies."

"They are? And we're free to go?"

"Yes. Is that so hard to understand?"

"We were just not expecting to be set free, that's all."

"What has happened to the Krocks?"

"A few went further west, some stayed. Most committed suicide. The older Krocks were disgraced to be defeated by what they felt was an inferior foe."

"Amazing."

"Many younger Krocks did not agree with the elders and wanted to abolish slavery. They stayed behind.

"So you represent them, too?"

"Yes, I do," Pele replied.

"Very well," Gurney said. "Return to your people and tell them that they may return home or stay here."

"I will deliver your message."

"What about you? Will you stay or will you return home?"

"I must spend time talking to the others," Pele said. "And, to you. I am curious about your motivations."

"Freedom for all is our motivation," Gurney replied.

"That may not be enough for the others."

"I suggest that you then set up a meeting for us. I would presume that the various groups have their own leaders."

"Yes, they do. I will set up a meeting as soon as possible."

"Please invite them to return here this afternoon," Gurney said.

"I will," Pele replied, bowing again to Gurney. "Until this afternoon, then."

The launch returned Pele to the waiting crowd on the docks.

"I doubt the Canis and Felis will have a problem with their liberation. They will, no doubt, return to their respective packs and prides," Spike said. He stood with Ling in the bow of the Swift.

"I would agree," Ling said. "However, they probably will want to sssee the way we interact with Humansss and each other here in thisss sssetting."

"And, you have no doubt Gurney is sincere?"

"Yesss. Completely," Ling replied. "He hasss alwaysss been truthful with usss. I sssee no reassson for him to lie to usss now, do you?"

"No," Spike said. "I don't."

"Since we don't know what they eat, it's kind of hard to set up a buffet," Bruno said.

"How about fruit and juice?"

"That might work," Bruno replied.

"No alcohol though," Gurney said.

"Not a problem."

The launch had to make two trips to bring all the representatives to the Swift.

"I encourage you to walk around and speak to anyone you like," Gurney said. "We have fresh fruit and juice, help yourselves."

The Canis and Felis immediately went to their respective groups. Pele came to Gurney with a group of Avians.

Gurney's first impression was that no two Avians were alike. They were a wild confusion of coloration and beak shapes.

"So, Pele," Gurney asked. "Where is your homeland?"

"All Avians come from one island off the coast."

"And, the Krocks came to your island?"

"Yes. They made a number of raids and took many of our people away. Many were killed, too."

"We are basically non-aggressive. We really had no way to defend ourselves," another Avian chirped.

"We know first hand that Krocks are formidable fighters," Gurney said. "We have lost many people to them."

"We morn your loss," Pele said.

"I'm surprised that they would give up so quickly," Gurney said.

"They are, were, a very proud race," Pele replied. "For them, domination of others and the search for food was the prime goal."

"I see," Gurney said. "Well, if any of your people want to return to Avian I will send a ship there as soon as possible."

"You would do that for us?" another Avian squawked.

"Certainly," Gurney said, turning to face him. "One of the things we value most is freedom of choice. You're free to stay or go."

"And, it's our choice," Pele said.

"Yes. It's your choice."

"I think we would like to talk amongst ourselves."

"If you like, you can go to the foredeck or I can have one of my men take you to a cabin."

"I think we would like to stay on deck," Pele said. "Many of us have been chained to oars below decks for a long time."

Gurney nodded. "Bruno," he called.

"Yes sir."

"Show our guests to the foredeck and see that they're not disturbed."

"Yes, sir," Bruno said. "If you'll follow me?" He led the Avians away.

Gurney slowly walked around deck, fielding questions from anyone who asked him to clarify something. He looked up at the foredeck. The Avians were having an animated conversation. Gurney continued on to the stern. The other cutters were in line behind the Swift.

"Excuse me, Gurney," Pele said.

"Yes, Pele. What can I do for you?"

"Many of my people want to return home," he said. "But, many want to stay here. This is the only home some of the young have ever known."

"I'll make the arrangements."

"Will you go along?"

"Perhaps. I have to see how things are here before I do anything else."

"I see," Pele said. "I would be honored to have you as a guest in my family home."

"I would be honored to do that."

Pele stood next to Gurney and looked back at the other cutters. "You are a man of great power, yet you do not appear to abuse that power. You are very open. Everyone speaks highly of you."

"The most important thing to me is the future of my people, actually, of all people. It is the right of someone to be able to control his or her own course in life. In the ancient past, my people were often persecuted just for being who they were."

"I think we could be good friends, Gurney."

"I think you could be right."

"And, I think I will stay here in Freetown for a while before I return home."

"Freetown?"

"If you have no objection, that is what we would like to call it."

"No. It sounds good to me."

"And, now, if you'll excuse me I will return to town and begin to put things in order for you."

"Sounds fine to me."

"Have a good night, my friend," Pele said. He turned and went down to the main deck. After a short conversation with some of the Avians, he climbed down to the launch and it returned him to town.

Gurney went to Freetown in the morning.
"Good morning, Gurney."
"Morning, Pele. I've come to tell you I have to return home."
Is there anything I can do for you?"
"If you are going to remain here, you could be the temporary governor."
"You honor me, Gurney."
"Then later, I'll come back and we can go to Avian together."
"I would like to do that, very much, Gurney."
"I'll see you soon."

Gurney headed upstream on the San Francisco. After a stop in Labrys and what seemed like an endless number of speeches and honors, he continued on to Lthrtown, where it started all over again.
"Good to have you back, Gurney," Kirby said.
"It's good to be back."
"Rommel is already at the house."
"Good."

A spring shower had recently passed over Gurney's house. The air smelled fresh and clean. "Have I found the peace I've struggled for all my like? Is this all there is to life?" he wondered. He sat on the deck facing west, a mug of tea in his hand, watching the sun as it disappeared behind the distant mountains. All he knew right now was that he needed to rest.
The sunset slowly changed, from red, to orange, to purple, and then to black.

In Search of a Vision

The early morning rain fell in a fine mist, almost like fog. It swirled around the house in the dim light before dawn.

Rommel was already busy in the kitchen, preparing Gurney's breakfast. It was a routine that they had fallen into months before, once Gurney had recovered from the stresses of his battle campaigns against the Krocks.

Rommel put his bread in the oven. Soon the delicious smell of the bread filled the house. He went into the great room and turned on the lights. Even though he knew it was well after sunrise it didn't seem to be getting any lighter outside.

"Morning, Rommel."

"Morning, Rufus. Sleep well last night?"

"I always do," he replied.

"I know," Rommel laughed. "I can hear you snore in my wing of the house."

"I do NOT snore," Rufus replied, indignantly.

"OK. You breath heavy," Rommel laughed.

"Are you two at it already?" Gurney asked from the doorway.

Rommel and Rufus smiled.

It was a familiar routine that they were all happy with.

"What's happening today?" Gurney asked.

"The usual, sir," Rufus replied. "People asking for favors or advice or both."

Rommel set Gurneys and Rufus's breakfast in front of them.

Since Gurney's retirement he, Rufus, Bruno and Rommel had been the only fulltime occupants in the house.

Gurney would see callers during the morning and right after lunch. The evenings were dedicated to research or relaxation. Gurney liked to go riding on his big, black gelding if the weather was good.

Rufus was always nearby in case he was needed. If someone new came calling, Rufus was in the office with Gurney.

Bruno would patrol the grounds. There was also a squad of Spartans at the main gate. Sometimes Rufus would join Bruno in his rounds after the last of Gurney's callers had gone. Bruno also saw to it that Gurney kept in shape, despite Gurney's protests to the contrary.

Rommel kept the house in order, handled all the paperwork, scheduled the appointments, and kept Gurney and the others well fed.

"The first appointment is due soon, sir," Rommel said.

"I'll be ready," Gurney replied. He got up from the table and went back to his wing of the house. He looked at himself in the bathroom mirror. His close-cropped hair and beard were almost completely white. His face was tanned and deeply weathered from his travels. Thanks to Bruno his body was still in good shape, but he was beginning to feel his age. He had seen many things, beautiful and ugly, good and evil. No matter how many times he thought the evil had been destroyed, it came back in another form, stronger and more evil than the time before. It seemed to be a constant fight, a constant theme in his life.

After a quick shower, he got dressed and went to his office to start the day's business.

"There's an official request for you to visit Avian," Bruno said, rubbing his big black mustache.

"Yeah, I know," Gurney replied. "I just haven't been able to find the time in my schedule to go."

"Here's a personal note from Pele," Bruno added. He handed the sealed envelope to Gurney.

Gurney broke the seal and read the letter.

"What does he say?" Bruno asked.

"He's found some old records in a hidden vault in Freetown he wants me to look at," Gurney replied.

"That's it?"

"There's got to be something more to it than that," Gurney replied. "Something he doesn't want to put in writing."

"Well. What are we going to do about it then, Gurney?"

"We?" Gurney smiled.

"You KNOW what I mean," Bruno grinned back.

The Hudson Theater was packed. A production of CATS with a full cast of Felis was opening that night.

When Gurney and his party appeared in his personal box the audience stood and gave them a standing ovation. He rarely appeared in public because of this kind of response. He didn't like to attract a lot of attention. Sometimes he was embarrassed by the hero worship of some of the people.

Gurney motioned for them to stop. Finally the uproar subsided.

Gurney enjoyed the show immensely. He met with Troy afterwards before going to the Nimbus-Unicorn collective to spend the night.

When Gurney had retired, Kirby took over day-to-day operations. He had seen to it that Gurney's house would always be his and that he had a good pension. Gurney also had a good income from his various business enterprises. The restaurant, the shipping company and shipyard, and a few small specialty shops all provided a good income for him. He paid his workers well, as always, and they worked hard for him.

As the Swift left port the following morning an honor guard of Spartans stood at attention on the dock.

Gurney looked back at the multicolored tiled roofs of Lthrtown as they sailed away. The Dome of the Rock towered over everything. Sometimes he felt each time would be the last time he would see it.

The following day, when the Swift docked in Labrys, the Amazons were out in full regalia, just as the Spartans had been. The golden dome of the Shrine of the Goddess reflected the suns glare. Gurney spent the night at M'Lenas house. They talked about the past and what was still to come.

The Swift slowly made its way down the River Styx. Now they were on the way to Libertyville. Then they would make a stop in Free Town and see what Pele had to show them.

"Gurney, It's good to see you," Pele greeted them at the dock.

'Good to see you, too," Gurney replied.

"I know you want to get right to business, but I'd like to show you around a little," Pele said.

"That's alright. I haven't been here since the Krocks were driven out," Gurney replied.

They climbed into a carriage and rode down the main street. Everyone knew who Gurney was. The ride turned into an impromptu parade. Crowds lined the street, waving and cheering.

Finally, they reached Pele's villa.

"I think you'll be interested in what we've found," Pele told Gurney after they were in the privacy of Pele's library. He indicated a pile of papers and tapes on a side-board.

"What's all this?" Gurney asked.

"This is what we found in the vault. It was airtight, so even the papers are intact," Pele replied.

"Wonderful," Gurney said, picking up a pile of papers.

"I thought we could go through them on the way to Avian."

Gurney sat down and quickly went through some of the material. "This is good stuff."

"Should I pack it up and get in on the Swift?" Bruno asked.

"I've already got the boxes ready," Pele said.

"Leave me this pile and get the rest on board the Swift," Gurney told Bruno.

"Yes sir."

Gurney was up late. The more he read the more excited he became. He felt there was more information than he could take it all at once. The voyage to Avian would give him time to go through it all properly.

The coastline disappeared in the distant haze as the Swift sliced through the water. Gurney slowly walked around the deck. The fresh salt air was invigorating to him. He had always liked the water. That was one reason his house overlooked the river, the sounds of the water over the rocks helped him relax and sleep better.

"We'll be in Avian in a couple of days," Pele said, as he walked up to stand beside Gurney.

"I'm looking forward to it," Gurney replied.

Pele started to reply when he was interrupted by the lookout. "SSSAIL HO!" he called from the crows-nest.

"Where away?" The first mate called up to him.

"Ssstarboard. A sssingle sssail," was the reply from the Felis crewman.

Another crewman scrambled up to the crows-nest. "It'sss not a Krock sssail, unlesss they've changed their desssign."

"Any ideas?" Gurney asked Pele.

"What shape is the sail?" Pele called to the lookout.

"It's triangular," he replied.

"That's a new one to me," Pele told Gurney.

"Captain," Gurney said, "I suggest you go to alert status until we know who we're dealing with."

"I agree, sir." The crew hurried to battle stations.

"Stay our course," the captain ordered. "We'll let them come to us."

Slowly the ships approached each other. The Swifts gunners were at their stations.

"Can you see anything?" the captain called to the lookouts.

"No, sssir," the other Felis replied. With their natural climbing abilities many Felis had taken jobs on Nimbus-Unicorn ships. They were fearless in the rigging.

Gurney and Pele stood in the bow. They watched the strange ship through their binoculars.

"I've got a bad feeling about this," Gurney said.

The distance between the ships continued to shrink.

"I can sssee a body on the deck," the lookout called. "But, I can't make out any detailsss. He's undersssomething."

Pele climbed partway up the rigging.

"What do you think?" Gurney asked him when he returned to the deck.

"It's a plague ship," he replied. "Sink it."

'Sir?" the captain said.

"You heard the man, captain," Gurney said.

"Yes, sir," the captain said. He gave the crew their orders.

Five minutes later the burning ship slid beneath the surface. Some floating debris was the only thing to mark its passing.

"How did you know it was a plague ship?" Gurney asked.

"The tiller was tied in place," Pele replied. "A sure sign."

"Any idea where it was from?" the captain asked.

"I'm not sure," Pele replied. "The design was not familiar. There's so much unexplored country. I know there are some islands east of Avian, but I don't know who, if anyone, lives there."

"You've never explored there?" Gurney asked.

"We never had a real reason to," Pele answered. "Once the Krocks began to raid Avian, we practically went into hiding."

"I wish we had been able to find out where they were from," Gurney said.

"Chances are there are more of them out here."

Two days later, the Swift approached the main harbor at Avian. The waterfront was deserted. Nothing moved. Even the flags hung limply in what little breeze there was.

"I think I had better go alone," Pele said.

"Don't you want to take a security detail with you?" Gurney asked.

"No. I don't want to run the risk of exposing anyone else."

"Do you think that ship was here?" Bruno asked.

"All I know for sure is that the waterfront should be very busy this time of day," Pele replied.

A small boat was put over the side and Pele rowed to the dock by himself. He disappeared down one of the streets.

Gurney stood on deck, waiting for him to contact them.

"Gurney," Pele voice crackled over the radio.

"I'm here."

"The town is deserted. No sign of bodies. I'll go to the council chambers and see if there's anything there."

"Do you want back-up?"

"Not until I know it's safe," was the reply. "No reason to expose a lot of people if there's something wrong here."

"OK. We'll wait until we hear from you," Gurney said.

Hours passed. Gurney was on the verge of sending a security team ashore when Pele reappeared. He rowed back to the Swift.

"Well?" Gurney asked.

"The town is deserted," Pele said.

"No idea where they went?"

"They may have gone to the southern end of the island," Pele replied. "That's the only place I can think of. It is kind of isolated there, too."

Slowly, the Swift followed the coast of Avian. They were looking for something that would indicate there was someone still alive.

"SSSmoke," called the lookout, pointing ahead.

The ship, ever more slowly, approached the island.

"I'm going ashore," Pele said.

"I'm going, too," Gurney said. "You'll need help."

Pele started to object, but he knew, from the look in Gurneys eyes, that he wouldn't change his mind.

Gurney and Pele approached the beach, looking for some sign that there was someone nearby.

Pele jumped out of the boat and pulled it up onto the smooth sandy beach.

Gurney picked up his backpack and tossed one to Pele. "Do you have a sidearm?" he asked.

"I don't think I'll need one. My people all know who I am," Pele replied.

"Better to be safe, than sorry," Gurney said. "I'll keep mine."

They headed towards the tree line.

Suddenly a voice rang out. "Stop right there!"

Gurney and Pele stopped their advance.

"Pele? Is that you?" the voice chirped.

"Yes. Yes, it is," Pele replied.

A parakeet-like Avian stumbled out of the thick underbrush. "Have you come to rescue us?" it chirped.

"What happened here?" Pele said. Gurney let him take the lead.

"Strangers came from somewhere. I'm not sure where," it chirped again. "Our people began to get sick with a strange disease that we had no cure for."

"How did you get here?" Pele said.

"We came overland. Many died. A few of those who got sick recovered," the Avian suddenly seemed to become aware of Gurney.

"Do you know what the shape of the stranger's ship was?" Gurney asked.

"Yes," the Avian replied. "It was triangular."

"That must be the ship we sunk then," Gurney said to Pele.

"How many of our people are here?" Pele asked.

"Two hundred or so."

"We can take some back to Avian with us. I'll have to have the captain contact Freetown and send out some other ships," Gurney said. "We don't have room on the Swift for very many."

"Let me take you to the others," the Avian turned and followed a path away from the beach.

As they walked, Gurney contacted the Swift and explained the situation. "I also want a decontamination team send to the main port on the fastest ship available. And get a medical team here, too. Ask for volunteers."

"Yes, sir," The captain replied.

The trio walked through the underbrush in silence. The path was well worn.

Finally, they emerged into a clearing surrounded by some rough shelters. It was full of Avians in a bewildering array of bright plumage.

The Avians saw Pele and rushed to him. They were all talking at once.

"Have you come to take us home?" asked one.

"How's the town?" said another.

"Calm down everyone. Calm down. I'll talk to you all in time," Pele replied

Slowly the crowd dispersed and the Avians sat and waited.

Pele and Gurney went from shelter to shelter. Pele spoke words of comfort and support.

"Where are the sick?" Gurney asked.

The Avian who had met them looked sharply at Gurney. "They are separate from us. Not too far. Why do you want to know that?"

"I want to see them," Gurney replied. "To see how they are and if they need anything."

"Aren't you afraid of contracting the disease?" He chirped.

"Everyone needs to be comforted. The sick more-so than the well," Gurney replied. "Besides, I have a feeling that I will not be affected."

The Avian bobbed his head, his blue and white feather crest stood-up. "This way," he said. He led Gurney and Pele to another clearing.

Pele once again spoke to everyone. Gurney stood silently behind him for support if he was needed.

"Sir," Gurney's radio crackled.

"Yes, captain?"

"We're at the first shelters. I have a medical team with me."

"Home in on my signal. We're not too far away."

A few minutes later the medical team entered the clearing.

"We need to take some samples, sir," the medic told Pele.

"I'll tell them what you need. They'll cooperate," Pele replied.

"I'll also want to get samples from someone who contracted the disease and recovered, plus someone who never got sick."

"Whatever you require," Pele said.

"I don't really have a well equipped lab here," the medic told Gurney. "   I can't do a really good analyst of the samples."

"We'll have to set up a lab in Avian," Gurney told him. "Get a list of equipment to the captain and have him contact Freetown."

"Yes, sir, Thank you, sir."

The Swift returned to Avian Town with the survivors.

Immediately, the Avians began to clean the city.

The Swift retuned to bring more Avians home.

"I think our physiology is different enough that this disease won't affect us," Gurney told Pele.

"I hope you're right," Pele replied. "I would hate for you to get sick because of us."

"I'm not worried," Gurney answered.

Volunteers from the Swift made a house-to-house search of the town.

They found a few dead Avians, but not much else. The town was just as they had left it.

"There will be a steady stream of ships with emergency supplies coming in to Avian," Gurney told Pele.

"We appreciate all you are doing for us," Pele replied.

"We'll also set up a field hospital just outside of town. The sickest will be taken back to Free Town. If necessary, and conditions warrant it, we'll take them all the way to Lthrtown." Gurney added.

"I don't know how to thank you and your people, Gurney."

"You'd do the same for us," Gurney said.

"I'd like to think so," Pele replied.

Over the next week the refugee camp was dismantled. Few victims needed to be taken to Free Town, but Gurney sent samples to all the medical centers for testing. He felt that the more people were working on a cure they would come up with an answer faster.

"We're still running some tests, but I think we have some good leads," the doctor told Gurney.

"Do you think there's the possibility of humans contracting the disease?"

"I don't think so. It's similar to some diseases I've read of in the old medical texts."

"You mean bird diseases," Gurney said.

"Yes. Even though the Avians are now bipeds, internally they are still really just large birds. Even the Canis and Felis are more related to their ancient ancestors then they are to us."

"I see," Gurney replied.

"It might be a good idea to develop a broad spectrum treatment for everyone," the doctor said.

"That would be quite a daunting task, I would think."

"I would hate to have to deal with a plague of some kind."

"Alright," Gurney replied. "Get your program together and let me know what you need. I'll pass it on and we'll get what you need as soon as possible."

"You'll have it in the morning," the doctor said.

"When things have stabilized here, I think we need to try and find out where that mystery ship came from," Gurney told Bruno.

"The Swift and the Shrike are on their way back," Bruno said.

"Good. Be sure the Swift is fully provisioned. It may be a while before we get back."

"Yes sir."

The Swift and Shrike were unloaded when they arrived. A few Avians who had left earlier came back, recovered from the disease.

"All the medical research teams are making progress on a broad spectrum vaccination," Bruno told Gurney.

"To be sure they get everyone, they are going to take a census. Since a majority of people work for a collective, at least in Lthrtown, it shouldn't be a problem," Gurney said.

For the next few days, the Swift was loaded for the expedition. The horses were the last things to be brought aboard.

"Any idea how long you'll be gone?" Pele asked.

"It's hard to say," Gurney replied. "First, I want to find where the plague ship came from."

"And then?"

"It's still a voyage of exploration," Gurney replied.

"That reminds me," Bruno said. "How are the young Krocks that stayed behind in Freetown?"

"Surprisingly well," Pele replied. They've found work and keep their claws trimmed."

"Good," Gurney said. "I'm glad they're fitting in well."

"So am I," Pele replied.

The rings reflection on the ocean was like a pathway for the Swift to follow. The water slapped against the hull. The rigging creaked as the sails moved.

Gurney felt very alone. He was in a very romantic location and had no one to share it with. Ever since he had broken things off with Troy he hadn't really had the time for a serious relationship.

"Good evening, sir," Bruno said from the shadows.

"Hello, Bruno."

"It's a beautiful night," Bruno said, slowly approaching Gurney.

"Yes. It certainly is."

"Can I ask you something, sir?"

"You can ask," Gurney laughed. "I may not answer though."

"Why haven't you ever settled down?"

Gurney thought for a moment. "I guess its part of the job."

"Part of the job?"

"You know my past record. Besides, I always feel like there's enough pressure on me, let alone having a partner and trying to maintain a relationship," Gurney sighed. "Always trying to better your last accomplishment, wondering if the decisions you make are the right ones. Struggling to be fair at all times, putting your own feelings, wants, and needs secondary for the greater good."

"I can understand that, sir."

"I'm tired. Tired of life in the public eye, tired of doing the right thing, tired of being the man with all the answers," he sighed again.

Bruno listened quietly.

"I want to make that one big find I've been looking for so I can rest. Withdraw from the public eye. Stay at home. Ride my horse. Maybe write a book."

"Do you remember a night, a while back?" Bruno asked. "You had a late night caller?"

"Yes," Gurney said, surprised. "I never told anyone about that. How did you know that?"

"There's only one way I could, sir," Bruno replied.

They stood, silently, close together.

"I don't think this is a good idea, Bruno."

"I think you should stop over analyzing everything, Gurney. Do something YOU want to do," Bruno replied, moving even closer to Gurney.

For once Gurney wasn't sure what to do.

Bruno stepped closer to Gurney. The younger man slowly raised his arms and folded them around Gurney, pulling him to his chest.

"Breakfast, sir," Bruno open the cabin door and came in with a tray.

"Uh, thank you, Bruno."

"Did you sleep well, sir?"

"I don't remember much of last night," Gurney said.

"Well, I certainly had a good time," Bruno grinned.

Before Gurney could reply, there was a knock at the cabin door. "Come, in," Gurney said, pulling the sheet over him.

"Sorry to bother you so early, but I've found something I thought you'd like to see," Pele said.

"What's that?"

Pele handed Gurney some papers. "I've marked the relevant parts."

Gurney scanned the paper. "If this is a real document, I think this is what we've been looking for."

"What's that, sir?" Bruno asked.

"In a nutshell, it indicates that there's a massive supply and database buried under a mountain, somewhere," Gurney said.

"If we can find it, we'll have the accumulated knowledge of the Ancients at our disposal," Pele said.

"The only problem I can see is that the surface of the planet has been changed so much, the site could be underwater or it could have been destroyed," Gurney said.

"I think the information you're looking for is on a different page," Pele said, "It indicates the site was in a geologically stable area."

"I hope you're right," Gurney said.

"There is some information on the location, but some of it is damaged," Pele said. "We need to find more information to confirm what we do have."

"We've got plenty of material to go through. There's got to be more information," Gurney said. "I can send a message on a secure channel back to Free Town. They can pass the message on to M'Lena and the rest of the research teams."

The ocean had changed character from the day before. Now the waves were higher, the troughs were longer. The waves often had foam crests.

"There's a storm coming," the captain said.

"It certainly seems like it," Gurney said, watching the wind whip the waves.

"We'll have to turn and run with the waves. If the waves keep getting bigger we're in danger of capsizing."

The lookout called down. "TIDAL WAVE!" he yelled to be heard over the noise of the storm.

"GET DOWN HERE!" the captain yelled up to the lookout.

"NO TIME," came the faint reply, as the wind whipped through the rigging.

The Swift turned to starboard, trying to get its stern to the wave. Sails ripped. Lines split and snapped from the stress. Gurney thought he heard wood splitting.

The full force of the storm hit them. Lighting flashed and thunder crashed almost constantly. The rain came down in curtains. They were soaked to the skin as soon as they emerged on deck.

"LOOK OUT!" someone yelled as the crow's nest came crashing down.

Gurney thought he saw the Felis that had been in the crow's nest fall overboard.

"SIR," The captain yelled to Gurney. "Please get below!"

Bruno grabbed Gurney and pulled him through an open hatchway. They fell to the deck in a sodden heap.

The deck tilted at a crazy angle. Gurney thought they were going to capsize.

Slowly, the Swift righted herself.

The deck was a tangle of torn sails, split rigging, and splintered wood.

"How bad is it, captain?" Gurney asked.

"Bad enough," he replied. "But, I think we can jury rig something. The main mast has been cracked, but we might be able to reinforce it"

Bruno joined them. "The radio is junk. Even if it was working we have no antenna without the masts."

"What about the spare?" Gurney asked.

Bruno shook his head. "Junk, too."

Gurney frowned. "Where's Rufus?"

"Below, trying to see what's salvageable," Bruno replied.

"Captain, this is your area of expertise," Gurney said. "Just tell my staff and I what we can do to help."

"The first thing is to get the main deck cleared up and take a roll call. Hopefully, we didn't lose anyone."

"I'm afraid we may have lost some or all of the horses," Bruno said.

"I hope not," Gurney said. "That would certainly slow us down once we make landfall."

"As soon as I know I'll let you know," Bruno replied.

"OK. I'll see what I can do up here," Gurney said, as Bruno went below to check the situation.

"Until we can get underway, we'll just drift," the captain said.

"I know," Gurney replied.

There was a crash on the deck. The rear mast had toppled over. It dragged in the water.

"Cut those lines and throw the junk overboard," The captain ordered. "But, keep anything that could be of use later."

The Swift drifted with the current. Until they were able to rig up a sail of some kind they were at the mercy of the wind and the waves.

Roll call revealed that they had only lost the lookout in the crow's nest. They considered themselves to be lucky that they had not lost more crew. There were a few broken bones and lots of cuts and bruises.

"The horses are a little shaken-up, but otherwise they're fine," Rufus told Gurney. "We were lucky none of them broke legs."

"We're going to have a little meeting in my cabin. Come down when you're ready," Gurney told him.

"Well," the captain said, "All things considered we're in pretty good shape."

"We've lost some supplies, but we were pretty well stocked," Pele added. I do not see any problems there. We can also rig up something to catch rainwater."

"We only lost the one crewman," Bruno said. "It's a miracle that we didn't sink."

"I want to get the crew busy on reinforcing the main mast," the captain said. "If nothing else, it keeps them busy."

"There's plenty to do, that's for sure," Gurney added.

"We've rigged a spinnaker so we can make some headway," Captain Ridge said.

"We're heading north?" Gurney asked.

"Yes. I think that's the best thing to do," the captain replied. "If any of our other ships search for us, following the coast would probably be what they would do."

Kadrovich contacted M'Lena from Freetown. "The Swift hasn't checked in recently."

"It could just be a radio problem," she replied.

"You know Gurney. There are at least two complete radios and parts to build another. He always has a backup system."

"Can you wait for me to get there?"

"Sure. We have to load the Shrike and get a fresh crew together anyway."

"I'll leave within the hour," M'Lena said. "I'll be there as soon as possible."

"We'll be waiting for you." Kadrovich got back to the details of outfitting the Shrike for the rescue mission.

M'Lena commandeered the Bronski, one of the fast mail packets. She knew she had to get to Freetown as soon as she could.

"M'Lena," Captain Melka said, shaking her shoulder.

"Are we there?" she asked.

"Not too much longer," Melka replied.

As the sun rose, M'Lena got her first look at Freetown. The single story, white-faced buildings were pink in the early morning light. She could see that the docks were already crowded with people.

"Ah, you're here," Kadrovich said as M'Lena walked into the office.

"What's the current status?" she asked.

"Still no word from the Swift," he replied. He handed her a hot cup of tea.

"What's the plan?"

"The Shrike will first go to Avian. After that it will head north to the coast and head east," he said. "Meanwhile, a mixed volunteer squad will be following the coast on horseback."

"When do we leave?"

He glanced at his chrono, "Within the hour."

"Well then, I guess we'd better get on board."

Kadrovich led the way to the dock.

"They left here a few days ago," the Avian said. "But, a few days or so after they left we had a very severe storm. We were shielded by the mountains, but the other side of the island took quite a beating."

"Well, at least that gives us a starting point," M'Lena said.

"We're taking in water," Captain Ridge said. "The pumps are just able to keep up with it."

"What do you think the problem is?" Gurney asked.

"Some hull plates probably buckled. If it doesn't get worse we'll be alright."

"How are the repairs to the mast coming?"

"We'll be able to put up some sail, but not much. If we overstress the mast if might break completely."

"Do what you can," Gurney said. "Even if we have to run the Swift aground."

"She's a good ship," The captain replied. "I'd hate to have to do that."

"I understand, captain," Gurney said. "I understand, completely."

The Shrike followed the coastline about a mile offshore. They were two days out of Avian. Kadrovich stood in the bow, constantly scanning for some sign of the Swift.

"See anything?" M'Lena asked.

"No. Nothing," Kadrovich replied. He continued to the scan the ocean.

"There's got to be something out here," M'Lena said, raising her binoculars.

"Well, I guess if we find nothing it means that they're all right," he replied.

Just then one of the lookouts called down. "I think I sssee sssome debrisss to port!"

Everyone strained to see if there was anything floating in the ocean.

The Shrike changed course to intercept the debris.

"Lower a boat," the captain called.

The crewmen in the boat attached some lines and pulled the wreckage back to the Shrike.

"Yes," Kadrovich said. "This is from the Swift." He held up a tattered piece of red and yellow cloth, Gurney's personal pennant.

"Do you think she went down?" M'Lena asked.

"There's not enough wreckage for a ship the size of the Swift," the captain replied. "There would be a much bigger debris field."

"So, there's a good chance they're OK," Kadrovich said.

"Well, at least they didn't sink here," he replied.

"I'm afraid to go to fast. We might rupture some more hull plates. The pumps are just barely able to keep up," the captain told Gurney.

"It's your call," Gurney said. "This is your area of expertise."

"Thank you, sir, for understanding."

"She's your ship, captain. Do what you need to."

"We've found a little debris on the beach," Spike said in to the radio. "But, it's not possibly enough though to be the Swift."

"Very well," Kadrovich replied. "Keep us informed."

"I will."

"LAND HO!" called the lookout. "Ssstraight ahead!"

The Swift shuddered.

"What was that?" Rufus asked.

The Swift began to list heavily to starboard.

"Another hull plate has ruptured," the captain said.

"We going to make it to shore?" Gurney asked.

"Hopefully at least to shallow water. We might be able to make temporary repairs if we can get close enough."

The Swift shuddered again. The list increased to an alarming angle

"Come on, you can do it," the captain muttered.

Gurney heard a grinding noise.

"That's the sea bottom," the captain said. "Not much further and we'll be OK."

The grinding increased and the Swift began to slow down. Finally, the Swift stopped.

"We made it," the captain said, he voice full of relief. "Get those repair crews to work on those hull plates."

"We keep finding small amounts of wreckage," Kadrovich said, "but it's not near enough to be the Swift."

"Well, I guess we just keep looking then," M'Lena replied.

"Any repairs we'll be able to make will not last very long," Captain Ridge told Gurney.

"I'm sure there must be search teams out looking for us. Since we've been out of radio contact for a while, I'm sure they know something is wrong."

"We found more wreckage," Kadrovich said. "And, something else."

"What else?" M'Lena asked.

"A drowned Felis," he replied. "He's been identified as a member of the Swifts crew."

"But nothing else?"

"No. There's still not enough debris to be the entire mass of the Swift," he replied.

"So, that's a good sign then. Hopefully they're out there somewhere."

"We'll keep looking," Kadrovich replied. He returned to his examination of the wreckage.

"Well, the plates are in pretty rough shape," Ridge told Gurney. "This might take longer than I thought."

"What do you have to do?"

"I've got a crew out finding a source of lumber. "We'll probably have to make some bucks and hand form the plates."

"What do you think caused it?"

"I remember an impact during the Freetown blockage," Ridge replied. " I think that's when in happened."

"Well, as I said before, this is your department. Do what you have to. And, if there's anything I or my staff can do to help, let me know."

"Well, sir. If you like, you could help put up some of the tents. I don't think it's a good idea to have anyone on board right now."

"OK, we'll take care of it."

They sat around one of the campfires. The Swift sat like a beached whale in the distance.

"I think we'll take the horses and do some scouting in the area tomorrow," Gurney said.

"Sounds like a good idea," Pele said.

"My supply of medical herbs is getting low," Rufus said. "That would give me a chance to restock."

"Some fresh food might be a nice change, too," Bruno said.

Gurney and his group spent the next few hours checking out the surrounding area. They found some fruit trees and a fresh water source.

Rufus found some herbs and Bruno was able to find a boar for dinner.

"We'll be back in sight of the coast soon," Kadrovich said to M'Lena.

"I hope we find them out here," she replied.

"The Pelican salvage and repair ship is following closer to the coast. We'll meet them and continue the coast together," he told her.

"What do you think," M'Lena asked.

"We'll find them. Don't worry," Kadrovich replied.

"We can't be sure how far off course we are," Ridge told Gurney. "All we can do is make an educated guess."

"How far off do you think we're off?"

"A hundred miles, maybe more."

"Knowing Kadrovich, they'll keep looking until they find us."

"You think so?"

"I know so. If he has learned one thing from me, it's persistence."

"How long will we keep looking?" M'Lena asked.

"Until we know for sure," Kadrovich replied. "Every possible ship is involved in the search. We'll find them. We're not going to give up until we know for sure."

The Swift's crew fell into a regular pattern of activity. Hunting, gathering, working on the ship, as they were needed.

In their off time they began to build more permanent structures. A watchtower was built on a nearby headland.

Work on the Swift went slowly, but morale was high.

The shipwright and his helpers hammered away on the damaged plates, attempting to return them to their proper shape.

M'Lena stood on the dark deck, watching the sea and the stars.

"I really think we'll find them alive," Kadrovich said, as he walked up to her.

"If Gurney was dead, I'd know it," she replied.

"How?"

"I just would. I can't explain it."

Gurney stood on a large rock the waves gently surrounded. The water slowly advanced and fell.

"Gurney," Rufus called.

"Yes Rufus."

"What are you doing?" Rufus joined him on the rock.

"Nothing really, standing, thinking, wondering."

"I'll never understand humans," Rufus said.

"Why's that?"

"Canis pretty much act on instinct," he said.

"Kind of like, if it feels good do it?" Gurney grinned in the darkness.

"Yes, I guess so," Rufus replied.

"They'll be here soon."

"Who," Rufus asked.

"The rescue team, tomorrow, maybe the next day."

"How do you know that?"

"Just a feeling I have," Gurney replied.

"A feeling?"

"Yeah, I know it sounds crazy," Gurney replied. "But, I'm sure they'll be here soon."

"Well, I guess we'll see tomorrow or the next day," Rufus said.

"Yes, we will."

"SSSmoke ahead," the lookout called out.

"Hopefully, that's where Gurney and the others are," Kadrovich said.

After a few minutes the beached Swift appeared. They could see crewmembers waving on the beach.

"Thank the Goddess," M'Lena said. "We've found them."

A boat was quickly lowered and headed for the beach.

The Swift's crewmen splashed out into the water and helped pull the boat onto the sand.

"Are we glad to see you!" Kadrovich exclaimed.

"Not half as glad as we are," Gurney replied.

"What happened?" M'Lena asked, looking up at the Swift.

Gurney quickly told them the story of the storm and their arrival at the beach.

"I knew you were all right," M'Lena said. "I just had a feeling."

"We're back together. That's all that matters right now," Gurney said."

"We've been going over the papers Pele found," Gurney said.

"Anything useful?" M'Lena asked.

"Some clues on the location," Gurney replied.

"I'm looking forward to finding it," Kadrovich said.

Captain Ridge joined the group. "With the Pelican to help us, we should have the Swift seaworthy in a few days."

"I think it's time for us to head inland," Gurney said. "Somewhere out there is the ultimate cache."

"Are you sure?" M'Lena asked as they sat in the Shrikes galley.

"Very sure," he replied as he pushed a pile of papers over to her.

"The problem is finding it," Gurney replied.

"It's like a puzzle," Kadrovich said. "Or a riddle."

"Exactly," Gurney replied. "The problem is finding the correct landmarks. Since we're not exactly sure how long ago all this took place, there could be massive changes in the topography."

"Well, the survey team should be here in a day or two. Maybe, they'll be helpful," M'Lena said.

"I would hope so," Gurney replied.

Cody, the survey team leader, looked up from the maps. "It's hard to say from these old maps. There are some mountains north of here that might be possible sites. There's something here about the mountain of four faces," Cody said. "I've heard of a place like that."

"Where is it?" Gurney asked.

"Quite a distance north," Cody replied.

"How can a mountain have four faces unless it's square?" Bruno asked.

"I guess we'll have to put together an expedition and check it out," Gurney said.

"I'll see to it, sir," Cody replied.

Gurney sat in the captain's cabin on the Shrike. He had set up a temporary office so he they could continue going through the papers Pele had found.

M'Lena sat across the room and looked through her own stack of papers. "Look at this," she said, walking over to the desk where Gurney sat.

Gurney took the book from her hand. "Mount Rushmore," he said. "Four faces. Four faces of men."

"Looks like we're on to something here," she said.

"Looks like," he replied. "The problem is, is Rushmore still there?"

"I guess we'll have to go find out," she said.

The Pelican and Shrike began the slow job of towing the Swift back to Free Town. There, they would make more repairs before taking her back to the main shipyard at Lthrtown.

Five survey teams headed north. Gurney rode in the center team with Cody. Kadrovich and M'Lena rode with two other teams.

"So, Cody," Gurney said, "Tell me about yourself. I've been out of touch for a while."

"Not much to tell really. I'm from Breederstown. Wife, a couple of kids."

"I see," Gurney said.

"I came to be in your service in a desire to help make the world a better place for my kids. My oldest son is in Lthrtown. If I can help you in your quest that's a bonus for me."

"Things seem to be in a constant state of flux," Gurney replied.

"So I've noticed," Cody said. He removed his hat and ran his hand through his brown hair. "I have a number of apprentices and students. We've been very busy lately, laying out street plans and building sites."

They continued to ride across the grasslands.

"When word of your disappearance got out, I knew I could be of some help."

"How so?"

"I've been keeping up with your exploits. I know you're a man of your word and consider all the possible angles. I know what you're looking for is important to our future and our children's future. And, I know you always take care of your people. No matter where they're from," he glanced back at Rufus. "I've even tried to do some of my own research."

"You have, eh?"

"Unfortunately, there's not much written information. All I had to go on was stories and hearsay."

"This Mount Rushmore seems to be the only information we have," Gurney said.

"Yes, it is. But, I'm sure we still have a lot of material to go through. Somewhere there has to be more information to go on."

"I'm sure there is," Gurney said. "The challenge is finding it."

"Sure, but you're not the kind of man who backs down from a challenge. Otherwise you wouldn't have done all you have," Cody grinned.

"True," Gurney grinned back.

Every night Gurney went through more papers. Just as he had been doing for days. He and M'Lena talked on the radio every night, too. They were trying to find the information they needed to locate Mount Rushmore. Gurney thought with the teams operating independently of one another they could cover more ground and learn more.

"I don't have much to report," M'Lena said.
"Nothing much here either," Gurney replied.
"So what do we do now?" Kadrovich's voice came over the radio.
"We'll rendezvous at the end of the week," Gurney replied. "We'll access our progress then."

"The terrain is quite different from the old maps," Cody said. "It looks like swampland ahead."
"Hmm," Gurney said, "I wonder if that means there are Krocks ahead."
"The climate is a little cooler here. It might be too cold for them," Rufus said
"I guess there's only one way to find out," Gurney said.

Pumpkin looked upstream from her perch in the ancient maple tree. She wasn't sure what she was actually looking for, only that she had been told to keep a lookout. She was dozing in the warm sun when she suddenly realized something was coming down the sluggish river.
She got her binoculars out, and looking upstream, saw a ship with a triangular sail coming towards her.
"Able bassse," she said into her radio.
"This is Able base," was the reply. "What's up Pumpkin?"
"I've got a sssighting," she replied.
"A ship?"
"Yesss," she replied. "It matchesss the dessscription of the plague ssship."
"Keep on eye on it. If it looks like they're headed for land let us know."
"Roger," she replied
"Able base, out."

"Should we contact Gurney?" Buddy said.
"They'll be here in a couple of hours," Eddie replied. "Write it up in the log."

"Able bassse," Pumpkin said.
"This is Able base, go."
"I can sssee the ssship better now."
"Can you make out the crew?"
"Yesss," she replied. "They have hornsss. Broad shouldersss, big chestsss, narrow waissstsss, and powerful looking legsss."
"Do they look like they might be headed to shore?"
"No. They're right in the middle of the river," she replied. "They don't look like they're planning on sssstopping."
"Keep them under observation and we'll pick them up down closer to us."

"Roger."

M'Lena and Kadrovich arrived at the base and were told about the ship coming downstream.

"Sounds like a minotaur to me," M'Lena said.

"Minotaur?" Kadrovich said.

"A mythical beast with the head of a bull and the body of a man," she replied.

"How could they pass a disease onto the Avians?"

"I suppose it's possible," she replied.

"Excuse me," Buddy said. "The ship is just around the bend and should be in sight in soon."

"Do you have someplace where we can observe it?" Kadrovich asked.

"Yes, this way," Buddy replied. He led them to a hidden shelter on the side of the river.

As they watched the ship appeared in the distance. The red and white striped sail hung limply in the hot, humid air. The sluggish current slowly moved the ship along.

M'Lena and Kadrovich watched the ship move past through their binoculars.

"Very interesting," M'Lena said. "What an unusual event."

"How so?" Kadrovich asked.

"Just think," she replied. "Of all the creatures we have run into, the Canis, the Felis, the Avians, the Krocks, none of them came directly out of old human myth. Except for the gods of a very ancient people, the Egyptians."

"I never heard of them," Kadrovich replied.

"I'm not surprised," she said. "Material on them is very, very old."

The ship slowly moved out of sight.

"Many of their gods were represented in multiple of forms. Quite often as animal headed men," M'Lena said.

"Interesting," Kadrovich said. "I'd say we need to get our information together. Gurney will be here soon."

"Only the one ship?" Gurney asked.

"Since we've been here, yes," Buddy said.

"We'll slowly head upstream. I don't want to run into a hostile enemy in unfamiliar territory," Gurney told them. "We'll head out in the morning."

"Yes sir."

The low, fast moving clouds periodically spit rain. Visibility was very low and slowed their advance to the north. They following the course of the river as it twisted and turned. A small squad led the way. Far enough ahead to give warning, but not so far ahead that they were out of touch with the main group.

"We've come to a sssmall sssettlement," Pumpkin reported.

"Can you see any movement?" Buddy asked.

"Not much," Pumpkin said into her radio.

"Stay where you are," Gurney said. "We'll be at your position shortly."

"Yesss, sssir," Pumpkin replied.

The members of the expedition sat in the bushes and watched the settlement. The rain had finally stopped, but the clouds were still low and threatening.

"Well, what do you think we should do?" M'Lena asked Gurney.

"We can't sit here forever," Gurney answered. "I was hoping to get an idea as to the culture here before we burst in on them."

No sooner had Gurney made his comment than a group of Minotaurs appeared around the corner of a building. They walked casually to a building and went inside.

"I sense no tension," M'Lena said.

"Well," Gurney said. "Let's mount up and head in."

Word was passed down the line and the members of the expedition prepared to head into the settlement.

Bruno and Kadrovich flanked Gurney as they rode the short distance to the end of the first street.

Their approach had been noticed. Doors opened and curious faces watched them.

A pair of Minotaurs came out of a nearby building and walked into the center of street, blocking the group's path.

"Welcome, strangers" the larger of the two said. His back was dark brown; his face and belly were white.

"Thank you," Gurney replied.

"How can we be of assistance to you?" the second Minotaur asked.   H e was solid black.

"We are explorers," Gurney said. "We come from a distant land."

"Come, we'll take you to a place when you can get a warm meal and a dry bed to sleep in after all this rain," the first Minotaur said.

"We'll need someplace for our horses, too," Gurney said.

"Not a problem."

"I am called Tarsis," the larger Minotaur said. "My companion's name is Cerebus."

"I'm Gurney, this is Kadrovich, Bruno, Rufus, and M'Lena."

"Welcome to Minos," Tarsis said.

"Thank you," Gurney replied.

"How long will you be with us, Gurney?" Cerebus asked.

"We are just passing through," Gurney replied.

"Are you on a quest of some kind?" Tarsis asked.

"Yes," Gurney said. "We are looking for a landmark. It will help us find what we're looking for."

"What landmark is that?" Cerebus asked.

"The mountain of four faces," Gurney said.

They walked on in silence.

"There is a place north of here that has one face," Tarsis finally said.   "It's possible the other faces were worn away."

"How far is it?" Gurney asked.

"About a week," Cerebus said.

"Here we are," Tarsis said. They stood outside a low rambling building. "You can spend the night here at my home. There is a building in the back where you can put your horses."

"How long have you been looking for this treasure of yours?" Tarsus asked.

"Over twenty years," Gurney replied. "But I don't think it's a treasure in the traditional use of the word."

"It's not?"

"It's a treasure of knowledge," Gurney replied. They sat in the dinning room of Tarsus's villa.

"Knowledge can be very valuable," Cerebus said. "In the right hands, that is."

"It can also be very dangerous in the wrong hands," Kadrovich said.

"Very true," Cerebus replied.

"If you like you can stay with us for a few days," Tarsus said. .

"I must ask you this," Pele said.

Tarsus and Cerebus turned their attention to him.

"We think it's possible one of your ships visited Avian and was responsible for a plague. Many of my people died."

"One of our ships is overdue," Tarsus said, "But we certainly would never intentionally take plague someplace."

Pele was satisfied with their answer.

"We'll spend a day or two here in Minos before we head north," Gurney said.

"Perhaps I can find a guide to go part of the way with you," Cerebus said.

"Thank you," Gurney said. "That would be very helpful."

As the expedition headed north the terrain changed from lush grassland, splashed with wild flowers and babbling brooks to heavy forests of evergreens. Fireflies dotted the night. During the day falcons and hawks could be seen high in the air, riding the thermals. The forest thinned out and the terrain got dryer and rougher. Even the clouds changed. From white and fluffy, to high, thin clouds, then to an almost completely clear sky. Even the wildlife changed from a variety of small animals and birds to little readily visible to the naked eye and those were mostly lizards. Now vultures rode the thermals above the expedition.

"We should be in sight of the mountain tomorrow," Aries said, as he walked beside Gurney's horse. He was a ruddy red color. His horns were lacquered in black and the tips were covered with silver guards, as was the Minosian style.

"Then we have the problem of finding the entryway," Gurney replied.

"That I cannot help you with," Aries said. "I have never seen anything that would indicate a tunnel entry."

"Look at the size of that thing!" Bruno exclaimed. They sat astride their horses and stared at the giant face in the distance."

"How could men make something like this? It's so big," Buddy said. "It looks like something only a god could do."

"Things that would seem like magic to us were commonplace to the Ancients," M'Lena said. "Their technology was on a much higher level than ours."

"Yes," Gurney replied. "It was made by men. It took a long time. Originally there were four faces."

"We are still a long way from the mountain," Aries said. "Wait until you see it up close. It's very impressive."

The expedition stood at the foot of the mountain and stared up at the massive face.

"You can see that there were other faces long ago," Cody said. "Look at the rock at the base of the mountain.

"This is as far as I can take you," Aries told Gurney. "I have not been any farther than this."

"We'll set up a base camp and explore the area," Gurney replied.

"Keep a look out for the Coyos," Aries said. "They are nomads. There is no pattern to their movements."

"Do they have territories?" Kadrovich asked.

"Not really," Aries replied.

"We'll have a watch schedule for everyone," Gurney said.

"I am returning to Minos," Aries said. "Good luck to you. I hope you return to Minos soon."

"If we can, we will," Gurney said.

"Good-by, my friends," Aries said. He retreated the way they had all come earlier.

Gurney stood and stared at the face that night. "If the Ancients did this, they should have been able to do anything," he thought. "Why couldn't they save themselves?"

"It's amazing, isn't it, brother," M'Lena said, appearing out of the darkness.

"Yes. Yes, it is," he replied. "The world must have been full of many wonders long ago."

"Do you think the cache is here somewhere?" she asked.

"This is the best clue we've found," he replied. "All we have to do is find the entryway."

"Any idea who that is?" she gestured at the mountain.

"A famous president, I can't recall his name at the moment," he replied.

"Well, we have a lot of work to do. I'm going to sleep," M'Lena said. "Goodnight, brother."

"Goodnight, sister. Sleep well."

Over the next few days Gurney and the others went over the documents they had brought with them once again. When one person was done, another would go over the same papers as they double and triple checked each other's work. Gurney was convinced that the cache was somewhere close-by. The problem was finding the way in to it.

"Everything says below or beneath the mountain of four faces," M'Lena said.
"To me, that means the cache is under the mountain. That would mean that somewhere there has to be an entrance. Maybe a tunnel a distance away or a hidden entry in the side of the mountain," Gurney said.
"I concur," M'Lena said.
"We'll begin a search pattern and see what we can find," Gurney said.

Cody's survey crews slowly worked their way around the mountain. They investigated every possibility.
Gurney and the others examined potential sites. It was slow, dirty work, but no one complained.
"Baker base," Cody's voice came from the radio.
"Baker base here. Go ahead Cody."
"Is Gurney nearby?"
"I can get him. Stand by."

"Gurney here. What's up, Cody?"
"We're at the eastern end of the mountain. We couldn't contact you before with the mountain in the way."
"Have you gone something for us?" Gurney asked.
"We've come across what looks like the remains of an ancient road.   I t goes to the mountain, but there's so much debris it's hard to tell if it goes all the way to the base of the mountain or not."
"OK. We'll come and take a look," Gurney replied.
"Yes sir. I'll have someone meet you and bring you right to the site," Cody said.

"Set up a relay station here," Gurney said. "That way we can talk to Baker base."
"Yes, sir," Kadrovich replied.
"How far is the site?" Gurney asked.
"A few miles, sir," Bickham replied.

"As you can see the road is buried," Cody said. "It looks like there could possibly be a tunnel entrance."

"We'll just have to climb over the rocks," Gurney replied. "This looks like our best lead so far."

"When do you want to get started?" Cody asked.

"It will be dark soon. We'll start in the morning. I want everyone to be fresh," Gurney replied.

They sat around the campfire and relaxed after dinner. Conversation was low and sporadic. Most were too tired to even talk. The perimeter sentries waited patiently for their replacements so they could get some rest themselves.

Somewhere, nearby, an animal howled.

"What was that?" Bruno asked.

Before anyone could answer Bruno, there was an answering howl. More howls came in quick reply.

"I don't like the sound of that," Kadrovich said.

"Some kind of pack animal," Gurney said.

"I wish Aries had told us more about the Coyos," M'Lena said.

"So do I," Gurney replied.

"Do you think that's what we're hearing?" Bruno asked.

"It could be," Gurney replied.

The howls increased in number and volume. They seemed to be closing in on the expedition.

"Call everyone in. I'm worried about what's happening here," Gurney said.

Suddenly they heard a wild yowl in the distance.

"That sounded like a Felis," M'Lena said.

Kadrovich and a couple of security men grabbed their rifles and hurried out of camp.

"Pack up and move back towards the mountain face," Gurney said.

Everyone scrambled to get their gear together.

Gunfire could be heard in the distance.

"What about the horses?" Bruno asked.

"Don't worry about them now," Gurney replied. He hurried over to his gelding. The horse snorted and pawed the ground. "Take the herd home, fella. Understand?"

The horse snorted again and then whinnied. The other horses looked in their direction. The gelding moved out of the circle of light from the campfire. The other's followed, disappearing into the dark.

The gunfire had stopped and the howls receded into the distance.

Kadrovich and the security men came back carrying two bundles.

"What have you got there?" Gurney asked.

"One's what I think must be a Coyo," Kadrovich replied.

"And the other?" M'Lena asked.

Kadrovich paused before he replied. "It's Pumpkin. We were too late to do her any good. I think we may have lost others, too. It's hard to say right now."

Gurney uncovered the Coyo. Even in death its lips were drawn back in a snarl. Its tongue hung from its open mouth. It smelled and its fur was matted and dirty.

One of the Felis came and took Pumpkin's body away.

The expedition clambered over the rocks, looking for a haven out of the reach of the Coyos.

The howling began to rise in volume. The Coyos were closing in on them from all directions. There were more of them all the time.

"I think I see a cave entrance," M'Lena said. "Over there."

"Where?" Someone called out.

"Back there," she replied. "See the arch in the cliff face?"

"I see it," someone yelled.

"There's a door here," M'Lena said.

Everyone scrambled over the rocks, dropping equipment in their haste.

Kadrovich and Bruno forced the door open enough for them to get through.

"Hurry," Bruno urged. "Get inside."

Soon only Gurney, Kadrovich, Bruno, Rufus and Buddy were outside the door.

"Gurney, please get inside," Kadrovich grabbed Gurney's arm. "We'll be right behind you."

Gurney stumbled through the opening, expecting the others to follow him through the door. But, when he turned around, they were not there.

Suddenly, Bruno stumbled through the opening. A moment later Kadrovich followed.

"Where are Rufus and Buddy?" Gurney asked.

"Right behind us," Bruno panted.

The noise outside got even louder. The Coyo pack was right outside the door, trying to get past Buddy and Rufus.

"Where are they?" Gurney went back to the door and tried to look outside.

Rufus and Buddy were fighting to keep the Coyos from the opening. They were in danger of being overwhelmed.

Buddy pushed Rufus towards the opening and Gurney's position. From somewhere Buddy had picked up a grenade.

Rufus stumbled as Buddy pulled the pin on the grenade. Buddy turned and threw the grenade over the cave opening.

"BUDDY!" Rufus yelled.

The grenade exploded. The shock wave started an avalanche. The rocks began to rain down on them.

Rufus fell down when the rain of rocks hit him.

Gurney pulled Rufus's limp form through the opening.

Buddy tried to get to the opening, but the avalanche buried him. Rocks clattered against the metal of the door. The opening closed up, buried beneath the fallen rock. Buddy disappeared.

Kadrovich picked up Rufus and carried him farther into the cave.

Gurney was suddenly aware that they were not in complete darkness as he had expected. Light panels in the walls and ceiling gave off a soft glow.

"Did everyone make it?" M'Lena asked.

"No," Bruno replied. "We lost Buddy. Rufus is injured."

"I'll get Bernard," she said.

Bernard, the Canis healer, was at Gurney's side almost immediately.

Kadrovich pulled Gurney away. "Let him do his job, Gurney."

Gurney sat down a short distance away, his back against the cool rock. He was exhausted, as was everyone else. He couldn't imagine why the Coyos would attack them without provocation.

Bernard came over to Gurney. "Rufus wants to see you."

"Is he," Gurney began.

"All I can do at this point is make him as comfortable as possible," Bernard replied. "His injuries are too severe."

"How, how long?" Gurney asked. His throat was constricted, his mouth dry.

"Not long, I'm afraid," Bernard replied.

Gurney went to sit by Rufus. The others all stayed where they were.

"Gurney," Rufus whispered.

"I'm here, Rufus. I'm here."

"It was an honor to serve you, Gurney," he murmured. "Both for my pack and for myself."

"You'll be ok. We're safe now." Gurney took hold of Rufus's hand.

Rufus weakly shook his head. "No, Gurney. I know that I'm dying."

"No. No. You'll be fine." Gurney blinked back the tears.

"Tell my sire Spike I loved him, Gurney," Rufus said, his breathing was irregular.

"I will, Rufus. It was an honor to have you as a friend," Gurney choked up

"I love you, Gurney. Just as if you were my father," Rufus barely managed to say.

"I love you, too, Rufus." Gurney's tears rolled down his cheeks, leaving a trail in the dust on his face.

"Don't forget me, Gurney."

"Never, Rufus, never."

"I wish I was going to be with you when you make the big find." Rufus's breathing was getting more irregular and shallower.

"You will, Rufus. You will."

"Good-by Gurney." Rufus's chest rose as he took one final breath, a smile on his face. He exhaled, slowly, one last time.

"Gurney," Bruno asked.

"He's gone," Gurney replied. He sat holding Rufus's hand.

"I'll take care of him, Gurney," Bernard said.

Gurney stumbled away, looking, in vain, for a dark corner where he could hide and vent his feelings. He fought to keep from crying.

"Here Gurney," M'Lena said. She handed him a steaming bowl. "Eat this."

"Thanks," he said. "How is everyone else?"

"They're OK," she replied. "Are you feeling better?"

"A little." His eyes were red. His efforts to keep from crying had not been totally successful.

"I've been examining the tunnel walls," she said. "They're obviously artificial."

Gurney looked around, finally seeing where they were. He could see the tunnel curved down out of sight. Light panels dimly lit the way. Some light panels were not working steadily, others were out completely. He could hear water dripping somewhere.

"There's not much in the tunnel," she said, watching him eat.

"Has anyone gone down it yet?"

"No. We've been waiting for you."

"How about the door we came through?"

"Sealed up," she said. "Buddy set off a grenade which caused an avalanche. The debris blocked the door."

"So, there's no way out then," he said.

"Well, at least not the way we came in," she replied, taking his empty bowl. "Buddy sacrificed himself for us."

Gurney rose to his feet. "I guess there's only one way to go. Ahead. There's no turning back now."

They followed the basically featureless tunnel. There were fewer and fewer light panels out as they went deeper into the mountain. Otherwise, there was nothing else, not even a side tunnel. The tunnel seemed to go on forever.

"No bats or rats," Kadrovich said.

"I've noticed that," Gurney replied. "I'd say that means there are no outlets."

"But, where is the fresh air coming from? And, how are the lights powered," Bruno asked.

"That's part of the riddle we have to solve," Gurney replied.

"That looks like a door," M'Lena said, pointing down the tunnel.

"It certainly does," Gurney said.

They all hurried to the door. The gray face was crisscrossed with reinforcing strips. In the center, where a lock should be, there was just a flat panel.

"Here's a key pad," M'Lena said. "But without the proper code, there's no way to open the door."

"Unless we can short it out and get the door to open," Gurney said. H e took out his knife and pried the cover off the unit.

"Look at that mess," Bruno said, surveying the mass of wires inside.

"Kadrovich, see what you can do here," Gurney said as he and Bruno stepped aside.

Kadrovich poked and prodded the wiring.

Suddenly there was a rumbling, grinding noise and the door slid open slightly.

"Nothing to see inside," Gurney said, peering through the opening.

"What do we do now?" M'Lena asked.

"I'm going in," Gurney replied. He squeezed through the small opening.

"You can't go alone," Bruno said as he followed Gurney into the darkness.

"Kadrovich, post a guard here and they rest of you continue on down the tunnel. See if there's a way out," Gurney instructed.

'How long should be wait?" Kadrovich asked, but suddenly the key pad erupted in a fountain of sparks and the door rumbled shut, sealing Gurney and Bruno inside.

"Well, that's a problem," Gurney said to Bruno.

"All we have is my pack," Bruno said.

"Do you have your sidearm?"

"Yes sir," Bruno replied. "Not much else though."

"Well since the door has sealed itself shut we need to find another way out. Hopefully the others will continue on their way and we'll meet up with them again."

"Yes sir," Bruno replied.

"Let's get going." Gurney led the way into the darkness.

"There's no way this is going to work," Kadrovich said. "The wires are all burned."

"Then they're on their own. We have to find a way out of this tunnel," M'Lena said. "If nothing else we'll have to return to Lthrtown and get a rescue party together."

"Gurney said to leave a guard here," Kadrvich objected.

"There's no point to it. The door is sealed. Let's get going."

The survivors gathered their equipment and continued down the tunnel.

Gurney and Bruno continued down the side tunnel, soon coming to another door.

"Let's hope this door works, "Gurney said.

Bruno pulled the door handle and they stood on the threshold of what appeared to be a control room of some kind, filled with desks.

"This looks promising," Gurney exclaimed. He surveyed the room. "These are work stations. I have a good feeling about this."

"Do you think we're close?"

"If this is what I think it is," Gurney replied. "Look here."

They walked to the far end of the room.

"What's out there?" Bruno asked, looking through a floor to ceiling window.

"See if you can find a light switch someplace."

Bruno fumbled along the walls. "Here!"

Lights began to come on outside the window, revealing a massive chamber filled with large rectangular containers.

"By the rock! We've found it! WE"VE FOUND IT," Gurney yelled.

"We have? This is it?"

"Yes, YES! The containers are what the Ancients would have loaded with their records and equipment for reuse after the crisis was over."

"Then all we have to do is find a way down there and figure a way to get out of here," Bruno said.

"Yes, but the search is over. I'm sure we've found the knowledge of the Ancients," Gurney grinned. He felt that all the pain he had gone through had finally been rewarded.

They found a stairway down to the main floor and then it didn't take long to find the massive door into the cavern.

"If we can get this door open, we'll have made it all the way," Gurney said.

They soon found a control panel, but there was also a smaller door next to it.

"Maybe this leads outside," Bruno said.

"If it does we'll have achieved my lifelong goal," Gurney replied.

"It's jammed," Bruno said, pressing his muscular shoulder against the metal door.

With a scream of metal the door opened to revealing the setting sun.

"We're out, we made it," exclaimed Bruno.

"Now the real work begins," Gurney said.

Biography

Growing up in Detroit long before there were such things as the internet, cable TV and game consoles, Michael was a voracious reader.

When he received an encyclopedia in junior high, he read about everything that caught his eye, from the first volume to the last. The library was an unending mine of information and exposed Michael to the science fiction of the Golden Era.

Later, auto racing became the focus of Michael's attention. Despite family objections he pursued his dream and became a winner in his second season. A class championship followed.

Always looking for a challenge, Michael began writing short stories and has over 50 stories in print.

"I enjoy a challenge," he says. "Don't tell me I can't do something, because that's the best way to get me to go out and do it, just to show you you're wrong."

Michael's latest challenge, besides continuing to write, is to embark on an acting career. He has recently worked in movies, on TV and in print.

Michael says he's "terminally single" and lives on the south side of Chicago.